NETBLUE

Glen C. Allison

YOKE PRESS

United States of America

FICTION

Cover design: Marie Owen
Cover photo: Stephanie Hood

Printed in the United States of America

ISBN 0-9718105-1-6

Library of Congress Control Number: 2004103698

To Jonathan,

my son,

my brother,

my friend,

my fellow warrior.

Acknowledgements

My thanks go to Kathy, whose patient support makes this work possible; to my faithful friends and readers: Carolyn Schreiter, Anna Fortner, Ann Benson, Cindy Ballard, Pat Vaughn, Randall Murphree, Jim Homan, Jamey Finley, Bill Smallwood, Peggy Carlton Jones, Christy Grissom, Rachel Luttrell, Mary Jo Tate, Virginia Carlton, Mona Byrd, and Bill Farrar; and to the librarians—at the Lee County Library and beyond—whose loyalty will be remembered always.

Chapter 1

Micah Cray watched through his rifle scope as its crosshairs crawled over the man's face in a window a quarter mile away.

The hatch marks centered on the man's forehead. Cray studied the man's features, compressed as they were by the telescopic lens, and felt the familiar calmness come over him. He caressed the curve of the weapon's trigger guard but trusted himself to come no closer to the actual action of the rifle.

Oblivious to any danger, the man in the window was bent over his kitchen sink, his lips moving even though he was alone in the house. Was he singing? Cray couldn't be sure. From this distance, he could only *see* his prey through the rifle scope, not hear him. Not that it mattered to him what noises the man made. He might as well have been an animal, for all he cared. The man in the window *was* an animal. They were *all* animals. The initial gut-bomb of disgust he always felt upon first viewing one of his subjects up close had long since been replaced with the detachment of an Orkin man surveying a roach.

Cray shifted in the crook of the royal oak tree which ruled over a vacant lot 400 yards from the man's house. He had hauled himself and the sniper rifle up into the tree just after dusk, his routine of the previous three evenings. He could have used a set of powerful binoculars for this surveillance, he realized. He preferred to watch through the scope of the sniper rifle. It kept him focused, he told himself. The tree hid the weapon well and afforded him several stout limbs from which to observe the back of the man's house. This particular spot gave him the best view of the kitchen window. Late summer leaves easily obscured his perch from prying eyes below.

The schedule varied little each night: the man arrived home in his white Toyota Camry from his job at the dry cleaners, made dinner for himself, ate alone, washed his dishes, then left the house surreptitiously. He cruised the neighborhoods on the opposite side of town, slowing his car to a walking pace when he noticed children playing in their safe yards or on lazy cul-de-sacs. So far, the man had not stopped to talk to any of the children. So far.

But he would stop. And talk. And more, if allowed. Cray was stone-cold convinced of that.

Sometimes men like his prey would hold out for weeks after being released from prison. Almost always they would give in to their perverse yearnings, however, and begin their rituals of stalking. Then, eventually, another child would be lost. Not killed, necessarily, but torn from any shred of the innocent, trusting life they once possessed. Just as his Jenny had been lost.

This target might be more difficult than the others, Cray realized. The law enforcement community had begun to take note of the killings. Cray slowly swung the rifle away from the house until he could spy through the scope the cars parked on the street in front of the house. He let the crosshairs travel over the cars until he found one a half-block from the house with two men in work clothes. The man on the passenger side was dozing, a newspaper scattered over his chest. The one on the driver side sipped coffee from a thermos and stared straight ahead through the windshield of the car. Cray guessed the policemen hated being assigned to stake out the man's house in case a killer came calling. They were merely going through the motions.

The man in the house knew the police were there. That was obvious to Micah Cray. Through the scope Cray had caught him peeking through the blinds at the unmarked cop car at the curb. When night had fallen, the man had gone into the den, turned on the television, and settled into his easy chair. The blinds were left open to give the stakeout crew easy viewing. Flickering, blue shadows from the TV played across the walls and ceiling of the den for the next couple of hours. To anyone watching, the man appeared to be swallowed in the chair. The police probably imagined him snoozing in front of the set.

Except he wasn't. Cray kept the scope trained on the back door of the house. After a few minutes, the door opened. The man skulked through the shadows of his back yard, walked through a neighbor's yard to the next street over from his. Cray watched through the scope as he strolled toward a brown van parked on the next block, just as he had done the previous three nights.

Cray looped the strap of the rifle over his shoulder and scrambled down the tree. He carefully placed the weapon between the front seats of his Jeep, turned the key in the ignition, and eased out from under the tree. He pulled out onto the street just as the man steered the brown van away from the curb.

The van made its way out of the neighborhood, and hit a larger artery which took it to an interstate bypass leading to the other side of town. Cray followed more loosely than he had the previous nights; he knew the man's basic pattern by now. He drifted to the far right lane as the van approached the same exit it had taken before.

Soon the van was trolling a neighborhood, an affluent area featuring a well-kept, well-lit park. On the playground, several children darted in and out of the red and yellow oversized plastic tunnels. A group of three girls, all about eight years old, were tossing a Frisbee to one another. The van slowed, as it had on previous nights. Tonight, no grownups were on the playground.

The van stopped.

A block behind, Cray immediately pulled over and let the Jeep idle. He twisted slowly in his seat to survey the closest houses on the street. As usual, the August heat had driven the neighborhood residents inside where air conditioners hummed away, blocking the hot, heavy reality outside.

Cray faced front again to focus on the scene being played out.

The girls took no notice of the van parked next to their playground or of the man watching them. They stood on a triangle of grass about 10 yards apart, singing a ditty; Cray could not make out the words. They seemed to be chanting something as they tossed the plastic disc. The fluorescent green Frisbee floated from girl to girl as they continued chanting.

The passenger door of the van opened.

Cray reached down and switched off the Jeep. He picked up the rifle.

Cray could make out the words of the ditty the girls were chanting now. "Eenie, meenie, miney, moe..." they sang as they kept the Frisbee in the air.

Cray rested the rifle on the rollbar of the Jeep. He put the scope to his eye.

"...catch a tiger by the toe..."

In the van, the man's hand appeared at the opening on the passenger side.

"...if he hollers, make him pay..."

Cray kept the rifle steady now, his breathing even.

The man slid out of the van on the passenger side.

"...fifty dollars, every day..."

The man called out to the girls.

They stopped chanting. The Frisbee hit the ground and rolled toward the man.

Through the scope, Cray could see the man's face clearly now. He was smiling.

The sensations of the night—the breeze whispering through the tree branches above, the tickle of the sweat sliding down his neck, the smell of grass fresh-cut—faded away from Cray as a chilling calm settled over him. His entire world was framed by the scope's viewfinder now.

The man stepped away from the van, bent down, picked up the plastic disc. The girls stared at him. Then the girl closest to the man laughed. The man laughed and held out the Frisbee to the girl.

The cool steel of the trigger pressed against the skin of Cray's forefinger now.

The girl stepped toward the man.

The scope showed the man's features in detail. The smile was changing, morphing into something else, not a smile but something masquerading as a smile—something twisted, something hideous.

The crosshairs steadied on the man's temple. Cray took a deep breath.

The girl reached for the disc.

Cray exhaled——slow, calm, steady—precisely as he had been trained.

The man's other hand darted for the girl's wrist.

Still exhaling, Cray squeezed the trigger.

A burst of scarlet and the man's body dropped to the ground.

It wasn't joy that flooded Cray's mind. He'd lost recognition of that emotion months ago.

But it would have to do.

Chapter 2

Perspiration trickled down the middle of Al Forte's back under the Kevlar vest as he crouched in the cave-black hallway. Forte held the Heckler & Koch submachine gun with one hand and pushed the night-vision goggles up with the other to wipe the sting of sweat from his eyes. Inside the abandoned building the dusty air seemed more stifling than the 98-degree east Texas midday outside. Without the goggles he literally could not see his hand in front of his face.

The heat and the darkness annoyed Forte but did nothing to crack his resolve: the baby must be found.

He flipped down the goggles. Behind him were the other two members of the Forte Security rescue team, Nomad Jones and Jackie Shaw. He motioned them to follow as he moved silently down the hallway. Pieces of torn wallboard dotted the floor as they advanced toward the corridor T-junction ahead. A quick peek around the corner showed no hint of light in either direction. At the far end of the hall to the right was a stairwell.

The faint hum of a radio drifted down the stairs from somewhere on the floor above them.

As the team slowly moved toward the stairwell, Forte reminded himself of the details of this mission. Escaped convicts had kidnapped a nine-month-old boy from a judge's home the day before. There had been no negotiations: the kidnappers refused to talk. They had made no ransom demands. They had simply left a note at the judge's home saying they wanted revenge against the man who had put them behind bars. Two of the thugs had performed the actual kidnapping, but another suspect had driven the getaway car. A strategic and forceful rescue attempt was the only hope for recovery of the child. The team had to be prepared for resistance from at least three men armed with shotguns.

The judge had insisted on using Forte Security for the rescue attempt because this type of mission was the sole reason for the company's existence: recovering and protecting children in danger. Not rich executives held hostage by money-hungry fiends, not diplomats plucked from embassies by terrorists. Just children who found themselves in hostile hands with little hope of a future. Saving them was Forte's life, one of the few reasons for living he had grasped during the past few years.

He motioned for the others to follow. The journey of 20 feet down the hallway took a full minute as the trio stepped through the debris of the old building in their rubber-soled boots. A tiny sound from a kicked piece of plaster could cause the kidnappers to open fire. At the bottom of the stairwell Forte signaled the other two to stop. The metal stairs seemed solid, but they were spotted with rust. Hopefully they would not creak. He tested the first two steps with his half-weight. They were silent. He flipped off the safety on his machine gun and slowly walked up the first flight of stairs. At the first landing he waited. He could hear the radio more clearly now. Above him, the faintest bit of light touched the wall next to the second floor hallway. If there was a sentry, he would be there.

He eased his face to the corner, took a deep breath, and looked quickly. A husky man in a dirty denim workshirt and camouflage pants was leaning next to a door that was cracked open to spill light into the hallway. He ducked back and held up one finger: *one guard.* He slowly stepped around the corner. The guard's head bobbed up and down as he fought sleep. Forte noiselessly covered the eight steps that separated them, clamped a hand over the man's mouth, and drew his Bowie knife across his throat. Forte held the guard, listening for any sign he had been detected, then lowered the man to the floor without a sound.

He stopped and listened again. No stirring came out of the room. The radio droned on. He waved the other two toward him. All three flipped off the night-vision goggles now that light was available.

From his belt Forte took a tiny electronic periscope with a flexible wand tipped with a lens the size of a pencil eraser. He bent the wand carefully and put the viewfinder to his eye. He repositioned the periscope twice along the edge of the doorway and repeated the process to get a full picture of the room. He extracted the wand from the doorway. He felt the others' eyes on him.

He rocked his arms over his chest to indicate the child was there, pointed to the left side of the room. He crossed his arms, held up two fingers, then pointed once to the center of the room and once to the right side: there were two other people in the room. He signaled again to remind them of the order of attack. They would enter on the count of three.

Forte watched as Nomad pulled a flash grenade from his belt. To his left, Jackie was crouched, her mouth grim but eyes calm.

He held up one finger. *One.*

Forte felt a drop of sweat glide down his earlobe.

Two fingers. *Two.*

A commercial for cell phone service blared on the radio inside the room.

Three fingers. *Go!*

Nomad lobbed the flash grenade into the room, tossing it high to give it time to explode before hitting the floor. The blast of the grenade was timed exactly with the crash of the door as Nomad rushed into the room. He rolled on to the floor and shot the man on the right with two quick bursts before the kidnapper could move. Forte, coming through the door behind his teammate, could see the man's mouth form a surprised "O" as he flew backward.

Jackie followed immediately. The remaining kidnapper had sprung up from his chair and kicked it backward. In a half-crouch he pivoted and grabbed for a shotgun on the chipped kitchen table. Jackie put a three-round burst into his chest, stitching him from waist to throat as her weapon rose from the recoil. The rounds from her weapon knocked the last kidnapper backwards. He lay still

The baby was screaming now.

Forte sprinted to the left corner and flung his body over the small cardboard box holding the child. Smoke from the flash-bang grenade drifted waist-high throughout the room.

"Target One down and out," Nomad shouted.

Jackie immediately called out, "Target Two down and out."

The baby's crying abruptly stopped.

Forte rolled away from the box and looked inside it. He reached down to pull out the tiny figure cocooned in its bundle of blankets.

It was a toy doll.

He kissed its smooth plastic forehead and placed it back in the box.

A loudspeaker blared somewhere above the room. "Exercise concluded! Well done, Team Forte." A man in fatigues carrying a clipboard stepped into the room from the hallway. "Strategy, excellent. Execution, excellent. Response time, excellent. Your scores keep getting better and better, Al." Forte lifted a hand to give a weak wave to the man with the clipboard. Even though the rescue had been a simulation, his adrenaline had spiked and was now draining, just as if the mission had been real. The fake kidnappers had risen from the floor, slapped the dust from their clothes, and removed their earplugs. They patted him on the shoulder as they trailed out of the room.

Twice a year, Forte brought a rescue recovery team for drills at the Blackthorn Training Center in the Big Thicket area of Texas just across the Louisiana border. Mike "Nomad" Jones came along for at least one of the training sessions each year. Nomad, a former Navy

SEAL teammate of Forte's, was leaning over with his hands on his knees, his head below the haze in the room.

This was the first time at the training center for Jackie Shaw, the thirty-something resident director of The Refuge, a shelter for endangered children that Forte had established. She had been hired a year earlier and had already experienced an armed attack on the shelter. During that incident, Jackie, an expert shot, had brought down one of the attackers with a shot to the leg. She deserved the extra training, Forte told himself. He grinned as he recalled her background.

"Quite a buzz, huh?" Forte asked. "Still wish you were a nun?"

Jackie was sitting at the table running a hand over the white streak in her closely-cropped black hair. She lifted her head. "Yeah, right. I'm going to act like I didn't hear that. My ears are still ringing from the flash-bang." She tossed a set of earplugs on the table. "Even with these things plugged in."

"Good job," Forte said. "Both of you." He pulled out a slightly dented pack of Checkers cigarettes from a zippered pocket on his fatigues. He was down to four smokes a day. The Checkers were nasty but they were all that was left of more troubled times. He shook out Number One and lit it up.

Nomad straightened up, his eyes white against the black-and-green streaks of camo paint on his face. "In the words of the Indian chief to John Wayne in *McClintock*, 'Good party, no mo' whiskey, we go home.'"

They all laughed and began extricating themselves from the special sensor-weapons provided by the training center, stacking them on the table in the middle of the room.

The whump-whump of helicopter blades penetrated the thin walls of the tattered building.

"Must be another simulation exercise," said Nomad.

The whirring of the chopper blades slowed as the craft landed outside. Suddenly, a voice came over the speakers. "Al Forte, please report to the heliopad. Al Forte, you have company outside."

Forte took off his gun belt and vest and handed them to Nomad before retracing his steps down the stairs and out of the building. A sleek blue corporate helicopter rested in an open area 50 yards away. A man in a business suit was walking toward him bent over as the blades whirled at half-speed.

The man extended his hand as he approached. "Mr. Forte?" The man pronounced his name "fort" instead of the usual "for-TAY" with which most people addressed him. "I'm Thomas Penderby with VillaCom, the telecommunications company. May we step inside for a moment?"

Away from the noise, Penderby came straight to the point. "Mr. Bryce Graham needs your help. His daughter is missing. She's 14 and Mr. Bryce wants the best help available. That's why I'm here."

Forte studied the man. Penderby's brow was creased as he stood stoop-shouldered in the dusty foyer of the building. He had looked smaller as he approached from the helicopter in his tailored pin-stripe suit. Now he merely seemed cowed.

"Has she been kidnapped?" Forte asked.

"We think so, yes."

"Any ransom demands?"

The man looked at his feet. His collar above the pink silk tie was stained with sweat. "No, not yet."

"So, she could be a runaway," Forte said.

Penderby looked up. "Please. Mr. Bryce just wants his daughter safe at home again." The man looked to be on the verge of tears. "He said to tell you Mrs. Christenberry recommended you."

That explained how the man had tracked him down. Ordinarily his office would not have released information on his whereabouts. Verna Griffey, his assistant, would have responded to the Christenberry name, however. Forte had recovered Mrs. Christenberry's grandson from kidnappers in Italy four years earlier—his first major case after opening the security firm. The Christenberrys, leaders in New Orleans social and political circles, had donated a large sum of money to make The Refuge a reality. Besides that, Louise Christenberry was his bridge partner.

"When was she last seen?" Forte asked.

"This morning, when Mr. Graham went to work," Penderby said.

"She's only 14 years old, right?"

"About to turn 15."

"So, she's not driving yet."

"Right. Well, she doesn't have her own car yet. A limousine usually chauffeurs her wherever she needs to go."

"How do you know she isn't at a friend's house?" Forte asked.

Penderby looked embarrassed. "Well, she was, sort of, grounded."

Forte sighed.

The pin-striped man hurriedly continued. "But there's evidence she went to meet someone from a chat group she had been visiting." Penderby paused. His Adam's apple bobbed as he swallowed. "We think she's in danger."

"She met someone from the Internet?"

"Right. We found some notes she'd left on her computer."

Forte gazed across the clearing where the helicopter sat. Beyond the aircraft, a hawk circled lazily above the pine trees. He wondered if the bird had a victim in view or was just biding his time in the hot August sky until something turned up. *We all seem to be waiting for something to turn up sometimes,* he mused. He turned back to Penderby.

"When does Mr. Graham want to meet with me?"

"As soon as you can do it," the man said. "He will be at his house, waiting for you. The chopper can have us there in an hour." The man's face was flushed now.

"Let me tell my crew," Forte said. "But you need to know that I'm not agreeing to find the girl yet. I'll meet with Graham and then we'll see."

Penderby grabbed his hand. "Fine, Mr. Forte, that's all we ask."

"Sure," Forte said. "That's what they all say."

Chapter 3

Some of the priciest run-down real estate in America can be found in the French Quarter. And as much as the land itself costs, the price of renovation is usually steeper. The shifting Mississippi mud of this romantic whore of a neighborhood makes for drunken foundations and cracked walls in century-old buildings that, if they could talk, would express tickled surprise, no doubt, at having survived such a self-indulgent past.

Some people, however, eagerly pay more for the historic debauchery than the actual value of the land. Bryce Graham was one of those. He had made his money fast and hard in the best part of the telecommunications industry: long distance service. Buying up one competitor after another, Graham had made VillaCom one of the top five telecom giants in the world.

Forte guessed that the automated security gate, with its black wrought-iron disguise, cost as much as a luxury automobile, maybe more. The limousine slid past the gate through the narrow alley leading into a parking garage. A courtyard at the center of the Graham compound led from the garage to the main house. The chopper had whisked Forte and Penderby across the state of Louisiana to a heliopad atop the VillaCom building in downtown New Orleans. The car had been waiting to whisk them through the downtown streets as the setting sun cast the concrete canyons in shadow.

As Forte followed Penderby into the house, he caught a movement on the balcony above the courtyard. A woman in an evening gown, wineglass in hand, watched him pass beneath her.

Penderby paused at the door and punched in an alarm code at the security panel. He led Forte through a foyer and into a sunken den surrounded by walls of artfully exposed brick dotting the plaster facade. Above the fireplace was a sprawling metal sculpture showing a school of metal fish on the verge of being engulfed in the gaping jaws of a shark. A wraparound leather sofa separated the room from a cluster of matching chairs in a reading area. A tuxedo jacket had been flung over the end of the sofa. The house looked like a high fashion model—a pretty face that hid the soulless void.

From somewhere in the house came the sounds of one side of a heated conversation. From the pauses, it was obvious someone was on the phone. "—it's not the payments...Yes, we do appreciate it, but you can't just...."

A door closed upstairs somewhere, cutting off their inadvertent eavesdropping.

"Mr. Graham will be down in a moment," Penderby said. "Thanks again for coming."

"You're leaving?" Forte asked.

"Mission accomplished," said the other man. He smiled and left.

Forte slapped the dust out of his fatigues and sat on the sofa facing a huge television that dominated an entertainment center set into the wall. The news was on but the sound was muted. He picked up the remote and turned up the volume.

"...was gunned down in a wealthy St. Louis neighborhood in what the FBI is calling a 'vigilante action.' The murder is the third of its kind this year, where men who have been recently released from prison for molesting children apparently have been tracked down and killed." The news anchor gave a few more details then moved on to another story.

Forte heard a rustling behind him.

"Bastard deserved it." Bryce Graham stood behind the sofa, his tuxedo tie askew, a glass in his hand. "Mr. Forte, can I get you a drink?"

Forte remained seated. "No thanks," he said. "Not my day for one."

"Whoops," said Graham. "I forgot about your—your problem. Or should I say your recovery." He walked over to the bar in the corner. "Louise Christenberry tells me you are doing well with that."

"Day at a time." Forte had learned in recovery that alcohol wasn't his major problem. It was just a trigger that launched him toward the white powder. Today he was clean and sober. Over three years and counting. He fingered the pack of Checkers in his pocket but didn't pull one out. The liquor hadn't gotten close enough to him to make him smoke his last one of the day. Yet.

Graham refreshed his drink, then sat down on the edge of a marble-top coffee table in front of the sofa. He was probably a half-foot taller than Forte, lean and hard-angled. His hair was prematurely gray and cut short. His eyes were puffy above a pink nose that seemed out of place on his tanned face. "Penderby told you about Exxie."

"He told me she was missing, that she might have met someone from the Internet," said Forte. "Was she mad about being grounded?"

Graham closed his eyes and sipped his drink. "No more than usual."

"Did she run away or was she kidnapped?"

"Does it matter?"

Forte studied the man's face. A father, he's a father, he reminded himself. "Yes, it could matter."

Graham poked at the air in front of him with the hand holding the tumbler. A few drops splashed out onto the carpet. "Look, I just want her back here. If you can't do it, just tell me. Louise said you were the best and that you kept your mouth shut when you needed to. Now, will you help me or not?" The words came out "hep-me-

or-no." The fragrance of the spilled liquor spread over the room. Forte wondered how many drinks the man had taken before he arrived.

Forte stood. "Mr. Graham," he said, "I came here out of courtesy to Mrs. Christenberry, who obviously referred you to me. To be blunt, this is not the type of case we usually accept. I am sure you are worried about Exxie. The police will be glad to investigate her disappearance if you file a missing persons report."

Graham's face was flushed as he stared at him for a beat. Then he carefully set the tumbler on the marble before leaning forward and placing his forearms on his knees. His head hung as he looked down at the carpet. "No, please sit down." he said, his voice hoarse and low. "I don't want the police. I want you. Please bring her home to us. Please help me."

Forte had no desire to beat up on the man. "Then you must answer some questions."

Graham nodded.

"Do you think Exxie ran away?" Forte asked.

"It's possible," Graham said. "But the girl is—adventurous. She may have met someone from one of her chat rooms."

"But you don't have any idea who it could have been?"

"No. We let her have her privacy about her computer. A lot of girls get together in the chats. They gossip about boys and each other and whatever. Her computer is password-protected and she is the only one who can get into it."

"Penderby said there was something on her computer about meeting someone."

"Yeah, it was a sticky note actually, stuck to the monitor, but she could have met anyone. She has a lot of friends." Graham picked up a rosewood box from the top of the bar and pulled out a thin brown cigar. "Smoke?"

Forte waved it away. "Do you know the name of one of her girlfriends, someone who knows about her chatroom?"

Before Graham could respond, the woman in the evening gown came down the stairs. The wine glass, now empty, dangled from her left hand. In the other hand she held a piece of paper. Forte stood up.

"Mr. Forte, this is my wife, Cheryl," Graham said. "She can probably help you with the names of Exxie's friends." He checked his watch. "I'm sorry but I must return to the reception for the board of directors." He picked up his tuxedo jacket and shrugged into it, facing Forte. "You will help us, won't you." It was a statement, not a question.

Forte watched a smile twitch across the woman's face then disappear. He turned to Graham. "Yes, I'll try to find her."

"Excellent. I'll call later." Bryce Graham walked through the den and out to the courtyard.

"He's used to getting his way," the woman said. She was bending as far as the black gown would allow, reaching for a wine bottle in a refrigerator under the counter. It looked as if she had been sewn into the designer gown. Outside, a white Corvette purred past the bank of windows facing the courtyard and went out the alleyway leading to the street.

"Mrs. Graham," Forte said, "could one of Exxie's friends know where she is?"

She sat on the opposite curve of the sofa, crossed her legs and sipped the wine. The slit of the gown revealed a length of toned, tanned thigh. "She's done this kind of thing before, you know." She tilted the wine glass back, drinking deeper this time. When she lowered it, her lips glistened with the liquid. Pink lipstick rimmed one edge of the wineglass. "It's a contest. When he grounds her, she always pulls something like this. She wins." She drained the glass. "And, please, call me Cheryl." She studied his face. "You know, your eyes may have the most interesting color I've seen. What is it?"

Forte looked away from the woman. Too many years of leniency had passed in this household for him to give parenting advice. He had to concentrate on what he could do, not what was needed here in the big picture. Outside the courtyard was nearly all in shadow. Only the tip of the garage roof caught the last glimmer of light. The day seemed darker to him now. But darkness was no stranger to him.

"Yellow," he said.

She tilted her head but said nothing.

"So, in the power struggle between father and daughter, Exxie wins. By running away?" he asked.

Cheryl leaned back against the sofa cushions and stretched. "For a while. He always finds her. Or has someone track her down. Or she shows up late in the night."

"At age 14," he said.

She gave a sleepy smile, her eyes closed. "You may not have noticed, but 14 is a lot older than it used to be." She picked up the piece of paper she had set on the sofa next to her. "See for yourself. Exxie took this with her digital camera." She held out the piece of paper.

Forte stepped around the coffee table. He could see now it was a photo of a blonde girl. She was wearing a cheerleader outfit and was draped over a huge pink teddy bear. The top button of her tunic was unbuttoned to show cleavage. Her head was tilted and her eyes half-closed.

He viewed the photo quickly then put it back on the coffee table.

"A whole lot older than it used to be," he said.

Chapter 4

The needles of scalding water washed the day's grime from Forte's skin. He closed his eyes and luxuriated in the shower at the workout room of The Refuge for another minute before turning it off. He toweled the water off his black crewcut, flipped open his locker, and dressed quickly in a black cotton T-shirt, black cotton slacks, black leather belt, black rubber-soled ankle boots.

The walk from the Grahams' to The Refuge on the northern edge of the Quarter had taken ten minutes. He had turned down the offer of a ride back to The Refuge from the lady of the house, giving the excuse of wanting to stretch his legs. In truth, he worried that she might be too wine-dizzy to navigate the narrow streets of the old neighborhood without knocking a few bricks loose from any building built too close to the curb.

Plus, it was his belief that the fewer people who knew the exact location of The Refuge, the better it was for the children inside who needed protection. Most tourists strolling past the block-long building saw a ramshackle century-old collection of townhouses converted into office space for Forte Security on one end and Forte's apartment on the other. The middle section appeared to be badly needing renovation. Inside, it was a different story. Walls had been knocked down, communication cables strung, bullet-proof windows and security systems installed to make The Refuge a specialized shelter for children in extreme danger. So far, no child entrusted to the shelter had been harmed.

Forte stuck his Glock nine-millimeter automatic in the back waistband of his pants. He walked out of the workout room, down the corridor that overlooked an enclosed courtyard filled with playground equipment. Overhead, the skylights had been opened remotely so the first stars twinkled through the bulletproof glass. *Home sweet home*, he thought as he jogged down the stairs to the shelter's playroom on the first floor.

Slumped in a beanbag was a teenage boy with a Nintendo control in his lap. Everything about the boy was relaxed except his hands, which slapped at the firing buttons on the remote and twisted the joystick. On the television display in front of him, several bad guys fell from a guard tower, the victims of a deadly, if computer-animated, James Bond.

Forte didn't care for the violence of the new video games. He'd seen enough of the real thing. But he knew that Fizer had, too.

"Good shooting," he said. He pulled a chair away from the desk in the corner and sat in it backwards.

The boy did not respond for a beat as he drilled two more video foes. Finally, he mumbled, "Thanks." He kept playing the game.

"Do you know Exxie Graham?" Forte asked.

The boy's hands stopped moving on the remote controls. On the screen, James Bond went down in a hail of bullets. Fizer slowly turned and looked at him.

"Exxie...Graham?" he said.

In the month that Fizer Beal had been under the protection of The Refuge, he had said little to anyone, refusing to let down his guard for a moment. His response to the question about the girl was the most emotion he had displayed.

Forte nodded. "You know her?"

The boy scrunched his eyebrows into a "you-idiot" expression. "Duh. Everyone knows Exxie Graham."

"Popular, huh?"

"Only like the hottest girl in school."

"Hot," said Forte.

"Lava," said the boy. He raised his hand to his face and absently touched a pimple on his nose as he gazed at the wall behind the TV set.

"Do you know who she hangs out with?"

"Mostly older guys." Fizer turned to look at him. "What's up with the quiz on Exxie Graham? She in trouble?"

"She's missing."

Fizer gaped, his cool broken. "Get outta town."

"Yup."

Forte showed him the photo of Exxie. "Have you seen this before?"

The boy took the photo. His face reddened. "Yeah, I've seen it."

"Really? Where?"

Fizer handed back the photo. "Couple of weeks ago, she started sending it out to guys in chat. A friend of mine snagged it and posted it on his website. It's all over the school now."

"Does she have a bad reputation?"

The boy studied him, his cool facade returning. "What do you mean?"

"You know what I mean."

Fizer examined a bare spot on the wall for a moment. "Yeah, I guess you could say that." He looked back at Forte. "You think she's in trouble?"

"Could be. You know any of the guys she chatted with?"

"Yeah, but she's sorta...selective. I mean, she likes the older guys." He reddened again. "Kinda tough to fool her."

Forte thought that one over for a minute. "You know any of her girlfriends? One who would know something about the chat stuff?"

Fizer pondered for a second. "Yeah. Heather Cobb. She goes by 'HoneyKiss' in chat."

"HoneyKiss?"

The boy shrugged. "Hey, I didn't make it up. She did." He touched the pimple again. "But she's really not too bad. It's just a name; I think she made it up to impress Exxie. Really."

Forte stood up. "Want to do some undercover work for me?"

"Hell no."

"That was quick. You don't even know what it is."

"Can't be good."

"It might help find Exxie."

Fizer pondered that one. "What kind of undercover work?"

"On the Internet."

"Doing what?"

"Chatting—with Heather Cobb."

"About what?"

"About who Exxie might have run away with."

"Man, everyone will know I narcked her out."

"Fizer, she could really be in danger," Forte said. "Besides, it's a chance to chat with HoneyKiss."

The boy took his hand away from the pimple. He grinned. "You got a point there."

Within ten minutes, Fizer had a name, a place, and a time when Exxie was to meet a guy from the chatroom.

Forte clapped him on the shoulder. "Good work." He started to walk out of the game room. He stopped and turned. "By the way, how'd you come up with 'CyberStud' as a nickname in chat?"

Fizer flopped down on the beanbag. "For me to know and you to be jealous of."

Forte smiled and walked out. At the end of the hall, he could see the light of Jackie Shaw's office. He stopped and rapped his knuckles on the open door.

The resident manager was at her desk, scribbling furiously on a form. Two wooden trays labeled "IN" and "OUT" in black block letters occupied the far left corner of the desk. Both boxes were half-full of forms. She kept writing until the last blank of the form was completed, then looked up. "Paperwork will be my very death one day," she announced.

Forte sat on the corner of the desk. In the year since Jackie had come on board, The Refuge had run more smoothly than ever in its four-year existence. She'd streamlined much of the reporting process and had earned praise from both the board of directors of the nonprofit shelter and the dozen or so government and law enforcement agencies with which The Refuge had to coordinate.

"But you are so good at it," he said.

"I'd rather get shot at."

"Well, you've had some of that fun, too."

Jackie leaned back in her desk chair, laced her fingers together, and propped her hands on top of her head. Her hands covered the white streak in her short dark hair. The hint of flowers wafted across the desk. She looked like she could still compete for a spot on the Olympic gymnastics team. "Come to think of it, I'm beginning to understand why you spend so much time away from your office."

"No rest for the wicked," said Forte. "How's Fizer doing?"

"Okay, all things considered," Jackie said. "He doesn't say much, but what 14-year-old boy does, even when his Dad hasn't skimmed money from the Mob." She stretched, her back arching and her arms straight above her head. It reminded Forte of his cat Boo. "I think he's worried about them getting to his father even if he's behind bars. But he's concentrating too much on being cool most of the time to show that he's scared."

"Yeah, I sorta get that from him, too. He's not beyond having his buttons pushed though. He helped me get some information about this Graham girl case. He was a little proud of being able to do it." He told her about the meeting with the Grahams and showed her the photograph of Exxie in the cheerleader's outfit.

Jackie studied the picture and turned it sideways. "Wow," she said, "how do they grow—like that...so young." She looked down at her chest. "Or ever, for that matter."

"I've wondered that," he said. "In a professional sort of way, of course."

"Right," she said. "So, she doesn't seem to be an innocent kidnap victim?"

"Nope."

"But you're going to find her and bring her home anyway."

"Yep."

"Because...?"

"Louise Christenberry referred the Grahams to me."

"And?"

"What do you mean 'and'?"

"That's not the only reason, is it?"

Forte picked up a thin book from the corner of the desk. The book cover had a photo of a man on the craggy summit of a mountain. The man on the cover was a speck in the distance, his hands held out to his side at an angle as if he were about to be launched into the sky. *An Arrow Pointing Toward Heaven* was the book's title. *If only it were that easy,* Forte thought. *Just launch yourself into the sky and be at peace.* He set the book down on the desk.

"No," he said, "that's not the only reason I'm going to bring Exxie back. The Grahams suck at being good parents as far as I can tell. But they want her back. Maybe there's hope."

Jackie was searching his face as he spoke, her head cocked to one side.

"What?" he said.

"Nothing," she said. "It's just that there seem to be indications of soft-heartedness somewhere inside that tough Al Forte shell."

Forte felt himself blushing. He absently touched the X-shaped scar above his right eye. It felt hot. *What the hell is this,* he thought.

Jackie laughed. "Don't worry. The secret is safe with me." She picked up a pink piece of paper from the desk. "By the way, Rosalind Dent called you about a half-hour ago." She handed the slip to him. "And it didn't sound like FBI business." She made her eyebrows go up and down, Groucho-style.

He took the phone memo from her, folded it, and put in his pocket.

"She probably heard about the new, softer Al," he said.

Chapter 5

All the money in the world couldn't buy true caring, Micah Cray thought as he strode down the gleaming hallway. It could buy 24-hour attention, 100-channel satellite, and a vase of fresh flowers on the bedside table every Monday morning. But a piece of their hearts? None to spare.

He didn't blame them. They weren't trained to love the people here, just keep them comfortable, keep them alive. Most of the people in the rooms wouldn't know it anyway, their senses long ago buried.

A nurse behind the desk gave him an antiseptic smile as he walked past. Her face held the expression for maybe a half second, then she turned back to her computer. Cray glanced back at the monitor screen. She was playing Solitaire, staring at the screen as the tip of her tongue touched her top lip.

He kept walking, the heels of his boots making clop-clop echos that bounced back to him from the end of the hallway. He found himself deliberately timing his gait to avoid matching the rhythm of the cloying instrumental version of "Wind Beneath My Wings" that flowed out of the wall speakers like syrup. *Damn, I hate that this is the best I can do.*

At first he had been too numb to notice it, the forced compassion and empty gestures that would have seemed well-meaning if they hadn't been so polished with practice. Was it only eight months since he had first floated through these germless halls with every last nerve drained of any hint of feeling? In the weeks after that first day, when the pain descended on him, he longed for those initial hours of non-feeling.

A tidal wave of guilt had nearly crushed him. Why hadn't he been able to prevent it, to protect her? All his life he had bent the world to his will, going after the next rung in the ladder and reaching it, never feeling the disappointment of true failure. When cancer had taken his wife, he'd been sad, for sure, but the illness had dragged her through so much misery that it was almost a relief when the end came. It was a loss, but one that he understood and with which he coped. This thing, this hideous unspeakable act, however, had torn a gaping, jagged hole in his life. He should have been more diligent about the computer, the Internet, those damn chatrooms. He should've known the kinds of friends she was making in school. And the girl who was with her, the one who escaped—he should have seen through her act right away. Before it was too late. But he hadn't.

The guilt subsided after a while, only because the anger needed room to grow. And grow it did, raging like a maelstrom through a forest until all his close relationships—all of his friends and family—had been burned away to ashes. The flames of anger still scorched anyone who came close. There were the fights, sometimes accompanied with a few glasses of beer, sometimes not. Most refused to press charges, recognizing that a chipped tooth or swollen eye was their donation to his misery and secretly counting their blessings that they were not in his place. Some insisted he spend the night behind bars but were cajoled by local police to drop charges if he would pay their hospital bills. Which he always did in a calmer moment.

Eventually the anger and hurt receded, however, and transitioned into something else, a numbness that gave him a few hours of sleep before his soul-ripping screams flung him into consciousness again. At least he got the few hours of rest. Life became bearable.

Then, after a month or so, the suffering became a friend, then a mentor that taught him how to endure the visits and phone calls and greeting cards full of sentiment that passed like a comet so far away in its mirage of nearness. After a while the calls had stopped, and he no longer had to wait in the darkness of his house while unannounced well-wishers dawdled at his door and knocked and waited and finally left their disposable aluminum pans of casseroles on the stoop and drove away.

He could begin putting his plan together.

The first one, the monster who had taken his Jenny away, had actually been plucked from him. He considered it some kind of a divine joke, the man being killed by a tractor, the victim of his own ego to think he could manhandle the machine across the ditch. Cray was glad to be able to witness the event, however, from his hiding spot in the trees two fields over from the pasture where the man was working. That day he had come merely to begin collecting tidbits of the man's habits so that he would be prepared to strike one day soon. The man's fluke accident had robbed Cray of the pleasure of revenge, leaving him ambivalent: he enjoyed seeing him crushed under the tractor, but the fact that he didn't make it happen was disappointing. For a week afterward, he drifted emotionally, aimless.

One day he saw the newspaper article about another predator, one who had also been released from prison after a second offense only to strike again. Cray thought it over for a few days and decided to make the man his first project in his new life's mission. If he couldn't be personally avenged, at least another family could be.

He smiled as he turned left at the next intersection of hallways. Remembering his projects—the planning, the logistics, the literal execution—brought him the closest thing to satisfaction he had experienced during the past eight months. A woman in white scrubs gave him her automatic smile as she pushed a metal cart of food past him.

This hallway was a dead end, coming to a halt at a ceiling-high bank of windows that overlooked a covered patio with wooden picnic tables and a barbecue grill bolted to the concrete pad. It was empty. Come to think of it, Cray had never seen anyone at the patio. He guessed that visitors spent little time here, and most of the residents would never know what it was like to feel the sunshine on their faces again.

Cray slowed at the last room on the left side of the hall. He paused and took a deep breath before pushing open the door.

The smell of Pine-Sol greeted him. Someone must have just mopped down the room. Everything was in its place: the afghan folded precisely across the foot of the bed, the picture aligned on the opposite wall to square with corners of the room, the vase of flowers placed exactly in the center of the bedside table. The TV was off, he was glad to see. The housekeepers might have watched it while they were cleaning the room, but at least they had the decency to switch it off when they left. On the rolling tray beside the bed, two greeting cards lay unopened. Earlier there had been dozens every week for him to open and read aloud. But time had a way of pushing the painful memories back to a place in the mind, even the minds of family and friends, where it was more comfortable to let those memories sleep than to run the risk of reglimpsing the horror that put them there to begin with.

He picked up the cards and opened them as he stood next to the bed. Nice sentiment, at least as much as one could buy for $2.95. He stuffed the cards back into their torn envelopes, placed them on the bedspread. Only then did he look at the head of the bed.

The girl's auburn hair fanned out against the yellow pillowcase. He reached over and smoothed the hair. It was freshly washed and fell from his fingertips as if the strands had been poured from a pitcher. She lay so still she could have been merely asleep. Except for her eyes which stared at a spot on the ceiling. Other visitors to the room kept busy as they chattered away, always avoiding the eyes. Not Cray. He bent over and kissed the girl on the forehead, looking into the pale blue eyes as he did it.

32

Though there had been some physical trauma from the attack, the coma did not show signs of physical cause. It was a complete mental and psychological shutdown at the horror her body had endured. The darkness was better than the light of her own experience, one psychiatrist had said. From the first, the doctors said she probably would not register anything she saw or heard while in the coma, which showed no signs of ending. On the other hand, they could not say with absolute certainty that her mind was beyond the point of receiving any signals from those who tried to penetrate the darkness. So, he kept his weekly vigil.

"Hello, my sweet Jenny. Daddy's here," he whispered.

He leaned closer, his face in her hair just like when she was a baby.

"I got another one for you." He raised up and peered at her face, its expression unchanged.

"And not the last one, either, my baby," he murmured.

Chapter 6

Exxie Graham stepped into the off-campus bar and stopped for a moment, peering through the cigarette haze as she hooked the thin strap of her purse over her shoulder. She reached into the purse, pulled out a cigarette, and lit it. It was impossible for anyone in the bar to guess she was anything but a college student. Her half-lidded gaze swept the room. He wasn't here yet. She could tell because none of the guys in the bar were looking expectantly at her when she entered. She was early for her meeting anyway.

Beyond the bar was a row of booths along a half-wall that separated the drinkers from the restaurant crowd. A few heads turned as Exxie went directly to the booth furthest from the front door and sat down. The bartender walked over. In his eyes she could see a question—would he card her or would he ask for a drink order?

"What'll you have?" he said.

She stretched and waved her cigarette as the smoke ribboned above her outstretched arm. "I'm waiting for my date." She gave him the smile that she'd practiced in the mirror a hundred times, the one that played with the corners of her mouth and made her eyes say something slightly warmer than a friendly smile intends. The bartender held her gaze for a beat, then grinned and snapped his fingers at her before going back behind the bar.

Works every time, she thought. Not that it mattered if he asked to see her ID. She was ready with a fake driver's license that cost $1,500 of her daddy's money. The game was fun though. She leaned back against the red cracked leather of the booth and released a rope of smoke which quickly became lost in the cloud near the ceiling. The strains of Hootie and the Blowfish poured out of unseen stereo speakers somewhere in the bar. The music took the edge off the occasional raucous outburst from the college crowd spread out in groups of three or four among the tables. Everything seemed about the same as when she'd visited the place a week earlier in anticipation of tonight: half-empty bar near the Tulane campus, not too rowdy, not too ritzy, not too scuzzy, plenty of noise and smoke and people who didn't care who came here or how young they might be.

Always pick the meeting place. That had become her number-one rule after her first meeting with a chat partner had nearly gone way wrong. She was in control now. It amused her that her parents thought they knew her so well. She'd overheard them talking a couple of weeks earlier about how they needed to supervise her activities more closely now that she would be in high school. Like most parents, they had no clue. Which was fine with Exxie. Let them drink themselves stupid. Just leave her alone.

At first the chats had been the innocent gathering places for her seventh-grade pals, like the malt shops of the past or the malls where kids hung out on weekends sometimes. They were a place where parents seldom visited; and if they did, they were easily detected and either avoided or exposed. Everyone knew their own crowd's nicknames. If someone logged on using another's name, the writing style usually gave them away quickly.

Exxie tired of the gossiping and bickering of her friends' chatroom after a few months. She'd hit puberty ahead of the others and had developed quickly. She had definitely discovered boys. And the boys had discovered Exxie.

An entire world opened up to her. She wondered how she'd ever been so ignorant of the other half of the human race before. Less than a year earlier she'd been invisible, the boys streaming past her in the hallways of school as she huddled against the door of her locker. That changed. The boys followed her everywhere and started phoning and e-mailing her constantly. It had been flattering. She'd started chatting with the boys, spending less time with her girlfriends. At first, it amazed her how easy it was to arouse a boy's awareness in the chats and over the phone. It didn't take long, however, to get used to the power she wielded in her new-found sexuality. And it took even less time to become bored with junior-high boys.

The high school boys fared a little better and, more to the point, they had cars. She never lacked for a ride anywhere after that. Despite her parent's half-hearted warnings, she soon crossed the lines that her mom had said were "reserved for people who really loved each other." Like the way you love Dad, she'd wanted to say that day as she looked into her mother's eyes.

The first time had been a fumbling disappointment after school in her parent's empty house, and she'd wondered what all the fuss was about. That first boy faded from view as quickly as he'd appeared, and she went on to others. Then to the college boys. And even to older men. Which had nearly ended it all for her. She rubbed the smoke from her eyes as she remembered how bad that had been.

But she was careful now.

She would meet her chat partner, spend the night with him, then let herself back into her house while her parents slept. In the morning, she'd promise never to run away again and all would be forgiven. After a few screaming threats and having her privileges taken away for a month. Que sera.

Exxie saw a figure walk past the front window of the bar. Was this the one? The door opened and a nice-looking man of about 25 looked around at the tables. Finally he saw her. She felt a pleasant chill at the back of her neck. *Let the games begin.*

He walked over to her. "Exxie?" he said.

"Rick?"

The man smiled and sat down. "Sorry I'm late," he said. "What are you drinking?"

"Rum and coke," she said, "but I was waiting for you to order."

"Oh, yeah, okay." He called over the bartender. "Two rums and cokes," he said, then gave a nervous chuckle. "Is that how you say it, or is it rum and cokes...whatever."

The bartender shrugged. "However you want to say it, pal. Coming right up."

He seems a little on edge, Exxie thought, *but not in a threatening way.* "So, you're a graduate student," she said, watching him carefully. He looked better than the photo he had e-mailed her. His brown hair was cut short and stylishly mussed. He wore a tan bowling shirt with a green logo of a palm tree that matched his eyes. Cute and easy to control, she mused.

"Yeah, second year in the master's program in sociology," he said. He let his eyes wander over her as he spoke. "You look better than your picture. Which I thought was impossible." He pulled out a pack of cigarettes and offered her one, which she waved away. He looked around the bar. "Nice place. Do you hang here much?"

She waggled her hand. "Off and on, when I'm bored. What about you? You been here before?"

"No. First time."

They sat without talking for a minute, listening to the music. The drinks came. Exxie picked hers up and sipped. *Strong enough for tonight,* she thought.

Rick broke the silence. "And, you're a freshman, huh?" Doubt flickered in his eyes.

She gave him her mature smile. "Yes," she said. "Or I will be when class starts next week. I've got Dr. Loring for Western Civ. I heard he was tough."

Rick's face relaxed. "Yeah, but there are plenty of cheat sheets around campus to prep for his exams."

"So, tell me," she said, "are you really like the guy I've been chatting with?"

He reddened but recovered quickly. "What do you mean?"

She pursed her lips and stared at a spot above his head as if she were thinking. Outside, a motorcycle rumbled past the bar and stopped nearby. She could barely hear the low tones of the bike's muffler above the music. "I think you know what I mean." She loved making them squirm. "All the things...you like to do. Is that just virtual reality...or real life?" Her eyes bore into his.

He didn't look away. "It can be real." His face was still flushed, but not from embarrassment at this point, Exxie guessed. "What about you?"

Exxie closed her eyes slowly then opened them. She said nothing for a full minute, a long time to stare at another person from two feet across a table top. "Only one way to find out. Is your place far from here?"

* * *

Al Forte waited outside the bar, leaning against his motorcycle, a Bourget FatDaddy with a black-on-black gas tank and a custom holster for the sawed-off shotgun mounted on the frame behind his left leg as he rode. He'd had a Harley-Davidson for years but had been talked into switching to the Bourget by an ex-Marine buddy of his. He could easily afford the price of the motorcycle—which rivaled that of some luxury automobiles—thanks to a hefty bonus from the grandparents of a girl he'd rescued in the Caribbean a year earlier. The new bike was more powerful than the Harley and more balanced, allowing him to concentrate on other matters when necessary. Such as yanking the 12-gauge pistol-grip double-barrel shotgun from the holster as fast as possible. Not that he'd needed to take that kind of action so far since buying the Bourget. But you never could tell when a half-second here or there could save his life.

Not to mention it was a mean-looking ride, he admitted to himself.

Peering through his 10x Zeiss binoculars, he had watched from several blocks away as Exxie went into the bar. The blonde girl, dressed in jeans and a pink cami top, easily passed for a college student. Forte wasn't too concerned about the guy she was supposed to be meeting. He'd take care of him when they came out of the bar.

After he'd spotted her, he drove closer to the bar and parked on the sidewalk across the street. He shook out Checkers Number Two and lit it up as he waited.

"Got one for me?" The voice came from behind him, about 20 feet away and to his right, making it more difficult to twist, draw his Glock from the back holster and fire away. He immediately recognized the voice. He maintained his pose and drew deeply on the smoke.

"Sure, Lucky," he said, "but you won't like it." He took out the pack and shook out a single white stick. His expression remained casual as he surveyed the area up and down the street.

Luke Battier stepped out of the shadows and took the cigarette. He leaned forward and lit it from the end of Forte's. Up close, the other man's icy eyes twinkled with amusement. "Don't worry. I'm here alone." He stepped a few feet away, deeper in the shadows as he inhaled and made a face barely recognizable in the dim light. "Damn," he said, "you're right. These taste like...."

"Live longer. Don't smoke it," said Forte as he took another drag. He'd started smoking during his two-month stint in rehab a few years earlier. The cheap Checkers brand would make it easier to finally quit. At least that was his theory. He was down to four a day.

Battier grimaced and puffed again. "Old age is highly overrated."

Dressed in a tailored light gray Italian suit, the man looked the same as the day he'd run over Forte for the winning touchdown of the 1981 Holy Cross–Jesuit High game, except for a couple of fine wrinkles across the forehead, a notch in the top curve of his left ear, and several bleached streaks in his longer hairstyle. He'd earned the name "Lucky" way before his high school football playing days. His father's gangster pals always thought he brought them good fortune on their deep-sea fishing trips or their Saturday afternoon poker games or anything else where they needed a fast errand boy they could trust. Al had first met him when the young Battier had been sent into his grandmother's liquor store on Magazine to fetch a fifth of Irish whiskey for a card game. Lucky had worn the same lop-sided grin then as now.

Forte had never trusted the man much, and it wasn't just because back in high school he'd been one of the few running backs in the city to regularly get past his linebacker position. No, he'd sensed a dark streak in Lucky since boyhood. *Of course*, he thought, *we all have those streaks at one time or another.*

"Guess this place looks a lot different from the outside," Battier said. "On a stakeout?"

"Something like that," Forte said. He turned to the other man. "You figure to give me a hand?"

Battier tilted his head back to study the hazy sky above New Orleans. "Not tonight, my friend."

"Then enlighten me."

Battier's face remained stonelike, but his eyes shone with some inner joke. "Same old Alvin. No B.S., just come straight to the point then get the hell out of my way." He drew deeply on the cigarette, making it glow red in the darkness before flicking it away. "Okay, here it is. We need to talk to the boy, Fizer, the one you've got locked away. Mr. Marchetti is prepared to make a substantial donation to The Refuge for five minutes with the boy."

A red Mazda Miata convertible drove down the street in front of them, slowing to a crawl as the pair of co-eds inside examined the two men by the motorcycle. Battier flashed a smile. The girls smiled back. Forte kept watching the front of the bar. The car sped away.

"You're a smart man, Lucky, no matter what anyone else says. You know it's not going to happen."

"He knows where that money is, doesn't he?"

"Doesn't matter what he knows. You aren't talking to him."

Battier chuckled. "I told him it would be useless talking to you. But he knows that we were...that we knew each other from way back. Wanted me to give it a shot."

"And so you did." Forte flicked the dying ashes from his cigarette and put the butt in his pocket. Forte never sensed that the other man had moved until he was standing next to him.

Battier stepped in front of him until he blocked the view of the bar. Forte tensed, then relaxed and let his arms hang naturally in a loose stance. With Battier's back to the neon sign across the street, his face was backlit, his eyes hooded in shadow. His voice, though soft, had lost all lightness when he spoke again.

"We won't stop, you know. The boy's father stole Marchetti's money and we'll get to him, even in lockup. The boy, too. Doesn't matter where he is, even in your safe little shelter." A black Lincoln Town Car pulled up and stopped several yards away. "I've always kept respect for you, Al, even when you went through your bad times. But this is business. Think about it. We won't hurt the boy if he gives them the right answers."

Forte still could not see the man's eyes. "Tell Mr. Marchetti I respectfully decline his request."

Battier sighed and reached for the pocket inside his suit coat.

Forte flinched, his hand plunging for the Glock at the small of his back.

The other man held up a hand and slowly pulled out a business card.

"This is Mr. Marchetti's number," he said. "Call him if anything changes."

Forte took the card and put it in his pocket.

Battier backed away toward the waiting car. The rear door opened and he turned back for a moment. "Be smart, podnuh. Don't wait too late to call. Avoid the pain for once."

"Right back atcha," Forte said.

Lucky shook his head and got in the car. It glided down the street and disappeared around a corner.

Across the street, the blare of a Kid Rock song spilled out of the bar as a man opened the front door and came out on to the sidewalk. The man weaved for a moment, leaned against the wall, ran a hand through his hair then wiped it on his pants. Blinking under the pool of light from the streetlamp, he straightened and hobbled down the street.

Forte thought he could smell the booze from across the street but knew it was just part of his imagination, the part that tried to take him places he could never even visit again. Unless he never wanted to come back. It didn't matter that the rational part of him clearly explained the rules to living sober every day. There was always that other part that whispered of draft mugs sweating in the muggy night and the sweet burn of white powder in his nose to take the pain and make it go away.

Then he could stumble down the crooked avenue linked arm in arm with the old man he'd just seen.

He shuddered. *Why did I smoke my last one for the night already*, he asked himself.

The door of the bar opened again. Exxie Graham walked out, followed closely by a tall man in his mid-twenties. The pair kept walking along the sidewalk until they reached a new blue Camaro parked on the curb in the next block. The man opened the passenger door to let the girl in.

Forte stepped back deeper into the shadows, watching. He slipped his hand into the pocket with the cigarette butt, wishing again it could come back to life. He threw one leg over the saddle of the FatDaddy and kicked the starter to a roar.

Showtime.

Chapter 7

The cars parked in front of the row of townhouses all sported logos from BMW or Lexus or Acura or the like. *At least he drives American*, Forte observed to himself as he watched the Camaro search for a parking spot. The driver hadn't noticed the FatDaddy trailing behind him like a shark after a plump tuna.

The car circled the block once before finding an empty space. Forte hung back on the bike, then swung in behind a sports utility vehicle a block away. He killed the motor and watched the man and girl climb the steps to an upstairs apartment in a renovated four-plex. The man said something to Exxie that Forte couldn't hear. The girl laughed. Neither paid any attention to the area around the apartments. The man didn't move like anyone who had been physically trained for combat readiness. Just a student, Forte guessed, in the wrong place with the wrong girl.

Forte dismounted the bike just as the couple let themselves into the upstairs apartment with a jangle of keys, a slam of the front door. The lights went on in the apartment. He counted to ten and slowly looked up and down the street.

Fifty feet away a slender white-haired woman in capri pants walked toward him with a small dog on a leash. The dog yipped twice when it got close. When she saw him in the shadows, the woman made an involuntary noise and backed away.

"Oh my!" she said. Her hand fluttered up to cover her mouth.

"Don't worry," Forte said. "I'm safe."

The woman's eyes were wide with disbelief. She stood on the grass on the opposite side of the sidewalk.

Forte reached down and picked up a roll of duct tape he had looped over the pistol grip of the shotgun on his bike. He put the tape inside his T-shirt, tucked the shirt back into his belt, then pulled out the short-barreled shotgun from its holster on the motorcycle. At the sight of the gun, the woman made a small moaning sound.

Forte started across the street. He turned back and pointed the gun at the dog. "And make sure that dog doesn't pee on my bike."

The woman made a yipping noise from behind her hand. She retreated the way she had come, half-dragging the whining dog along the sidewalk behind her.

Forte smiled into the shadows and sighed. *Humorless people.* He continued across the street.

At the top of the landing he paused at the man's front door and listened. From inside came the rhythm of normal conversation. *Good,* he thought, *I'm right on time.* He hoped that the deadbolt had not yet been locked.

He stepped back and kicked hard at the door next to the doorknob.

The frame of the doorway splintered but held.

And now for plan B. He pointed the shotgun at the lock and blasted it loose. The door swung open.

The graduate student, his face a puzzled mask, was frozen in a stooped position as if he had just risen from the sofa. Forte pointed the shotgun at him. He couldn't decide if he would describe the guy as a man or a boy. "Facedown on the floor," he yelled, louder than necessary. A yelp and then a thud as the student dropped to the carpet.

A boy. Definitely a boy.

At the other end of the couch sat Exxie, her mouth a perfect circle of surprise. "Who are you?" she asked.

Forte put his knee in the middle of the man's back, drawing an "UNNHHH" from him. He pulled the man's arms behind him, held them together with his left hand, and bound his wrists together with the duct tape. He turned to the girl. "Your dad sent me after you. Let's go."

She looked puzzled, then anger replaced the fear on her features. "My dad sent you...you...you bastard!" she screamed as she flung a cushion at him. She lunged for the open door of the apartment.

Forte caught her by one arm and pulled her back. Across the landing, a couple peered from behind their cracked door.

"Domestic squabble," he shouted above Exxie's screams. The door slammed shut.

He pinned her flailing arms and dodged all but one of her kicks to his shins. After pushing her facedown on the sofa he taped her wrists and ankles. "Sorry about this but we must be departing swiftly," he said. He picked her up and threw her over his shoulder. She bellowed a string of obscenities. He put her down. "Okay, have it your way," he said. He pulled out the tape and plastered a strip over her mouth. He looked down at the figure on the carpet.

"Are you a student?"

The boy opened his mouth but nothing came out. Slowly his head bobbed up and down.

"What's your name?"

"Please, I'm sorry...I didn't know...."

"Just tell me your name. Now!"

"Rick. Rick Gaffney." The boy's voice was edged with tears.

Forte studied his face. "When the police come, tell them anything you want," he said, "but the truth won't sound good for you at this point. I'll be back shortly to talk to you and we will decide at that point what to do."

Forte picked up Exxie again and went down the stairs. At the Bourget, he carefully draped her over the gas tank as she continued to struggle. In the distance were sirens. He started up the bike and roared away. The girl stopped wriggling.

Once out of the immediate neighborhood, he slowed the bike and pulled over to listen. The sirens weren't following him. He started up again and drove normally as he zigzagged his way through the Irish Channel streets back to the French Quarter. He slowed his pace so that he wouldn't have to stop completely at stoplights. Most of the locals ignored the sight of a bound and gagged girl across a motorcycle. The few tourists who spotted it twisted their heads to see more. But by then he was gone.

Finally he pulled up at the security gate outside the Grahams' compound. He pressed the button and spoke into the intercom. "Mr. Graham, I've got your daughter here." There was no response on the speaker. The gate buzzed and swung open. Forte puttered down the alley and into the courtyard.

He lifted Exxie off the gas tank of the FatDaddy. "This is going to sting," he said.

He snatched the tape away from her mouth.

She screamed an obscenity, her voice hoarse with fury.

He picked her up and carried her toward the French doors of the house.

Bryce Graham opened the doors from the other side. "What in the...."

Forte brushed past him. The intricate notes of a Wynton Marsalis solo flowed out of the sound system. The music seemed unworldly now as the girl's bellowed curses nearly blotted it out. Forte dumped the girl on the leather sofa, pulled out a knife, and cut the tape from her ankles first, then her hands. He dodged her thrashing limbs and stood back.

She rolled away, then ran for the far corner of the room, picked up a vase and heaved it at Forte's head. He sidestepped it and watched it crash into the sound system behind him. The music stopped. He yawned and sat on the sofa, rubbing his shin where Exxie had kicked him back at the apartment.

Exxie stood still now, her hair a tangled mass over her face as she gulped air. She leaned forward, gripped the back of the sofa and began to sob.

Graham looked back and forth from his daughter to Forte. He carefully bent down and put his empty glass on the coffee table. "Oh, baby," he said. He held out his hands toward her. She ran to him and buried her face in his chest, her crying pitched higher now as she slumped against him. Bryce Graham smoothed the hair on the back of her head with his hand. His eyes bore into Forte as he cooed reassurances into the girl's hair.

Finally he said, "Go up to your room now, please." Exxie hugged her father a moment longer, then pulled away and moved toward the stairs. Once out of her father's line of sight, she stopped and offered a brilliant smile at Forte as she flicked a crude hand gesture in his direction. She resumed her sniffling and slowly ascended the carpeted steps.

Graham strode toward Forte and towered over him, his face crimson. "You...you...you damn junkie, if you harmed a hair on that girl's head...." He released a stream of invective, using some of the same expressions his daughter had. But he stepped no closer to the seated man.

Forte remained slumped on the leather cushions, his arms draped along the back of the sofa. His face was calm. His eyes, however, were not.

Once upon a time, Mr. Graham, he thought, *you'd already be flat on your back right now.* He kept his eyes on Graham's face.

"You're welcome," Forte said.

Graham swayed slightly then sat on the opposite leg of the sofa's "U." He picked up his empty tumbler from the coffee table, looked into the bottom of the glass to see if it somehow had been magically replenished with liquor, then set it back on the table. He flopped backward on the sofa and rubbed his eyes. "I'm sorry. About the junkie remark. Thank you for finding her and bringing her home." He sat up straight. "How did you do it? And where is the man who

47

lured her to meet him?" Graham whirled as if the culprit were in the same room with him.

"Don't worry about him," Forte said. "I'll take care of him."

Graham leaned forward. "Like hell you will. Mr. Forte, I appreciate your help with this matter, but I intend to have the man who took advantage of my daughter prosecuted and put away." His brow furrowed. "And if you choose to try to protect him, you will be dealt with also."

Forte took a deep, slow breath. He blew the air out even more gradually. Why had he smoked his last one of the night already?

"Mr. Graham, shut up."

The tall man leaped to his feet. "You can't talk to me like that in my own house, you little...." He stepped over the low table and grabbed a handful of Forte's shirt.

And found himself flat on his back on the carpet, fighting for breath. He had never seen the quick jab to his solar plexus.

Forte knelt beside him on one knee and gently raised him to a sitting position. "Just relax and breathe slowly. It will come back to you." The taller man's eyes streamed tears. He hacked twice and began taking ragged breaths, his nose and eyes still streaming. Slowly, he teetered to his feet, supported by Forte. "Take a few more breaths," Forte coached him.

After a moment, both men returned to their spots on the sofa.

"I'm going to say this once, Mr. Graham." Forte studied the other's face. The belligerence had been replaced with fear and caution. "You'll do nothing about the young man who was with Exxie. If anything, the evidence indicates that he was the one who was lured into the meeting, not her. I'll guarantee that he won't meet with her again and that will have to be good enough for you. If you choose to prosecute, then we'll just have to let the media in on the story."

Graham said nothing, his breathing still ragged.

Forte continued. "Here's my advice to you: take away all of Exxie's privileges and put her under house arrest until she shows some respect for your rules." He rose to his feet and walked toward the door leading to the courtyard. With his hand on the door handle, he paused. "And one more thing, if Exxie runs away again, don't call me."

Graham raised a hand to wave him weakly from the room. His head flopped backward on the cushion.

Forte started to open the door and caught a movement from the corner of his eye. To his left a corridor ran along the courtyard to a another suite of rooms.

At the end of the hallway, Cheryl Graham leaned against the wall. She mouthed the words "I told you."

On the last word, smoke curled out of her pursed lips.

Chapter 8

"...and I'm proud to have witnessed this first birthday of Raymond, a man I never thought would reach a week of sobriety, much less a year," said the wiry snow-haired man as he let his ocean-blue eyes wash over the group of thirty people seated in folding chairs in the crowded art gallery. The people in the folding chairs laughed at Manny Leard, none louder than the honoree.

The gallery, off an alley near Julia Street, was one of many that dotted the new arts district of New Orleans. Dozens of warehouses and abandoned storefronts had been gutted and had the grime blasted off their shells to make way for artisans and craftspeople. Tourists poured through the area like herds of sheep, not wanting to leave the Big Easy until they put their hands on that one perfect piece of artwork that summed up their vacation experience. The owner of the gallery, himself once a semi-famous watercolorist whose hand had become unsteadied by alcohol, hosted meetings in his upstairs gallery three times a week.

"Seriously, I'm glad to have shared in Raymond's recovery so far because it reminds me that, by God's grace, one day at a time, I can keep going in my own journey and even give a tiny bit of hope to someone walking in the same direction." The group clapped loudly as a black man with a weightlifter's build got up from the first row and hugged the much smaller Manny, enveloping him in bodybuilder arms. The crowd tittered again. The big man took over the podium and began sharing his story in a stuttering bass as Manny took a seat.

Forte stood at the back of the room and inhaled the last of his third cigarette of the day, then blew the smoke toward an open window nearby. Since he had started cutting down on the Checkers, they had never tasted so good. He looked at the butt. *Why do you have to be so bad for me?* He ground it out in a ashtray that resembled a hubcap, then walked over to the back row of chairs and sat next to Manny Leard. The older man leaned close. "You almost missed it," he whispered.

"Sorry," Forte said. "I was out getting kicked by a teenage girl, a client, and for dessert, I punched out her dad."

Manny kept his head forward and cut his eyes to the side. "Alvin Forte," he said. "Master of customer service."

Forte nodded but said nothing else as the man at the podium told the story of his first year of sobriety. As always Forte thought of his own recovery. Four years and counting, day by day, breaking down the pride that kept him from seeking help to begin with—after Ruth's death. *Those lost couple of years after that,* he thought. And then the rehab center, the group discussions, the slow realization that all his ex-Navy SEAL toughness wasn't going to pull him through his problem, his weakness. *Weakness can kill you,* the SEALs had drilled into him. Now he knew that everyone had crumbling, wounded parts inside them, no matter how capable or smart or rich or beautiful they seemed.

"...so, admitting my problem was the first step to getting better," the big man at the podium said. "Yeah, me, big bad Raymond, had a problem." The hulking figure at the podium paused and swallowed hard. He brushed a tear from his cheek and continued talking, his voice rumbling along in a tale of ups and downs, broken dreams and recovered hope.

After Raymond finished his talk, the meeting broke up and people gravitated toward the coffee pot and a huge pan of cake decorated in white icing with the words "You go, Raymond!"

scrawled in blue. From audio speakers hidden among the gallery's easels came the tones of Harry Connick, Jr. A few people immediately took their coffee and cake to the landing at the top of the outside stairs to mix a little nicotine with their other vices.

Forte stood in front of an abstract painting.

"So, is this a monkey holding up a bank with a banana, or is it Moses leading his people out of the wilderness?" Manny asked from his side. "I never could make sense of abstract art."

"Moses never made it out of the wilderness," Forte said, his eyes still on the painting.

"So, you actually were paying attention in Sunday School."

"Us Catholics didn't exactly call it that."

Manny was silent, a condition he could comfortably maintain for hours, for all his natural glibness.

Forte glanced down at his sponsor. "Wanna get your Step Twelve merit badge and hear about my day?"

Manny's blue eyes studied the painting a few seconds longer then flicked to his friend's face. "If you want to tell it."

Forte told it. The request of the Grahams to rescue their daughter Exxie. The encounter with Lucky Battier about the boy Fizer Beal and his knowledge of money stolen from men who would kill without hesitation. The snatching of Exxie from the college boy's apartment. The blowup with the girl's father at the Graham home in the Quarter.

Manny listened quietly, his only movement the sipping of his coffee from a chipped green mug with the faded purple message "laissez le bon temps rouler."

"You told the father, Mr. Graham, not to call you again."

"That about sums it up."

"But you felt free to give him advice on raising his daughter."

"Yep. He needs some advice."

"And you didn't give him the name of the college guy the girl was with."

"Nope."

"Why not?"

"Wouldn't have helped."

"Probably not, but the boy wasn't exactly an innocent victim himself."

"No, but he wasn't exactly a villain either."

"The girl lured him? She's only 14 years old."

"Like her mom said, 14 is a lot older than it used to be. Anyway, that's my best guess, that she set the guy up to meet her. Apparently, she's done it before. When I came through the door of that apartment, the scene looked pretty cozy. Exxie wasn't scared of the guy. She was a willing participant, at least."

Manny went quiet again. Somewhere deep in his eyes danced a tiny sparkle, like the glint of sunshine on a distant ocean wave. "You want to give the college boy another chance." It wasn't a question. "Something about him must've touched you."

Forte turned and gazed above Manny's head at the smokers congregated on the landing beneath the hazy halo of a street lamp. One of the puffers was a recovering junkie, an X-generation hi-tech counterfeiter who once had helped him track a killer. *What was his name? It was...Benny, that's it. About time for Checkers Number Four*, he mused. He took his last cigarette of the day and lit it, took a deep drag, and tilted his head toward the ceiling to release a plume of smoke.

Manny pointed to the "No Smoking" sign on the wall. Forte snubbed out the cigarette.

"Even though the girl doesn't seem so innocent to me, she's still a minor. The college boy could get hammered by a judge wanting to make a point if the parents get their claws into him," Forte said. "Do you still let that group of perverts meet at your church?"

Manny's eyebrows hooded his eyes. "You mean the Purity Group?"

"Yeah."

"I believe they prefer the name 'recovering sex addicts' instead of 'perverts.' And yes, they still meet there." The older man glanced at his watch. "In fact, they'll be there tonight, in about 45 minutes." He paused. "If you happen to take the college guy there, you might avoid the term 'perverts' around them."

Forte nodded and toyed with the shirt pocket that held his cigarette pack. "Yeah, I guess everybody's got something."

"So it seems," said Manny. "By the way, this urge of yours to help this boy reminds me of something I've been needing to bring up. Again."

Forte stopped fiddling with his shirt pocket. "Oh?"

"Yes. When are you going to sponsor someone in the program?"

"I don't know. I told you...."

"That you don't feel ready."

"Yeah."

"And I told you you'll never feel ready. It's not about being ready or steady enough or capable. You just have to be there." Manny's eyes coolly appraised him. "You've been helped by allowing others to help you walk your walk. And you are willing to help others in this whole bodyguard arena where you live your life. It's part of the program to make your pain worth something to someone else who's trying to dig their way out."

Forte held the other man's stare for a long moment, then looked down. "I know."

"You may not feel like it, but it will help you as much or more than it helps the person you're sponsoring."

"So they say," Forte said. He looked at his friend. "Does it help you, having to be my sponsor?"

Manny cocked his head slightly. The weatherworn face slowly formed itself into the semblance of a smile. "More than you can know, my friend."

Chapter 9

Micah Cray slashed at the air, the edge of his left hand a calloused weapon that could smash a much larger opponent to the ground. Instantly his right fist stabbed three times at his shadow assailant, his own guttural shouts punctuating the arm pumping that came so fast that most bystanders witnessing the fight would not have been able to count the number of times he struck. Leaping into the air, he twisted full circle as his left leg feinted and his right foot swung at astonishing speed at a spot six feet above the ground, the exact spot where his enemy's head would have snapped back into unconsciousness.

Cray landed lightly on the carpet in his workout room, an extra upstairs bedroom in his new, two-story suburban home in Metairie. The entire room was padded both for soundproofing and his own protection as he flung himself about to practice his own brand of martial arts. Along one wall of the room, a ceiling-high mirror showed his reflection. He watched now as he stood exactly as he had landed from the kick, poised to resume another imaginary attack. His breathing came relatively easy.

He had moved into this house two months after the attack on his daughter, after carefully constructing a new identity for himself. The family home where he and his wife and daughter had lived remained exactly as he'd left it three months earlier, locked up with the utilities still running. Some clothes had been left scattered in his bedroom—more than he would ordinarily allow himself—to indicate to any unwanted visitor that he had merely left the house earlier in the day.

His new abode was untraceable to his new identity. Cray had no doubt that the FBI would eventually connect him to the murders. Until they did, however, he was determined to make their pursuit as difficult as possible and to take out as many of the perverts as he could. *If they'd done their job to begin with and not coddled them, my Jenny would still be whole. The only justice is that which I execute with my own hands, see with my own eyes.*

Immediately upon moving into his new house—he thought of it only as a house or a base of operations, never a home—he had switched his sleep patterns to the day, working through the nights to outfit the house for his missions. State-of-the-art sensors guarded every corner of his property, allowing him to detect any visitors long before they reached his front door. He had even installed remote cameras on the street lamps at both ends of his street, disguised as a city utility worker doing midnight repairs. His control room contained monitors for the surveillance cameras, a network of three computers set up to monitor local, state, and federal law enforcement radios, and his own computer connected to the Internet with the fastest broadband access available. A closet contained a bin full of untraceable, disposable cell phones. Hidden in the walls were two separate gun closets each containing a cache of weapons capable of wiping out dozens of attackers, if necessary.

Whatever it takes.

In the mirrored wall of his workout room, he examined his form, the muscles of his chest and abdomen where the true strength of a man resides. *Men are fools who build heavy biceps to impress people*, he mused. The pose continued, stock-still, as he studied his form. Would he be ready? The sting of sweat burned his eyes but he continued to watch himself. He peered into the eyes of the man in the mirror. *Fierce enough.* The pain was there, yes, but it was controlled now. By what? Anger? Purpose? Vengeance? *Are you ready?*

Cray kept his stance, his legs bent slightly, arms poised to strike, his body turned diagonal to the mirror. After a full minute, he relaxed and breathed deeply. Taking a towel from a rack on the wall, he wiped it over his face and the brush-cut hair soaked with sweat. He clicked off the light and walked through the dark house, stopping only briefly at the refrigerator for a quart bottle of water. He stopped and tipped back the bottle, then continued to another bedroom. This one had been converted into an office of sorts.

He sat at a black-and-chrome U-shaped workstation and tapped out his screen-saver password on the keyboard. The CNN website was already open. On the top news list, the third item was the headline: Serial Murderer Kills Another Pedophile. He scanned the story until he was satisfied that the authorities had developed no further leads on the case, then he stretched and slowly rotated his head, his eyes closed against the blue glow of the computer monitor.

Immediately after shooting the man two days earlier, he had driven to the most crime-ridden area of St. Louis and left the Jeep with the keys in it. He'd hefted the black nylon bag with his rifle inside and jogged two blocks to the decrepit apartment where he had lived for ten days while stalking his victim. A roach resort, but one with a redeeming feature—the one-car lockable garage. There he had kept his van, packed and filled with fuel.

During the drive back, he experienced little of the emotional rollercoaster he had ridden after the first murder. He wondered if the lack of feelings now was a good sign or a bad one. He shrugged and clicked on the radio. It only took twenty minutes for the first news flashes to begin interrupting the music. He shook his head. *The media scum probably beat the cops to the scene.*

He hit the scan button until a talk show came up. "...and if you ask me, the guy should be given a medal for killing those perverts...." He listened for a while as the pro-killer callers poured into the radio station and out through the speakers in his vehicle. One caller meekly wondered if justice was being served by praising such vigilante acts. He was rapidly hooted off the air by the talk show host.

Obviously you've not had a daughter or niece or nephew molested by some lower-than-lowlife who should've stayed locked up.

Cray had clicked off the radio and drove in silence through the night. He had arrived home in the early morning hours and had slept all day. Upon awakening, he had worked out the stiffness of the long drive with an hour-long routine of the martial arts exercises he'd developed in the past few months. He had concentrated on the tactics and fight sequences specifically designed to kill an opponent.

No more B.S. about the honor of leaving an opponent alive in order to learn from his disrespectful mistakes. At the keyboard, Cray opened his eyes. That time was past.

He turned to the computer again and brought up the database he had developed. Throughout the nation, police departments and law enforcement buffs had posted lists of known pedophiles who had been released from prison after serving their sentences. Cray had pulled those lists into his own computer and had augmented their basic information with his own carefully collected data. Along the walls of his office were book after book on the behavior and patterns of the deviants, those men who stalked children to satisfy themselves. He had spent hours poring over the reports and psychological journals until he had been satisfied that he understood their behavior as much as he needed.

Not to help them. But to kill them.

Before his daughter had been attacked, he had never noticed the way the courts handled sex offenders. Like most people, he had assumed they were prosecuted and locked up, never to harm a child again. Like most people, he had been ignorant of the system. Sex offenders, even multiple child molesters, were often given chance after chance to mend their ways. They were separated from the general prison population or, more often, assigned to cushy federal mental hospitals where they roamed at will inside walls surrounding park-like grounds. Their days were filled with group meetings and counseling sessions with sympathetic psychiatrists determined to help them rebuild their self-worth because, as everyone knew, these men were simply acting out their impulses in an attempt to escape their own pain and fear.

Meanwhile, Cray knew, *their future victims played in their yards or neighborhood parks, blissfully unaware of their own future pain and fear at the hands of men without remorse in pursuit of their own perverse satisfaction.*

He quickly clicked through the screens of his database program until the computer screen displayed a list of thirty men he had analyzed as most likely to strike again after being released from prison. So far, he had guessed right: the first three on his list had chosen to approach children within three weeks of their release, despite their close supervision in outpatient psychiatric programs. He had been waiting for them, saving the children that the men had targeted.

His only regret was that he couldn't kill them twice.

Scanning the list on the screen, his eyes stopped at his next victim. This one was not next in line on his probability list. But there were other factors that attracted Cray's attention. He lived in the New Orleans area and, although he'd not attacked any innocent children since he'd been released from a non-resident sex offender program two years earlier, he had been visiting under-age prostitutes regularly during the past few months.

Cray had the feeling he would strike again. And soon.

And when you do, I'll be there with your just reward.

Chapter 10

The apartment door had been hastily repaired, the ragged hole around the lock covered with a piece of cardboard box with the words "Crown Royal" showing between the gray strips of Duct tape.

Forte rapped on the door frame.

Nothing.

"Gaffney, open up. Now."

From inside the apartment came the sounds of scurrying.

"Gaffney?"

The movements stopped but still no response.

Forte looked back over his shoulder at the apartment across the landing. Everything was still quiet. He leaned close to the door he'd smashed a couple of hours earlier. "Rick, I'm not going to hurt you. But there will be trouble for you if you don't let me in. I have to talk to you. Now." He listened again then put his mouth near the hole where the doorknob once was. "Open up."

Inside, he heard the sound of furniture being moved away from the door. He pushed the door and it cracked open. He stepped into the den. The smell of whiskey swarmed over him.

Across the room, Gaffney stood staring at him wild-eyed, a butcher knife hanging from his right hand.

Forte casually moved to his left, then closed the door. He lowered himself into an overstuffed love seat in the corner of the den.

Gaffney watched him silently. His eyes were rimmed red.

Forte jerked his head toward a chair. "Sit down."

The boy remained standing.

"Do it. Now!"

The boy jerked involuntarily, then slowly sat down, his hand still on the knife.

Forte exhaled slowly and slumped back in the loveseat. "You didn't know Exxie before tonight?"

The boy blinked. "No. We'd chatted...online...but I didn't know...."

"You didn't know what? That she was only 14?"

"Hell, no. She said she was a college student."

"But when you met, did you ask her how old she was?"

Gaffney closed his eyes and rubbed them with his fingertips. "Yeah, but she lied. Hey, you saw her. Does she look 14?"

Forte studied the boy's face for a moment. "No. No, she doesn't look 14. Whatever 14 is supposed to look like these days."

The liquor fumes lapped at his nostrils like flames, reminding him of other rooms long ago where new friends with no names shared empty pleasures. *But they seemed so right at the time, didn't they?*

"But Exxie is 14. That means you could be charged with statutory rape," Forte said.

Gaffney grimaced. "We didn't do anything. You came in before...."

"You could have done something though. You don't really know what Exxie would say if the police were called in and eventually she was called to testify in court. And it would be up to a jury to choose who they would believe—you or her."

"Man, you should have seen the things she said in the chat room. She knew what she was doing, I swear."

"But she is 14. The law calls it rape."

Gaffney put his head in his hands.

"I didn't give Exxie's father your name."

Gaffney looked up, astonished.

"But you have to do what I tell you."

"What? Tell me. Anything."

"There's a support group. You have to meet with them."

"What?"

"It's called the Purity Group. I'm going to take you there right now."

"Man, this is crazy."

"Yes," said Forte. "It is."

* * *

Manny Leard's church was actually a gutted old store in the French Quarter with cracked plaster walls and the everpresent perfume of Lysol. Every Sunday night, a concoction of humanity wandered through the peeling double doors and sat in metal folding chairs to worship. Once a pastor of an established wealthy church in the midwest, Manny had been relieved of his duties for refusing to acknowledge his alcoholism.

After a decade of aimless wandering and self-delusion, Manny had faced his problem, sobered up, and taken the assignment in New Orleans. Before he arrived, three young pastors had quit the inner-city ministry within 18 months, none of them able to stomach the stench of misery that wafted past the doorway of the church. Manny thrived on it. "If you believe Christ's promise that the lowly would receive grace, what better place to be?" Manny had said, his cracked-leather face arranged in a grin.

The old man lived above the church, which was available for use by any group needing it.

"Al Forte?" A wiry man with green eyes and rimless glasses extended his hand. Forte shook it, noticing the rippling of the man's forearms. *Shortstop. Maybe second base.*

"It's For-TAY."

He was half a head shorter than Forte's six-foot-even. The smaller man's grip was strong. "I'm David Jones. I lead this group. Manny called me. Said you might show up with a guest."

Forte had made Rick Gaffney follow him back to the Quarter in his car. He had parked his motorcycle at The Refuge's garage nearby and walked back over to Manny's place. Gaffney stood next to the two men and stared at a point on the wall, saying nothing and giving no indication he heard them. In the far corner a half-dozen men stood next to a folding table, drinking coffee from Styrofoam cups and making small talk.

Forte waved Gaffney to the area near the coffee table, then motioned the group leader to another corner of the room. They sat in folding chairs.

"Tell me about this group."

Jones smiled and gave a single appreciative nod. "Manny said you liked to come to the point quickly. Not much for small talk. Which is fine." The man leaned forward, rested his forearms on his knees and continued talking, his voice low but steady. "I'm a certified counselor and work with clients struggling with addictions of all types. I specialize in helping those wanting to overcome sexual addiction. This group started up a couple of years ago."

"Sex addicts," Forte said.

"Yes."

"I guess I didn't think...."

"That there actually was such a thing?"

"Yes. I mean, I know about addiction. I'm a recovering cocaine addict."

Jones was watching him intently now, his expression unchanged, still pleasantly neutral. "But you don't buy the whole 'sex addict' label."

"Well...."

"A lot of people think it's just an excuse, just a load of psychobabble designed to pamper criminals and perverts. Then again, some people think the same thing about programs for recovering drug addicts."

Forte searched the man's face for a sign of sarcasm and saw none.

Jones gave a small jerk of his head toward the men around the coffee machine. "These guys come from all walks of life—doctors, lawyers, accountants, teachers. We even have a cop who comes to the group. They've all gotten caught up in some type of addictive sexual patterns and they want to break free. But it's tough because they feel like there's no place to turn for support.

"On one hand, we are bombarded daily with the stereotypical 'men will be men' mentality, where guys joke about sex and women and try to act like that's just the normal way men should behave, if they are so-called 'real' men. That kind of mindset says, 'Hey, what's the big deal? Sex, any kind of sex, is okay. Don't worry about it.'

"On the other hand, you have people who think sex is only right for heterosexuals who are married. Church people. Unfortunately, too many churches turn their backs on men, or women for that matter, who struggle with sexual 'acting out.' It's almost as if they are afraid it's infectious. Not physically but spiritually." Jones paused and rubbed his eyes. "They think that if a guy only had enough faith, he wouldn't be drawn into unhealthy sexual patterns."

Forte waved his hand. "Not interested in what churches think about sexual addiction. Just tell me how your group helps these guys."

Jones smiled but his blue eyes seemed to fade to a shade of steel. "But the thing about churches plays a part in it for most of the guys who come to the Purity Group. What they are wanting is to learn what it means to be sexual in the context of their religion, or more accurately, in the context of their relationship with Christ. This is a Christian program, not just a 12-step addiction recovery program.

"Because of that, we deal more with the actual chemical high that a man's brain reaches in the sex act, whether that sex act happens with his wife or whether it happens in what we would call an unhealthy situation—with a prostitute or through self-manipulation after viewing Internet pornography. What we are really dealing with are intimacy issues. These men have developed destructive patterns that block intimacy. To paint it with a broad brush stroke, they've substituted porn or hookers for the real kind of intimacy we all need from the human relationships in our lives."

Forte said nothing, letting the man's words soak in. *What if you're so numb inside that you have no kind of intimacy, even false intimacy.*

Aloud, he said, "Where do you draw the line?"

Jones cocked his head. "What do you mean?"

"Is there any type of sex addict you don't allow here?"

"Good question. It's tough to draw that kind of line, actually, even though within the group itself sometimes we have a guy with one type of problem who looks down at a guy with another type of problem. I do personally draw the line with repeat sex offenders who've done jail time. There are some guys who come to the group under court order sometimes. But they don't usually hang around long. Does that answer your question?"

"Well, almost. Here it is, bluntly. Do you let child molesters come to the group?"

Jones held Forte's gaze steadily for a moment, then took off his glasses, polished them with a napkin drawn from his pocket. He carefully put them back on before answering. "That's a tough question, Mr. Forte, especially with all the crimes going on in our country involving young kids being sexually abused, some murdered. Mainly we try to help men who come here to deal with their problem before it becomes some type of criminal offense. There have been men who come to the group after having been charged with touching a child illegally. They are first-time offenders who have been ordered by a judge to attend the group in lieu of jail-time. They also must be seeing a counselor on a regular basis. I know it may sound like liberal bull-crap to a lot of people, but believe me, I'm as far from liberal as you can get.

"I just have a hard time saying that the healing grace of God is not big enough for any offense, as heinous as that offense might be. So, that's what we try to be here—a place, a safe place, where we can be accountable to one another and encourage one another to do the right thing."

Jones glanced over at the group who had wandered over to a circle of metal folding chairs. He stood up to shake the bodyguard's hand again. "Having said that, if a man chooses to molest a child again after having attended this group, I bar him from the group after he does his jail time and refer him to a psychiatric outpatient program specializing in dealing with pedophiles."

Forte looked over at the group in the chairs as he shook the counselor's hand. Gaffney sat with his head slumped, his arms folded tightly over his chest. "Thanks for talking with me." He motioned toward Rick Gaffney. "He might not open up too much. It wasn't his idea to come here, but he didn't really have a choice, if you know what I mean."

Jones smiled, his eyes blue again and each framed with a tiny fan of wrinkles. "He will be fine. It's a safe place."

Forte looked around at the stained walls and the cracks zigzagging across the floor. Somehow, under the bluish brightness of the flourescent industrial-strength lights hanging from the ceiling, it did seem like a safe place, for those who needed safety.

He turned and walked out into the night.

* * *

Micah Cray slumped in a doorway across the street from Manny's place and watched the man leave the meeting room. The man was a bit broader in the chest than Cray and his movements were fluid, like an athlete. But there was something else. He seemed ready, as if he'd had training to be continually aware of his surroundings. Police training, maybe. Or military. *Why was he leaving the meeting after just arriving with the younger guy?*

66

As the man drew close, Cray watched carefully from beneath his disguise. He seemed familiar. Had he seen him somewhere before?

Cray had hoped to follow his new quarry tonight. He knew the pervert had attended the meeting a couple of times in the past month, by court order. As if that was going to help him. Cray had donned the smelly rags he'd chosen to stake out the meeting and had driven down to the French Quarter from his new house in Metairie. After parking his van six blocks away, he had taken out the bottle of cheap wine and weaved his way to this empty doorstep. He splashed some of the wine on himself to blend in with the rest of the stinking Quarter and waited in the shadows, listening to the faint blaring of the club bands on Bourbon Street a few blocks over.

But the pervert hadn't shown.

He had watched the man with the black crewcut go into the meeting, his hand clamped on the arm of the younger man as if he were escorting him. The younger guy wasn't resisting, just shuffling along with his head bowed. A few minutes later, the black-haired man came out and walked at a steady pace down the sidewalk toward the north part of the French Quarter.

Cray watched him walk past without glancing at the bum swaddled in grime in the doorway. Two blocks down, the man turned the corner.

Immediately two men popped out of their own hiding places in the next block and scurried after the black-haired man. In the block past the corner, another pair of men hurried toward an alleyway about 20 yards from the spot where the man had turned.

Ahhhh. Looks like trouble.

Cray looked toward the open door of Manny's church meeting room, then back toward the direction the man had gone. He got up and shuffled down the sidewalk.

Chapter 11

Forte meandered back toward his apartment.

He had noticed the bedraggled figure slumped in the doorway across from Manny's. The man reeked, for sure, and for a brief moment, something about him seemed out of place. Almost too perfectly grimy even in a town where the perpetually unwashed homeless congregated in the Quarter and carried their shopping bags and precious five-gallon buckets everywhere they went.

Forte had kept his weight forward and his arms loose at his sides as he had walked past the bum. The man hadn't budged as he walked past, however. *Hmmm...guess I was wrong.* Forte trudged back toward his apartment and forgot about the man, his thoughts wandering back to what the counselor had told him at Manny's church meeting room.

Jones had called the Purity Group meeting *"...a safe place, where we can be accountable to one another and encourage one another to do the right thing."* Forte pondered that. That might be fine for the men struggling with their problems, but what about the others, the victims? He had founded Forte Security with a single mission: protect and rescue children in trouble. Among the dozens of clients he had helped were several children who had been abused, physically and sexually. Were some of those perpetrators like the men at the meeting?

He heard himself sighing in the sticky night. A brassy snatch of "The Basin Street Blues" came from some street corner nearby. He ran a hand along a sore muscle in the back of his neck. The struggle with Exxie Graham and the spat with her father had taken more out of him than he had admitted to himself. It had been a long day. Just this morning he had been sweating through the rescue exercise at the Blackthorn Training Center. Then the adventure with the Grahams, the encounter with Lucky Battier, the reminder that Fizer Beal was in serious danger from some of the most dangerous people in the Big Easy, if not the entire country. *Oh for another cigarette.*

He turned the corner. From here he could see the balcony of his apartment in the next block. In the dim light two stories above the street, the outline of a black cat on the balcony rail seemed darker than the night itself. "Boo kitty," he said aloud to the cat. "You are the black panther of the Quarter."

The nearly silent footstep of the man behind him was his only warning. Nearly silent, but not quite.

Forte bobbed to his right as a man's boot grazed his back. The speed of the kick let him know he would have been dropped to the gutter if it had connected.

He whirled to face the man and saw there were two of them. The closest man, the kicker, was his height but more muscle-bound. His partner, leaner and taller, was circling to his right. Both were dressed in black and moved like they knew what they were doing.

As he backed toward the wall of the building, Forte shuffled to his left to cut off the tall man and prevent himself from being outflanked. The kicker was moving closer, bouncing on the balls of his feet like a boxer. On the balcony above them, Boo the cat emitted a guttural growl. The kicker glanced up. Forte punched him in the Adam's apple. The man went down, gurgling and clutching his throat.

Forte turned to face the tall attacker who had lunged at him. He dodged the roundhouse punch intended for his jaw and caught it on the shoulder. The man was thin but strong. Forte pretended to stumble slightly and the attacker lashed out again. This time, Forte caught his arm, drew him forward, and smashed an elbow hard into his ribs. *Snap.* The man went down with a broken rib.

A hard punch from behind sent Forte to his knees. A streak of pain tore through his lower back from the sucker punch to his kidney. He managed to partly deflect a kick from one of the two other attackers who had snuck up behind him. He knew he would not be able to dodge another kick.

Suddenly a flurry of rags and the smell of sour wine swept past him. A man squared off against the man who'd kidney-punched him. His new defender feinted once with a jab which the attacker slapped away only to find himself slapped twice by the new opponent's other hand. Forte recognized the man. It was the bum he had passed on the sidewalk. Now, however, he looked neither drunk nor listless.

Moving easily, the bum slammed one of the attackers with a roundhouse kick, putting the man on the sidewalk. The other attacker swung a billy club. The bum let the club whoosh past him and, using the momentum of the swing, grabbed his attacker's arm and slammed him against the side of the building. Dust sprinkled from a ledge above at the impact.

The bum leapt forward across the sidewalk to the fallen man, knelt, and drew back his fist. Forte had seen the move before. It was meant to kill.

"No," he croaked.

The bum stopped, his arm cocked back, fist poised. "He was going to kill you. He deserves to be taken out." His face was covered in grime and hidden in shadow under the bill of a dirty ball cap. Forte couldn't see his eyes.

Behind them, a door opened at the end of the building. "Hey," someone called out. "Al? Al Forte, is that you?"

The bum stood up and silently backed away toward the opening of the alley.

Forte dragged himself up on one elbow and watched the men who had jumped him haul themselves down the street and around the corner, the man with the broken rib clutching his side and swearing. Forte shifted on the sidewalk and turned back to the alley.

The bum was gone.

* * *

Stupid, stupid, stupid. Cray sprinted through the alley to the next block. Slowing, he peered down the street and then dashed across to another alley. A voice called out from a pile of cardboard boxes as he passed. "Spare a dolluh?" He ignored the plea and kept moving as he made his way back to his van.

Why had he joined the street fight? That kind of mistake drew attention to him, attention that could only hurt him in the long run. He had vowed to wipe out as many perverts as possible before being discovered. Even then, he knew he would not allow himself to be captured.

But this—this was simply stupid.

When he finally got back to the spot where he'd parked the van, he stopped to watch and listen. It was after midnight, but revelers were still streaming along the street toward the clubs on Bourbon Street a few blocks away. The foot traffic seemed normal as groups in twos and fours tripped along chatting. Typically, none of the tourists even glanced at a bum leaning against the wall. No one was paying any particular attention to the van parked on the street. And no one seemed to be following him. Good.

He stumbled over to the van and walked around to the passenger side. When the pedestrian traffic waned, he quickly let himself into the vehicle. He shucked off the rank clothes, hat, and beard and stuffed them into a garbage bag. He lowered himself onto the carpet in the back of the van and took a deep breath. In the darkness, he felt himself smiling.

He put a hand up to his mouth and let his fingertips trace the curve of his lips as he touched the grin. *What was so funny?* How long had it been? How long since anything seemed remotely amusing to him? He realized it wasn't humor that caused the smile. But what was it?

He hadn't intended to become involved when the four men tried to mug the man with the black crewcut. He shook his head. It wasn't a mugging, he decided. They were sent to beat the man into submission. But for what?

After he had noticed the men shadowing the guy, he had followed along to see what would happen. *Al Forte*, that was the name the woman had called out at the end of the fight.

Forte had showed prowess against the first two attackers. He knew how to fight, definitely. The second pair of men had sucker-punched him. Cray had surprised himself with his reaction. He found himself defending the man, a man he had never met and even suspected of being soft toward the perverts who came to the meeting.

No, it was nothing about the man himself or the fact that Cray had saved his life that conjured this smile in the van's solitude. Maybe it was the fight itself.

He had always stayed in good shape since his military days with the Rangers, even after he'd taken the desk job with his father-in-law's trucking company. He had worked out regularly and still could easily outpace most men 15 years younger in a five-mile run. Since the attack on his daughter, he had stepped up his martial arts training, spending hours sharpening his skills until the exercise mat was soaked with sweat.

But all of his kills had been from a distance. He had used the sniper rifle exclusively, picking them off from a hundred yards or more, a ridiculously easy shot compared to the kills he had made from four and five times that distance with the Rangers. Tonight, it had been close contact fighting and he had come out on top. He had felt the impact of his punches and kicks and it had flooded him with adrenalin. He was euphoric.

Maybe the next kill won't be from such a distance.

He sidled between the front seats of the van and sat behind the wheel. He hit the switch to lower the window on the driver's side, then turned the remote control knob for the outside mirror, positioning it so he could see his face. Taking a handkerchief, he wiped the fake grime from his face and watched his appearance change back from a filthy, homeless loser to a 40-year-old man with sharp features and short-cropped sandy hair.

* * *

Lucky Battier sat perfectly still on the balcony across from The Refuge, his feet propped on an old mission bench, his hands laced over his vest. If someone in another building did happen to notice him, they would have assumed he was sleeping. He had not budged in more than an hour.

He had remained perfectly still as his men attacked Forte, knowing that his old high-school football opponent would put at least a couple of them on the ground even though the men he'd sent were a cut above the regular leg-breakers he would normally use. Mr. Marchetti had been infuriated and had ordered the attack. He had merely nodded, then had made it happen.

But he wanted to see it first hand. *Never hurts to scope out the competition,* his daddy had often said. He might have to face Forte himself one day.

Forte had dispatched the first two men fairly easily, just as Lucky had predicted. That's why he had sent two waves of attackers.

When the bum showed up, he still didn't move, except for the arching of his right eyebrow. *Who was this guy?*

He obviously knew what he was doing. If the fight hadn't been broken up, his men would have been seriously injured, if not killed. He'd seen the man put his knee in one of his thug's chest and rear back for a killing blow. But Forte had stopped him. *The bleeding heart.*

The man was undercover. Was he a cop? No, he would've hung around and flashed his badge. That's what cops did. The bum had dashed away through the alley. Lucky had phoned his men to follow him but they were too beat up to do any good tracking the guy.

He shrugged. *Let him go.*

Lucky watched as Forte was helped into the offices of Forte Security in the next block. The kidney punch had stunned him, he could tell.

You won't win this time, Al. I'll find the boy before you do.

Chapter 12

Forte looked up from reloading the clip for his Glock and watched the target jerk at the end of the next lane of the firing range. Round after round punched through the featureless head of the man-shaped target in a half-dollar-sized grouping. Finally the shooting stopped. The target slid forward on the mechanized pulley until it stopped directly in front of the shooter next to him. The unmistakable smell of burnt gunpowder seeped over from the next stall.

He leaned around the back of the partition and tapped on the shoulder of Jackie Shaw. She turned from examining the target she'd decimated, pulled off her ear protectors and grinned. "Guess he won't be bothering the schoolmarm again."

"Guess not," Forte said. "Good shooting."

"Thanks." Jackie popped out the magazine on her own nine-millimeter Glock and clicked another into place. She replaced the torn paper target with a fresh one and sent it back out. After slipping on her ear protectors, she settled into a shooting stance again: legs apart, knees slightly bent, arms extended but bent at the elbows, not locked. Her right hand, the shooting hand, was wrapped around the pistol grip while her left palm cupped the butt of the grip, steadying her shots. Her hair was cut short and Forte could see the muscles in her neck contract, then release as she began shooting again. The results were the same, if not better. She took off the ear protectors.

"Your dad ever want you to join the force in Boston?" Forte twinged as he felt the bruise in his lower back. He sat in a folding chair and leaned back.

"Nah, he said one cop in the family was enough. He wanted me to be the next Olga Korbut." She set the pistol on the small, wooden shelf across the front of the shooting stall. "But he didn't mind it that I learned how to shoot."

"I bet." Forte couldn't put his finger on what it was about Jackie Shaw that amused him. *Intrigued him?* He had seen the gold medals for both target shooting and gymnastics, two areas in which the woman had excelled. Maybe it was the fact that she had decided to become a nun after her no-account husband had left her.

He shrugged and winced in pain.

"What are you thinking about?" Jackie asked. "Are you okay?"

"Nothing. And yeah, I'm fine."

She rolled her eyes. "Macho man. Your spleen could have been ruptured with a punch to the back like that." She brushed her hair off her forehead, sat in the chair next to him and studied his face. "You're pretty sure they were sent from Marchetti?"

"No doubt about it," he said, his words disappearing into the room. The four-lane shooting range on the bottom floor of The Refuge was so insulated that no shots could be heard in the adjoining rooms. The only sound in the range came from the hum of the air conditioner vents.

"Why didn't you call the cops?"

"What good would that've done?"

"The police would have at least known that it happened. They could've questioned Luke Battier or his boss."

Forte gave a snort of a laugh that jolted his bruised back. "Believe me, the cops have bigger fish to fry when it comes to Marchetti."

"But the D.A. wants to keep Fizer safe so he can testify...."

"Marchetti's men weren't trying to get to the boy last night. They were just delivering a message."

"To let you know that Mr. Marchetti was still very interested in the boy."

"Right."

The room went silent again for a moment, as if all sound had been sucked out of the air. Forte closed his eyes and tilted his head back against the wall of the hallway that bordered the shooting booths. *Somewhere there are people who get up and have breakfast and kiss their kids goodbye and whistle as they drive to their safe, normal office jobs.* Then again, Manny had reminded him repeatedly that normality was a myth, that no matter how much a person seemed to have it all under control, it was an impossibility; there was something going on under the surface, always. Us addicts, Manny proclaimed, just have the blessed opportunity of dealing with our weakness right out in front of God and everybody. The thing was, Manny wasn't just joking around when he said it; he really believed it.

The fragrance of flowers floated through his mind, bringing a smile to his lips. Ruth had smelled of fresh petals: he never could remember the name of those...what were they? Funny he'd never noticed those kinds of smells before her; his world had been filled with the fragrance of locker rooms and hair tonic and gunpowder. But never flowers. It was her scent now drifting through his consciousness, the sensation of his face buried in her hair as they lay in bed while he wondered how she ever chose him to spend those few short years with and why he never told her the deep thoughts, the dammed up emotions he had for her, that love he felt but never fully expressed. "Ruth, Ruth...."

"You falling asleep on me?" Jackie's gentle voice jolted him back to the present. Her face was close enough for him to take in the floral scent of her shampoo.

He rubbed his eyes. "Not enough sleep. Sorry."

"No problem. A girl can tell when she has lost a man's attention."

Forte chuckled. "One of my first rules of life: never ignore a woman with a gun."

"You got that right." She paused. "I thought you accidentally called me...by her name."

He turned to face her. "What was I saying?"

"Her name...you said it twice. 'Ruth, Ruth'...."

Forte rocked his head back and forth on his shoulders. "I must've dozed off."

Jackie nodded and let a minute of silence pass.

"You think of her a lot?"

Forte stopped rocking and considered her question. *Do I think of Ruth much?*

Jackie leaned forward to stand up. "I'm sorry. I'm being nosy."

He put out a hand. "No, it's okay. I'm just thinking."

She sat back again, waiting.

"It's like this," he said. "In some ways, it's like she's never far away from the surface of my mind, even after five years, like the way the sensation of a nice dream sticks with you for a while even when you aren't consciously trying to remember the details of the dream.

"But in another way, I try not to concentrate on the memories because...." He paused, thinking.

"Because it still hurts too much," Jackie said, her voice a whisper.

Forte felt his throat constricting. He coughed and cleared it. He suddenly felt like escaping. *Why are we talking about this?*

She reached over and squeezed his arm briefly then released it.

"You think Fizer knows where the money is?"

He cleared his throat again. "I think he does," he said, thankful she had changed the subject. "I'm just not sure why Marchetti is coming after him instead of getting it from his dad, Teddy."

"Even though Teddy is in federal prison?"

"Hey, that's no problem for Marchetti. He could send a half dozen guys after Theodore Beal within an hour."

"Maybe he thinks it's easier to force the boy to tell it instead."

"Maybe. But it's a lot tougher to get to Fizer here than it is to get to the dad in jail."

"Hmmm...maybe there's something else."

Forte turned to face her again. "That's what I'm thinking. But I can't figure out what it could be."

Her brow was furrowed. "Me neither." She stood up and offered her hand. "Need help up out of that chair?"

Forte waved her away, then leaned forward. "Unhhhh...." A groan crept out of his mouth. "On second thought...."

She grabbed his hand and pulled him up, putting an arm around him to steady him. "C'mon, old man, I'll go get the wheelchair for you."

Forte could feel the definition of her muscles along her shoulder and back as she leaned against him.

"I can make it," he said.

"Yeah, but we can't have you gimpin' around at that shindig with Ms. Rosalind Dent tonight."

He grinned. "How'd you know about that?"

Jackie batted her eyes. "Oh, word gets around."

"Yeah, loose lips sink ships and all that. It's just a local law enforcement banquet anyway. She needed an escort." Rosie Dent was acting Agent In Charge of the FBI office in New Orleans.

Jackie nodded seriously. "Of course."

"That's right."

"And it probably doesn't hurt that she looks like a model."

Forte rubbed his chin and studied the ceiling of the shooting range. "Wonder where she's going to keep her gun?"

Chapter 13

Just where I need to be...on top of the world, mused Exxie Graham as she balanced precariously on one leg atop the pyramid of cheerleaders.

"...and we're the ones to beat!" The cheer ended with a synchonized collapse of the pyramid as the girls tumbled into the ending formation for the cheer. Exxie rolled on the mats in the gym and sprang up into an athletic kick to punctuate the yell.

The cheerleader's choreographer picked up her bullhorn. "That's it for today, girls. Be here for practice same time on Monday. And work on your dance steps!"

As usual, the rest of the freshman pep squad gathered around Exxie, the team captain, after practice. The first football game was exactly two weeks away, and there were three new routines to polish.

"You meeting us at Zany's?" a thin, orange-haired girl asked her. "The guys are coming."

"Not today, Brianna." Exxie felt no need to give an excuse. She was clearly the leader of the cheerleaders in every way. In fact, no girl in school had developed like she had. She doubted that some of them ever would.

She pulled out her cell phone and called her driver for the day, a man assigned by her father to pick her up after cheerleader practice. "I'm walking out now. Be at the curb by the south entrance," she snapped. "And you better have it cold in that car." She popped the phone back into her leather backpack. She was bent on making anyone from her dad's company feel her wrath as much as possible.

At the end of the gym near the exit to the street, a group of older football players leaned on the wall and watched her pass. When she looked directly at them, not a single boy was looking at her. She knew, however, their heads would swivel when she turned and swayed toward the door. Even in her workout sweats, she knew she would draw their immature glances. But these boys were a thing of the past for Exxie Graham.

Outside the gym, August in New Orleans wrapped itself around her in hot dampness. She immediately felt the tiny sweat drops pop up on the back of her neck beneath her swaying ponytail. The limousine pulled up to the curb and the driver leapt out of the car to open her door. She didn't make eye contact with the older man, but she sensed he was aware of her. Without a word, she got into the back seat.

Immediately she hit the button to raise the opaque divider between the front and back sections of the limousine. She despised making small talk with most of her father's underlings.

As the car made its way to her home, the girl replayed in her mind the previous night's adventures. "Exxie honey, are you okay?" her dad had whispered last night after throwing that bully out of their house. She had positioned herself face down among the pillows and stuffed animals on her bed, waiting for him to come up the stairs. At his words, she whirled and screamed at him through her tears, "How could you do that to me? That man...that Forte man hurt me!"

Bryce Graham's face was ashen after the encounter with Forte. She could tell he'd been drinking. Again. He held out his arms to his daughter. "Oh, baby. I was worried sick about you. I thought you had been...."

"You thought what?" she hissed. "That I was so stupid and young that I couldn't take care of myself, that I couldn't go out with a friend for a few hours?" She threw a stuffed bunny at him and watched it bounce off his shoulder and fall to the carpet. She burst into tears again.

Graham gathered the girl into his arms and patted her. "No, I don't think you are stupid. But, honey, you were supposed to be grounded. We didn't know where you were." Her tears soaked the front of his shirt.

Her mother appeared in the doorway of her bedroom, watching father and daughter. She said nothing but locked eyes briefly with Exxie before walking away.

The night had ended with her father's pronouncement, delivered almost apologetically, that her grounding would be extended another week. She had protested enough to let her parents feel they had delivered just punishment.

But she knew she would have other plans. Soon.

Such idiots to think they could control her. They had no clue whatsoever. Exxie barely remembered a time when her parents planned regular family outings. For years she had laughed at some of her friends when they moaned about "family night" at their homes, where mom and dad and the kids all played board games or watched old movies while piled up on the sofa together.

Her parents had drunkenly laughed at their cocktail parties while their precious Exxie had slurped the wine from half-filled glasses and careened around the room to the amusement of the rest of the rich sots. Not to mention the groping she received from her dad's pals after being cornered in some remote spot in the house. *Those were the days.*

She had grown up fast and was proud of it. She'd reached the point where she could take care of herself and nobody—not her parents or her teachers or the police—was going to tell her what to do.

Thump! The limousine hit a pothole in front of the Graham house, snapping Exxie back to the present. The car pulled through the driveway leading back to the courtyard. She hopped out without a word and skipped into the house. *Ahhhhh—freedom.*

The maid had left the house spotless. A single sheet of paper lay on the countertop that divided the open layout of the house between the den and the glass-and-metal dining table and chairs.

"Out for a dinner banquet.—Dad and Mom" the note read.

"Good riddance," Exxie said aloud in the empty house.

After grabbing a bottle of wine, some Pringles, and a KitKat bar from the kitchen, she went upstairs to her room. Moving the laptop from her desk to bed, she flipped it open and typed her password to log in. She waited as the hard drive whirred, the antivirus software did its thing, and her special anti-snoop software popped up to tell her no one had logged on to the computer while she was gone. Her parents were so trusting. *The fools.*

And now for a little cruisin' music. She ran her fingernails over the CD rack next to the bed, listening to the *clickety-clickety-click* until she came to a Limp Bizkit disk. Crank up the volume, zoom through the Net to her special places, those hidden cyber-caves where you can be anything you want to be and say anything you want to say. Nobody looking over her shoulder, no rules, no restrictions, total control. All at her fingertips.

She logged in to her favorite chat room as one of her pet net names, XXXgurl. She recognized most of the other names in the room. A couple of boys from her school hung out here along with some other guys from the universities in the area.

XXXgurl: Kisses to all the REAL men here.

StudTuffin: Heyyyy gurlllll. U smokinnnnn.

BadBoy: Mmmmm, been missing those x-kisses.

FriskMe: Now it will warm up in here, hahahahaha.

Exxie bantered with the boys in the room. Several secret requests for private chats popped up. She ignored them all and continued to trade small talk in the general public room. She knew all the boys here and had teased them unmercifully over the past few months. Tonight, she wanted to meet someone new.

She scanned the list of user names currently in the chatroom. There was a new one. MuchoMan. Actually she'd seen him lurking in the room a couple of times before. He said little. *The quiet type huh.* She decided to check him out.

XXXgurl: Hey MuchoMan...are you? ☺

The metal guitar riffs crashed around her in the sanctuary of her room. She didn't hear them. She was in another place. A place she controlled. She waited to see if the guy would take the bait. *Ahhhh, come on now....*

MuchoMan: No brag. The name says it all.

Exxie smiled. *Gotcha.*

* * *

Micah Cray propped his feet on the computer desk and watched the cyber-scene unfold as his quarry met the girl in the chatroom.

The man calling himself MuchoMan was actually in his early 40s but was posing as a college student, flirting with the girls until he could lure one into a private chat. There he would engage them in the filthiest of scenarios, pushing all the right buttons to make them feel understood and flattered in ways they hadn't experienced from the fumbling high school boys in their young lives. After warming them up and desensitizing them to the danger of meeting strangers, the pervert would ask for an address to send gifts. From there, he would arrange a meeting in a public place and politely give more expensive tokens of his affection.

Eventually he would lure them into a private meeting.

So far, three girls had succumbed to that final invitation and had emerged bruised and traumatized by the physical and sexual attacks. None of the girls, all of them 15 to 17 years old, had reported the incidents to the police. They'd been ashamed of their involvement with the man.

Gradually, Cray had pieced together the stories during the past few months from his sources on the Internet. He had tracked the

84

man through several chatrooms where high school students hung out. But he had been unable to break into the private chats his quarry had arranged with the girls.

Until now.

He had discovered the names of the system administrators for the online company that operated the chatrooms. Eventually, after dropping strong hints that there was big money for the right kind of access, he had found a System Administrator, or SysAdmin, willing to give up the information. It had cost Cray $10,000 but now he had the username and password that allowed him to spy on anyone in any private chat across the chat system of the online company.

Now, he was watching MuchoMan and XXXgurl in their virtual rendezvous, involved in the most sensual of acts, hidden, or so they thought, from prying eyes.

Cray turned his head for a moment from the filth. The girl seemed far from innocent. She was underage, however, a fact he had gathered from other chat participants during the past few weeks. And that was good enough for him. It was the man he was after, not the girl.

Chapter 14

"She don't look like no cop I ever saw," said Mack Quadrie as he tried to hide his massive frame behind the kitchen doors while peering out into the restaurant that bore his name. "Wonder where she keeps her gun?"

"Mack!" exclaimed his tiny wife as she swatted her husband on the bicep. "Ow!" she cried, shaking her hand. "Now shoo, so I can look." She stood on tiptoes and peeked through the window in the top third of the door that separated the dining area from the kitchen where they stood.

"You are right, Mack, she looks...." Renee Quadrie looked at Al Forte as she searched for the word. "She looks...H-O-T." She touched a finger to her hip and made a sizzling sound. The Quadries looked at each other and giggled.

Forte leaned against the stainless steel wall as he listened to two of his oldest friends tease him about his date. He had played high school football with Maurice "Mack" Quadrie at Holy Cross and had teased him about catching all the running backs at his linebacker position that Mack let slip past him at defensive tackle. His gigantic pal's athletic prowess took him to Louisiana State University and eventually to the NFL, where he earned a half-dozen All-Pro honors before retiring to open his restaurant in the French Quarter. Forte had spent those years as a Navy SEAL on missions that seldom appeared in Congressional reports on U.S. military involvement in troubled areas around the world. He remembered lying under rotting logs in Central American jungles reading the newspaper clippings on his buddy as he waited for the go signal on some covert sortie. *Seems so long ago now.*

"Are you two goofballs finished so I can go to my table and pay attention to my grub?" Forte held his stern face for a moment, then grinned.

"Grub?" Mack's broad features looked stricken. "Honey, you hear him call our fine cuisine...grub?"

"Such a connoisseur," said Renee. She called back into the kitchen. "C'mon, Katie, stop bugging Mr. Jeffard and come say bye to Uncle Alvin."

Around the corner stepped a chef holding a small girl with a mass of curly black hair. The tall chef's hat perched on her head. "I was teaching Princess Katie to make a roux sauce." The chef's elaborate moustache turned upward as he surveyed Forte. "Honey, aren't you looking scrumptious tonight in your black-on-black silk ensemble."

"Thanks, Damon. It must've literally taken minutes to put this look together." Forte studied his reflection in the stainless steel finish of the refrigerator: black silk jacket over a black silk crew-neck T-shirt and black silk slacks. He leaned over to kiss his goddaughter Katie. She touched the X-shaped scar above his eyebrow and said, "Unka Alvey, you got a hot date?"

Forte looked at Mack and Renee, who maintained expressions of total innocence for several seconds before bursting into laughter.

Forte waved at his friends and walked through the door into the dining area to his table where Rosalind Dent awaited him. He gingerly lowered himself into his chair.

"Old age catching up with you?" she asked.

"Just hard living and a bad memory," he said. "My sparring partner forgot to hold his punch and my kidney forgot to get out of the way."

She eyed him over the top of her wine glass. "Why do I always wonder if you're telling me the whole story?"

"Because your investigative prowess is always on duty, Rosie. It's what makes you such a great agent."

"Right. I spend half my days now pushing paperwork and the other half in meetings." She set down her wine glass, and a waiter appeared at her elbow instantly to refill it. "Thanks for being my date tonight. These inter-agency shindigs get old after a while." She unconsciously tugged at the hem of her little black dress.

Forte motioned to the waiter for a glass of water. "You look sharp. I think my friends used the word 'hot' and that was just from a distance."

"Yeah, I saw them peeking through that little window in the door." She started to brush her fingers through her hair then stopped.

"Letting your hair grow out some?"

"Yeah, the butch cut was good for field work, but it promoted too many lesbian jokes around the office." She sipped her wine. "Not that that's a bad thing; may the keepers of political correctness be praised."

Forte raised his eyebrows. "What? Am I hearing Miz Liberal Openmindness poke fun at her own political persuasion?"

Rosie set down her glass. "Mercy, you sound downright intelligent at times, especially when you're not walking the streets with your knuckles dragging the floor." She stood up abruptly. "Let's dance."

"Dance?" he said to her back as she walked away from the table.

From the corner of the restaurant a four-piece jazz combo spun out the opening notes of "It's a Wonderful World." Two other couples swayed out onto the cramped dance floor.

"What the hey," he mumbled as he followed his date.

As they passed the kitchen door, Mack Quadrie gave a big thumbs-up.

Forte slipped his arm around the woman and glided to the music.

"Your pals seem to be quite intrigued with your love life," she whispered. In the black heels, the FBI agent was nearly as tall as he. He could feel her breath against his neck as she leaned close to him.

"First date in a long time," he said. "A long, long time."

She leaned back to look at his face. "Is this a date, really?"

Her eyes are prettier than I noticed before, this close, he thought. "I didn't mean...like DATE date....I just meant...."

She put her head on his shoulder again. "Oh hush, Al Forte, I was just teasing you."

He hushed and was conscious of her body against him and the feel of the silk dress under his touch on her back as the fabric slid against her skin. It had been a long time since he had even touched a woman. Like this. There had been several encounters during the time he was being slammed against the rocky shores of reality by his addiction, women who had come in and out of his so-called life to give and take a bit of sensual pleasure. Pleasure? More like selfish gratification, the mutual sharing of sex to meet a physical need. Nothing like he and Ruth had shared. He thought of what the counselor, David Jones, had told him about the men in the Purity Group who used illicit sex to patch the holes in their hearts that only true intimacy could fill. Had he ever really allowed himself to be as close to another person as he could have been? Had he ever completely let down his guard and let another person in? *Even with Ruth?*

"Earth to Al," a voice puffed the words into his ear. "You were a galaxy away from here just then."

Rosie's perfume was tinged with the smell of powder and soap and softness. "We're two tough people," she whispered, "but right now, I don't feel so tough, and you don't either."

"No," he murmured, "I don't feel too tough either." He felt the skin of her cheek on his, the heat of her body mixing with his.

He took her hand and led her out through the side exit of Mack's, into an alley.

Away from the music, away from the other cops, away from the prying eyes.

He pulled her close and kissed her softly at first, then more frantically, hearing a moan come from deep inside her. And then another, this one from deep inside himself. Feeling the rush of heat lick against his skin like flames from a runaway fire as her body met his and the feel of silk sliding against silk in the darkness, rustling under his fingers as he fell deeper and deeper, losing control, losing all resistance, losing....

He pulled away from the kiss, panting, as Rosie's head lolled backward, her eyes still shut. "Whewww," she gasped, her voice thick and hoarse. "Why...did you...stop...."

"I...I...just can't," he said, his voice barely audible. His arms still held her but he felt her body stiffen now and pull away. He let go and she stood in front of him, swaying slightly.

He never saw the slap coming until he felt the shocking sting of it on his cheek.

"You bastard tease." She swung again,but he deflected this one and pinned her arms against her side.

"I'm sorry," he whispered in her hair. She cursed him in a voice edged with the threat of tears.

The abrupt sound of another voice broke through.

"A spasm of conscience?" said Lucky Battier. "Or just plain damn foolishness?"

Both Forte and the FBI agent whirled to face the sound of his voice in the alley. Instinctively, they had moved apart to give any adversaries a more difficult target. Forte caught a glint of light on metal in the corner of his eye. Rosie had a small pistol in her hand.

"Freeze!" she shouted.

Lucky chuckled softly, a cigarette dangling from his mouth. He said nothing for a beat, inhaling the smoke. The tip of the cigarette went from a dull orange to bright red as he sucked the flavor from it.

Behind him, three men were scattered in what a normal citizen would consider an unplanned arrangement. Forte knew they were strategically positioned for maximum firepower, if needed. Forte turned his head toward the other end of the alley. Four others had closed off that end, weapons in hand. From where he stood, he could see three shotguns and four automatic rifles.

Battier slowly extended his arms and turned over his hands to show they were empty.

"Miss Bigtime FBI Woman, I believe you will agree that it's not against the law to walk down an alley or, for that matter, to startle someone, even if they are in the clutches of..." he stopped and blew two streams of smoke from his nostrils, "...familiarity." The sound of soft, deep laughter drifted up from the alley behind Battier.

"But even if it were," he continued, "you might be wise to notice that my cohorts have somehow discovered themselves in possession of some mighty powerful hardware." From behind him came the sharp shuck of a shotgun pumping a shell into its chamber.

No one moved. In the distance, the mournful trumpet melody from a street musician floated above the French Quarter.

Rosie kept her small automatic pointed at Lucky. "That may be true, Mr. Smartass Smalltime Hoodlum, but this little bullet will still be rattling around inside your skull." Her long legs were bent slightly, making the short dress ride an inch or two higher and stretch tighter than normal. The effect, Forte had to admit, looked like something from a movie. Except that he'd seen the woman shoot a suspect before when it became obvious that force was needed. Her voice was low and steady now, adding menace to her message. "Now, what do you want?"

Battier's smile had disappeared. "We want nothing from you, Agent Dent." His words to her had nothing of the thick Cajun accent he'd been using up to this point. He turned to look at Forte. "How you feeling tonight, podnuh? A little sore maybe?"

Forte could feel Rosie's eyes on him. Her pistol stayed on the gangster in front of her.

"I feel just peachy, Lucky. Thanks for asking,"

"Just checking, podnuh. Heard you had a bit of a tough workout last night."

"Nothing too tough. Nothing I couldn't handle."

Lucky made a clicking noise with his mouth. "Oh, not what I heard. I heard you might've gotten your little behind kicked pretty good if someone hadn't shown up to save your little do-gooder hide."

"And how'd you hear about that?"

"Al, baby, you know how people love to tell me things." Battier puffed again on the cigarette. "Who was your helper?"

"Don't know what you're talking about."

Rosie broke in. "Yoo hoo, boys, I am the one who really doesn't know what y'all are talking about, but I'm standing right here."

Forte held up a hand. "If there was a helper, and you saw him, you must've been close by."

"Could be."

"I understand that you and your punks want to keep sending messages to me, but it's got to end sometime, you know that, Lucky."

The gangster's voice took a hard edge now. "I know that, Alvin, and people higher up than me know that, too." He took one last drag off the cigarette and flicked it away. "Believe me, you do not want to make us take it all the way."

Forte smiled in the darkness. "I'm not making you do anything, any more than you'll be making me hurt you, if it comes to that."

Battier shrugged. "Your choice, podnuh. See you in the funny papers." He motioned to his men, then walked past them out of the alley. Two of the armed thugs with him walked ahead of him out of the alley. The rest of the men followed until only the one nearest Forte remained. He recognized the man as the one he had chopped in the throat the previous night. The man stared at Forte for a long moment, then turned and followed his boss out onto the street.

"I don't suppose you're going to fill me in on what all that was about," said Rosie Dent. She stood facing him now, her arms folded over her chest with her hip cocked. The gun she'd been holding was out of sight once again.

"Can it wait until tomorrow?"

"It can wait forever as far as I'm concerned, as long as it doesn't turn into something that falls within the jurisdiction of the FBI."

"Listen, about earlier..."

Rosie held up a hand. "No need to talk about that either. Let's just blame it on the wine and let it go." She touched her finger to her lips. "You got a clean hankie?" He handed her one and she carefully patted her smeared lipstick. "This okay?"

Forte nodded and put his hand on the side door of the restaurant and swung it open. He paused.

"You had a gun. Where did you...."

She smiled sweetly as she walked past him. "I guess you won't get the chance to know, Mr. Forte, will you? At least not tonight."

Chapter 15

Forte's first choice of transportation out to Larue Hebert's barber shop would have been to hop on the streetcar and rattle along St. Charles to Felicity where he would get off and stroll a few blocks over the brick streets to the shop. He had ridden the old trolleys since he was a kid, running errands for his grandmother at her liquor store on St. Charles, scooting downtown to collect paper wrappers for the pennies, nickels, and dimes that piled up quickly from the scores of customers who came in with bandanas slung low with coins. In those days, the streetcars were only half-filled during the business hours when he went downtown; the tourists were in evidence but nothing like now. Back then, the cars overflowed in the evenings with maids and secretaries and security guards making their way home as they rode the old rails past the Garden District to the smaller homes farther out.

But this morning was not the time for one of those relaxed jaunts. In fact, if he hadn't been insistent on two things—keeping Fizer Beal close to him and keeping his self-promise to have Larue cut his hair and give him his weekly shave every Saturday he was in town—he wouldn't have ventured away from The Refuge at all, given Lucky Battier's recent warnings.

He caught enough of Fizer's facial expression in his peripheral vision to know that the boy was miffed at being up this early. *Tough.*

The van's radio crackled.

"FatDaddy checking in. All clear at the eagle's nest. Over," came Nomad's voice over the speaker. He had borrowed Forte's motorcycle for the task of checking the area surrounding the barber shop for any sign of trouble.

Forte lifted the radio's handset and pressed the transmit button. "Cute, Point Man. This is Unit Two. We're approaching Lee Circle. Should be there within five minutes. Unit Three, anything to report behind us? Over."

"Negative, Unit Two. Everything looks normal. We'll be on your tail up until one block from the nest. Then, we'll help greet you, as planned. Over."

Forte set the handset in its cradle. He could imagine his crew's joking about his insistence on the weekly trip for the haircut and shave. They said nothing about it, however, in his presence. True, he could've gotten his hair cut anywhere. The weekly ritual was merely a way to keep contact with the man.

He remembered the first time he met the old Creole barber.

"Hello, cher, I am La-Roo Ay-bayr," he said solemnly. To his grandmother, he said, "Lurleen, I see you got yourself a bodyguard to help you mind the store." The slight man seemed ancient even then to seven-year-old Alvin Forte, fresh from his parents' double funeral in Gulfport. The words themselves were unintelligible as they were forced to come out in Larue's soft French Creole accent, sounding more like "Ahsee yo gotchosef dem boddagard to hep mine da sto."

Little Al peered over the counter and the man's eyes told him that—even though the boy understood none of the words coming from his mouth—the man was a friend. The next day he had roller-skated from the liquor store to the barber shop to deliver a six-pack of soft drinks, back in the day when they still came in refundable bottles.

When his grandmother passed away six years later, it was to the old barber's home he fled from the state social services people. It was the only home he knew now.

The van weaved its way through the Irish Channel neighborhoods where the yuppies were busily buying up property, living in homes while they renovated them to re-sell for a fat profit. Every street, it seemed, was half-blocked with painters' trucks or piles of gravel. He passed Prytania twice before doubling back down St. Charles a ways; he then turned back toward the river and made his way to Felicity. He checked with the other units again. Still all clear.

He slowed the van to turn the corner next to the barber shop. The street was empty except for the Unit Three van at the next block down. The vehicle was parked at the curb, the driver behind the wheel and two other Forte Security men standing on each side of the street with automatic rifles. Another man, he knew, was stationed behind the shop. Forte scanned to his right and saw Nomad sitting sideways on the motorcycle smoking a cigar. He made an A-OK sign with his forefinger and thumb. Forte parked the van in front of the barber shop. "Let's go," he said to Fizer.

He put out a hand and rubbed the old barber pole as he went through the front door into the comfortable world filled with the smell of old-fashioned hair tonic and aftershave. Larue was standing next to his barber chair. A fresh strip of duct tape covered a torn seam along the back of the leather chair.

A young Forte had once remarked to the old World War II veteran, "Why don't you just buy a new chair? You got the money."

"Just 'cuz a man got money don't mean he got to spend it on making things look pretty," the barber had answered. "Do Old Mr. Chair he still work good?" Young Al admitted it did. "Do Mr. Chair feel good wrapped around you?" The boy again nodded. "So, you t'ink Mr. Chair, even though he still doing his job just fine and dandy, he just looks...what you call it...tacky, then? You think 'cuz he not shiny and new no mo', he need to be put in the garbage dump?" Al said nothing at that point and the old man bent down and gently touched the side of the boy's face. "Bemember sumpin', cher, ain't no need to t'row way an old chair if he still sit well, no matter how he look." He had gone back to work on his customer that day and may have quickly forgotten about the conversation. But Forte never had.

He came back to the present as he ran a hand over the duct-taped leather.

"Bonjour, mon fils," Larue said, his voice softer than ever. "You out early this fine day."

Forte gripped the man's hand and sat in the chair. "Oui, oui, mon amie. But we wanted to be out of your way before your regular customers come banging on your door."

Larue pumped the chair's lever a few times to adjust the height and tilted it back. The buzz of the electric clipper filled the room for a few moments. If the barber noticed the armed men in front of his shop, he gave no indication.

Through slitted eyes, Forte watched Fizer thumb through the stack of magazines piled on the leather sofa where customers waited their turn. The boy occasionally glanced toward the barber to check the progress of the haircut, then went back to his magazines. When Larue finished the haircut and began lathering up Forte's face for the shave, Fizer put down the *Popular Mechanic* he was perusing and watched intently. His hand wandered absently up to his smooth cheek. When he saw Forte watching him, he quickly dropped his hand back in his lap and looked out the picture window at the front of the barber shop.

The weathered barber pulled his head back to the headrest. Forte closed his eyes as he listened to the *shrappp shrappp shrappp* of the straight razor being run back and forth over the strop. Then the razor gliding over his skin.

What could the boy be thinking? He'd witnessed his father being beaten by Marchetti's men and had been seconds away from receiving the same treatment before the cops had shown up. Theodore "Teddy" Beal had been the computer whiz for Marchetti's crime syndicate for 20 years, since the advent of personal computers made it much easier to keep up with the millions of illicit funds flowing into the coffers. When Teddy tried to leave the crime group a decade earlier, his wife, Fizer's mother, had mysteriously disappeared. The authorities had little sympathy for the plight of the little techno-crook, so Beal had shed a few weeks' tears over his wife and had gone back to work. When she showed up a month later, she was a shell of her former self, never revealing where she'd been. Within a year, Julie Beal was committed to the mental asylum at Whitfield near Jackson, Mississippi, where Teddy and Fizer visited her weekly for six months. Until she was found dead in her room one morning, overdosed on heroin, a drug she had never been known to use.

And Teddy had gone back to work again. This time, however, he had a plan. For revenge. It took ten years to make it work. Patiently he learned all the new software that the accountants would be needing to take the Marchetti operations—drugs, prostitution, gambling fixes, and now, Internet pornography—into the twenty-first century. He hadn't skimmed a penny of the operation until he was satisfied that everyone in the crime group was totally convinced of his loyalty again. In just the past three years, he had funneled $10 million cash into his own pockets. Or, more accurately, into some hideaway that only he knew about.

Not that any of that information had come to Forte from Teddy Beal himself. The sketchy details of the caper had trickled down through the labyrinth of snitches in the N.O.P.D., eventually winding up in the hands of retired cop Archie Griffey, husband of Verna Griffey, the one-woman wonder who handled the daily office work at Forte Security and The Refuge. The Griffeys had been longtime friends of Al and Ruth Forte before Ruth's death. They had stuck with him through his stay in the treatment center, paid for completely by Larue Hebert, and helped him get back on his feet. Verna could be ornery, he thought, but she and Archie were great to have on your side. As Larue once told him: *A pound of loyalty is worth a ton of talent.*

Forte stirred from his reverie as he felt the old barber lift the hot towels off his face. The cool air hit him, followed by the even colder slaps of Clubman Aftershave.

Throughout the haircut and shave, Larue had said nothing, as was his habit. Customers might babble away in his chair, but he offered little to the conversation apart from a murmured "hmmm" from time to time. As Forte had seen more than once over the years, he was a man who believed the value of a man was measured by his action, not merely his words.

"How much do I owe you?" It was their running joke.

Larue whipped the cape off him. "Don't piss off the old gator while you swimmin' in his swamp, boy." The old man's moustache twitched, the closest he ever came to a smile.

Forte put a hand on the man's shoulder and squeezed it. He motioned to Fizer who carefully put his magazine back on the stack and stood up to leave.

"Boy," Larue said.

Fizer stopped. He was about the same height as the wizened barber with his shiny, wavy salt-and-pepper hair and pencil-thin moustache.

"Boy, you stay close to Alveen, and listen to him. He keep you safe."

Fizer seemed to be caught, not by the soft words but by the look in the old man's eyes. The twinkle had vanished.

The boy nodded and whispered, "Yes, sir."

Forte waited at the door with his hand on the knob. "You ready?" he asked Fizer, who nodded.

They went out and got back into the van. A block down, Nomad kick-started the FatDaddy and the caravan was on its way again.

They rode in silence for a few blocks.

"He gave you a place to stay," the boy said.

"Yeah."

"Why?"

Forte sped up to keep the lead van in sight. "Who told you he gave me a place to stay?"

"Jackie...uh, Miss Shaw. She said you had a tough life and that the state was going to put you in a foster home before Mr. Hebert let you come live with him. Why did he do it?"

"Good question."

"You don't know?"

"No, I guess I don't. But I'm probably not the best one to ask about why people do the things they do, good or bad. I've never been too good at figuring that out."

"Yeah," Fizer said. "Me neither."

The trees and sleeping houses glided past the windows of the vehicle. A man in a tattered, lavender bathrobe yawned as he watched his Jack Russell terrier water a bush in someone's front yard. At this hour, the city still rested in slumbering recovery from the night before. Forte didn't miss those shards of light stabbing his eyes after a night out to God-knows-where.

He took out his pack and popped Checkers Number One into his mouth. He lit it and cracked the window.

He could feel Fizer's eyes on him again.

"Why do you do it?"

He sucked in the smoke and exhaled it toward the slit of space at the top of the window. "What?"

"This...you know, this thing you do. The Refuge and all. To tell the truth, you don't seem much like a...kid person."

He glanced at the boy, who was turned in the seat now, facing him.

"You sure have come awake. Who tipped over your chatterbox?"

"Huh?"

"My grandmama used to say that, when I started asking a bunch of questions."

"Yeah, well, tell me. Why do you do this?"

Forte inhaled deeply and held it for a beat, thinking. *Why do I do it?* He remembered the group sessions in rehab treatment. He had known he needed help, that the cocaine had taken over his life and that all his toughness and self-discipline weren't going to get him back in control. He hadn't realized how much he thought he had an excuse for his addiction, after seeing his wife murdered by the gang punk who thought the gun wasn't loaded in a gang prank gone horribly wrong. The group leaders in rehab hadn't let him get away with hoarding that as an excuse, devastating as it was. *You think you still a hero, Mr. High-and-Mighty Navy SEAL? You think 'cuz you not a pimp or a whore or a drug dealer who dipped his pinky one too many times in his own product that you got a good reason for why you let the monster smash your pitiful life? You b'leeve this is just a little time-out so you can get back on your feet and let your true big-time hero-self come to the rescue, don't you? Well, I got news for you, pal, you just like the rest of us—weak and without hope if you think you gonna get through this by yourself.*

His first impulse was to smash the man's face. After detoxing, his nerves were raw, the drug-induced sheath around his anger now gone. The group leader would never know what it was like to feel his wife's blood ooze through his fingers and see the light in her eyes go out and to hold that gun against the boy's head, hammer cocked, finger on trigger, pressing and feeling the pressure build and seeing the fear and hopelessness in the boy's eyes and knowing he could never make sense of this and feeling his sanity slip-sliding away....

In the end, it was just one more excuse, he realized, to use again.

To use and keep using.

"Why do I do it?"

Fizer waited.

"Because it gives me a reason to get up and face another day. And because I *can* do it." He sucked the flavor out the last of the cigarette and ground it out in the ashtray. "That's the best answer I can give you."

Fizer nodded, searching Forte's face for a moment. He finally turned to watch the houses flash by again.

"Good enough," he said.

Chapter 16

Cray watched the streams of people waving their black-and-gold banners and pompoms as they poured into the SuperDome. The mid-August heat baked the sidewalks, but the Saints fans would not have missed this exhibition game, no matter how badly their team had fared in the past few years. They were playing the hated Pittsburgh Steelers, a rowdy bunch with even rowdier fans.

"Go to hell, Steelers!" a man yelled, almost losing his plastic helmet with two beer cans mounted on each side with flexible tubes running down to his mouth. The tubes popped out of his mouth and spurted beer briefly. The beefy man carefully replaced the tubes and took a deep draught before continuing his rowdy trek toward the gate.

Cray leaned against the fence near the ticket gate and resisted the urge to scratch his scalp under the black wig. He wondered if the costumer's glue for the fake moustache would hold up in this heat. Of any day to have to wear a disguise, this had to be the worst. But it couldn't be helped. He had yet to pursue a target in his hometown; the chance someone would recognize him was far too great. So he would wait and itch for as long as it took.

He had decided to wait for the man here after watching the conversation in the chat room the previous night. The back-and-forth flirting and sexual double entendres had sickened him; he even felt a flicker of doubt whether the girl was worth rescuing from the monster she was playing with. But he would do it. The girl was stupid but young, he could tell; she didn't deserve to lose everything. Whoever she was.

The pair had agreed to meet at this gate. Cray fingered the ticket he'd bought, enabling him to go into the stadium if his quarry went in. Or if he simply escorted the girl to his car, Cray would follow. He reached to scratch his back and let his fingers travel over the .45 automatic stuck in the waistband of his jeans. His oversized T-shirt was pulled over the gun instead of being tucked in like he usually wore it. After September 11, 2001, the security at the SuperDome had tightened up for a while. He noticed that the ticket-takers weren't checking for weapons at this gate. He didn't think he would need the gun, but it was the smart thing to carry a backup nonetheless. In his left boot was strapped a 7-inch hunting knife. He planned to take care of this one close-up and personal. With his hands if possible. *And you can look into my eyes and beg for your life, you worthless piece of crud. Then you will know how it feels to be the one without hope, to be the one at a killer's mercy.*

A pair of cops, a man and woman, strolled past him and stood at the gate, watching the crowd. The woman stopped scanning and fixed on him for a moment. Cray kept his hands folded over his chest and watched the cop from behind his sunglasses. He raised a hand and waved at an imaginary friend in the crowd. A 40-ish woman in black shorts and a Saints jersey waved back, thinking that maybe she knew him. She kept walking.

When Cray glanced at the cops again, they had continued scanning the crowd. After a few more minutes, they walked down to the next ticket gate.

He kept watching for his quarry.

The crowd had thickened now with kickoff getting closer. Hundreds of dads and sons and moms and daughters and uncles, brothers, sisters, nieces, nephews, friends. All laughing and shouting and traipsing through the sunshine on their way to a fun-filled afternoon, making memories and if not that, at least getting away from their humdrum existence for a few hours.

Cray remembered having a life like that. Or had he? He and his daughter had come to a few games before it became uncool to be seen with daddy. But it seemed like they had fun then, hadn't they? Cray blinked away the sting of sweat in his eyes. *Had it been fun?* That life, back then, was bubble-wrapped somewhere in his mind, a place where he could see the memories but when his mind reached out to touch it, to feel what it was like back then, he could only see the picture through the plastic. It was as if he knew something about that life, as if he had been told about it but someone else had actually lived it.

And this existence, if that's what you called it, this was all that was left to him.

How long would it last? He didn't know. He held on to the hope that his Jenny would come out of the coma one day. Then, maybe, she could get her life back and grow up into the beautiful woman she would become. Until that time, he would continue his mission for as long as he could. He had no doubt he was saving other families' little girls by eliminating the predators one by one.

If only someone had taken out the pervert before the man had damaged his daughter for life.

Jenny had been a good kid, never causing him a minute's worry. Until she turned 13. Overnight, it seemed to him, she had grown up, her body taking on the proportions of a woman. And the boys took notice, flocking to his house like so many dogs. He'd been too strict, he knew that. Eventually his daughter spent less time at home after school and on weekends, making excuses to do this or that with friends and spending more time with girls whose families Cray barely knew. She started spending hours in the chatrooms on the new computer he had bought her for school work. She and her junior high girlfriends loved flirting with the boys in the room, a practice she claimed was perfectly innocent. Until one of her pals convinced her to meet one of the boys in person. Cray had found an email to

Jenny from the girl, who promised they would go together, to make it safe. The boy they were to meet turned out to be a man. The other girl lost interest quickly and wandered away from the table at the bowling alley where they were to meet. When she came back for Jenny a few moments later, she was gone. The girl had shrugged and called a cab to take her home. She never reported anything to the police.

Later that night, the police called Cray, however. His daughter had been found, bloody and torn, in a park not far from the bowling alley.

The culprit, a 45-year-old insurance salesman who dabbled in his family farm in south Louisiana, was identified by others as the man last seen talking to Jenny. He had a prior arrest for child molestation that had been thrown out due to improper questioning of the suspect by the police. And the justice system was to falter again on this case. The man had been very careful, leaving no DNA or fingerprints on Jenny or at the scene of the rape and beating she received. The girl with Jenny had been no help at the trial, insolently telling the prosecutor she never looked close enough at the man at the bowling alley. The last time she saw Jenny, she said, her friend was laughing with the man. The jury, lacking that evidence and any eye-witness to the actual assault, found him not guilty.

Cray had sat in the courtroom, his hands gripping the back of the seat in front of him, the knuckles drained of color, feeling as if the breath had been punched out of him. It was at that moment, not when he'd endured the actual attack against Jenny, that his world changed, his heart and soul ripped from him like his daughter's innocence had been torn from her.

For weeks he'd stared into the darkness in his cold house, feeling helpless in the face of the absurdity of what had occurred, unable to grasp it and make any sense of it, like any other man in his position. But he wasn't like most other men.

One day, he walked over to his desk and found the key to the gun closet. He carefully took out the Remington Model 700 sniper rifle like the one he had used as an Army Ranger. The feel of the weapon, after years of idleness, comforted him. He took it apart and began cleaning it.

Seven weeks later in San Diego, he took out his first target. The man had managed to stuff a ten-year-old girl bound with duct tape into his trunk. She was found moments later, scared but otherwise untouched. Cray had waited almost too late on that one, his timing rusty after years away from his sniper duties.

That night, after watching the news reports of the killing on all the major networks, CNN and Fox News, he had enjoyed his first full night of sleep since Jenny's attack.

After his second save—the man had been dragging a five-year-old girl kicking and screaming from a neighbor's yard—the talk shows began hailing him as a hero, taking up the slack where, in their opinion, law enforcement had failed. "The PerverTerminator," he was dubbed. Panels of so-called experts in sniper tactics began appearing on "Larry King Live" and the network news shows as they bandied about the pros and cons of his vigilantism. A group of mothers whose children had been molested and murdered offered a reward—not for information leading to his arrest but to give to him, for "his contribution to ridding the world of the criminals" he had murdered.

From what he gathered from the news, the FBI suspected that the serial killer had special forces or SWAT experience, based on his sniper tactics. Cray knew that it was just a matter of time before they narrowed down the search to ex-Special Forces personnel whose children had been molested. When they came to knock at the door of his house, they would hit a blank wall in their investigation. He had left no trails to his current whereabouts.

Above the SuperDome, a wispy cloud high in the sky made the bright blue day even brighter. The crowd had reached its zenith now, swelling and backing up into the plaza around the ticket gates. Cray stood straighter, trying to survey the hordes of people as if he were looking to meet a friend for the game.

Then he saw the man.

He was wearing a mustard knit shirt and black chino slacks. A black leather bag was slung over one shoulder. As he shifted the bag from one side to the other, his biceps bulged in the short-sleeved shirt. Cray hadn't noticed the quarry being quite this physically fit before, having seen him only in dress suits up to this point. The revelation didn't faze him, however. He would be no match for the training Cray had put in.

Cray carefully tracked the man as he strolled through the crowd's sea of gold and black, being careful not to lose him. The leisurely pace of the man made it easier. *So arrogant, no rush, just walk right up and take a child away.* Cray felt his face flush with anger. He calmed himself, waiting. In a few moments, the girl would arrive. Cray would follow them back to the man's car and, before he could get away, would deliver justice, swiftly and without remorse.

He watched as the man made his way to a spot on the opposite side of the gate from where Cray stood. His quarry leaned against the fence there as he watched the crowd for the girl.

Inside the stadium the crowd began working itself up into a tumult. The Saints had apparently taken the field.

The first strains of "When the Saints Go Marchin' In" came over the loudspeakers. The mobs around the ticket gates joined in screaming the lyrics rowdily, their black-and-gold pompoms thrashing the air in time to the music.

The man bobbed his head slightly in time to the music, a pleasant smile on his face.

Enjoy life now, scumball, because it's almost over.

The music was deafening now. Cray kept his eyes on the man.

Something about the music seemed a little bit off, a little discordant. Someone was playing one of the instruments off-key a bit. It almost sounded like a beeping noise.

Beep, beep, Beep, beep. Cray turned his head slightly. It sounded close by, the beeping noise.

Then it hit him. It was his beeper.

He unclipped it and held it up to his face. Who could be paging him?

It was the number for the long-term healthcare facility where Jenny lived.

Cray held the pager close to his face.

Behind the phone number were three additional numbers.

9-1-1.

Cray stared at the numbers and felt chilled in the torrid summer sun. He sprinted across the plaza toward his van.

Chapter 17

Exxie checked herself one last time in the mirror. A lavender criss-cross stretch camisole top was just short enough to create the perfect gap between the shirt and the top of her low-rise sandblasted jeans. The suede open-toed clogs made navigating through the crowds at the stadium a bit of a challenge but what's a girl to do? They looked cute with this outfit. Besides, it's not like she would have to do any running in the shoes.

The outfit was exactly what she'd told the MuchoMan she would be wearing. He would be happy to see her, she had no doubt.

She scooped up her diamond bracelet watch from the bedside table. Almost game time. Her date would be waiting for her already, if he was on time. Just as it should be. Make them wait.

Exxie scribbled a note for her parents—"Gone to the game with a friend." She probably would be back before nightfall. Maybe even before her dad got back from his office where he usually spent his Saturdays, that is, when he wasn't sipping martinis in some airplane on a transatlantic flight to check on his European subsidiaries. Mom might be back from her usual weekend shopping forays. Maybe not.

The buzzer for the front gate went off, alerting her that her taxi had arrived.

"Be right out," she said into the intercom. "Wait for me."

She snatched a bottle from the top of her dresser and misted herself with her favorite sexy scent, HotFunk. *Mmmmm, baby baby you so hottttt.*

She grabbed her shoes and ran down the stairs. At the back door, she put on the clogs and sauntered up the driveway to the locked security gate, punched in the code and let herself out. "To the SuperDome," she said to the driver as she hopped into the back seat.

The Quarter had already filled with tourists in spite of the August heat. Many families had crowded into New Orleans today, taking the children for a weekend outing before school started. Two women, each gripping the hands of toddlers, stood at the corner of her street, waiting to see if the cab would stop. *You lose,* thought Exxie. *Never make eye contact with a cab driver; they can see indecision in your eyes a mile away.* The cabbie plowed through the stop after lightly tapping his brakes. The women and their children watched him pass, then gazed with apprehension down the street again to check traffic.

Dozens of cabs, buses, and limousines converged near the stadium, all jockeying for a spot closest to the game. Exxie threw a twenty into the front seat and chirped, "Just let me out here" a block away from the SuperDome.

As she walked, she reviewed the chat she'd had with MuchoMan online. He seemed more mature than other guys she'd chatted with, more willing to draw her out, more attentive. But he had not allowed her to control the conversation, to push him around in the virtual fantasy they had shared. He had been secretive about himself, sure, but that had just added to his intrigue. He declined to describe himself, even after she had sent him a digital photo of herself online. *You won't be disappointed,* he had told her.

A confident man. I like that, Exxie mused.

Something about him made her know that she was graduating to a whole different level of adventure. At the corner, a couple of college boys watched her approach, both smiling at her. She realized that she must have been smiling as she thought about meeting

MuchoMan today. *Hmmm, I must be looking forward to this more than I thought.*

A rumble of cheers and the chatter of the play-by-play announcer rolled out of the stadium as she crossed the street. The game had already started. Exxie deliberately slowed her pace as she crossed the street and walked across the plaza toward the ticket gates. She could feel the eyes of the college boys she'd passed at the last street corner. As she walked, she caught the eye of several men and boys who were hurrying toward the gates. Every few steps, she gave a tiny toss of her hair and looked around the plaza. She could feel the attention of the males all around her. She deliberately ignored all of them. She had learned early how to play this game. And she was good at it.

MuchoMan had said he'd be wearing gold and black. *Triple-whoop*, she had told him in the chatroom. *So will every other guy at the game.* Her chat partner had assured her that he would recognize her.

She hadn't liked it, the loss of control to the man, but she'd decided to trust him. If she didn't like his looks when she met him, she could just walk away in the crowded area outside the stadium.

She slowed her pace even more, the swivel of her hips becoming a lazy movement that still drew covert glances from the men surrounding her. She chose a spot about 30 yards away from the gate where they had agreed to meet and stopped. Which one was he? About a dozen people were waiting their turn to go through the ticket gate. A pair of policeman were walking along the concourse inside the chain-link fence that surrounded the massive concrete bowl that was the SuperDome. No one seemed to be waiting for anyone. No one had that familiar stance, their heads rotating back and forth as they searched the crowd for the person they were to meet.

She checked her watch again. It was 15 minutes past the time they were to meet. Would he have given up so quickly and left? She felt a chill of disappointment run along her back. *Did I wait too late?* She would never have admitted to anyone that she was not in absolute control of any male on whom she had decided to focus her charms. But this one...he had his own charm; maybe he wasn't in the mood to cater to spoiled little rich girls.

Exxie tossed her hair again and sighed. *Oh welllll....*

She felt, more than saw, a presence beside her. Glad she didn't jump, she turned to face the person next to her.

"Oh," Exxie said. "What are you doing here?"

* * *

Cray's mind was racing ahead of the Jeep as it careened through the traffic on I-10. *FASTER, GO FASTER.* He wanted to scream at the other cars but that would've just wasted time. He dodged around them, pushing the Jeep to its limit.

The facility administrators caring for his daughter were the only people who had his pager number. Their instructions had been explicit: you can page with any question concerning his daughter, but if an emergency arises, put the number 9-1-1 after the phone number.

He refused to let any possible scenarios go through his mind as he drove. *Got to get there, got to get there NOW.*

The doctors at the facility had been solemn in their prognosis for Jenny when he first brought her there, after her physical illnesses had healed enough for her to travel. "You do understand, Mr. Cray, that Jenny very likely will never regain the state of consciousness she enjoyed in the past," the older doctor had said. Cray had gazed at the man for a full minute at the doctor in his lab coat crisp with starch and unblemished by any sign he had actually made a patient healthier that day. Cray knew it was unfair to think about the doctors that way, but at the time he wasn't in the mood to be fairminded.

The state of consciousness she enjoyed in the past. His auburn-haired preschooler in her tutu and aluminum halo prancing across the den and tapping his head with a makeshift cardboard wand. His third-grade cutie in her new spectacles winning the spelling bee with "effervescent" and squealing with astonishment at her victory. His young lady standing on the steps of the junior high looking back at his car with a mixture of bravado and terror on her first day of adulthood.

He'd wanted to reach across the gleaming slab of oaken desktop and slap the doctor. Not out of anger but just to relieve a bit of irritation that anyone, even those in the business of caring, could pretend to know what he'd lost. *She enjoyed in the past.*

He took the last corner nearly at full speed and felt the Jeep begin to tip. He tapped the brakes; it regained traction. The vehicle slid into the circular driveway and skidded to a stop beneath the overhang of the front entrance. A security guard came around the corner of the building. "Hey! You need to park over in the..." the guard shouted. But Cray was gone. He tore off the fake moustache and wig and vaulted out of the car.

He banged through the front doors, sprinted down the hallway. A pair of nurses flattened themselves against the corridor wall. Another guard came around the corner from another hallway. He raised both of his hands, motioning for Cray to stop. *No weapon in his hands.* Cray feinted left, then sent the guard sprawling with a shove of his hand. At the intersection of the hallways ahead, he bumped an aide out of the way, sending the aluminum tray in his hands skittering down the corridor. Cray kept running, hearing the echo of his boots on the cold tile walls.

The nurses' station loomed ahead, a group of nurses huddled there. One turned and murmured "Mr. Cray" as he passed, the rest jerking their heads toward him, eyes wide with surprise. *Jenny my Jenny. No no no....*

Ahead was the room, a doctor just now stepping out of his daughter's room. The man wisely moved aside, his face a professionally neutral mask with just the appropriate hint of sadness around the eyes.

No no no, not this, not this....

He stopped at the door to her room. He could feel his chest rising and falling as his lungs refilled. But...no noise. Had he gone deaf? Every sound seemed to have slipped away. No phones jangling from the nurses' station down the hall, no shouts from the guards rushing toward this end of the building, not even his own ragged breathing. He raised his hand to push the door open.

His arm wouldn't move. He examined his hand, puzzled. *Move, damn you. OPEN THE DOOR.*

The doctor reached over and pushed the door open.

A nurse was smoothing Jenny's hair. Another stood at the life-support equipment next to the bed. She turned it off.

"So beautiful," Micah Cray said.

The doctor moved beside him. "Mr. Cray, we believe she passed peacefully in her final...."

Cray turned to face him, his gray eyes so cold that the doctor stepped back involuntarily. The man said nothing else.

On Jenny Cray's face was a smile, the first her father had seen in nearly a year.

Micah Cray brushed her cheek with his fingtertips. "Sleep, my Jenny. Sleep now, Honey." He bent over the bed and kissed her forehead. A single, racking sob shook his body and was gone.

He walked out of the room and down the hushed hall.

Chapter 18

"Why do you think they painted this room such a hideous blue?" Jackie Shaw had her nose crinkled as she glared at the walls of the family visiting room of the Benson Federal Prison.

Forte said nothing as he sat with his back to the teal metal-and-plastic picnic table. His eyes remained focused on Fizer Beal and his father, who sat at an identical table across the room hunched over, whispering back and forth.

The hour's drive north of New Orleans had been uneventful after the van broke free from the concrete restraints of the city and crossed Lake Ponchartrain with its gnarled cypresses beckoning from the swamps. Just a few days before they'd been on the training exercises out in the Big Thicket just across the western border of Louisiana. It seemed like months since he'd been out in the countryside.

He noticed Jackie had stopped peering at the walls of the visiting room and had focused on him.

"Thinking about your date last night?" she said.

He kept his gaze on the Beals.

"Nope."

She made a tiny puffing noise. He turned his head slightly. She was looking out of the wall of windows into the visitor's yard next to the building.

"What did that mean?"

"What?"

"You know. That puff thing you did with your mouth."

"What puff thing?"

"Oh, c'mon, you know." He made the noise. "That puff thing."

"I didn't do that." She folded her arms over her chest and turned to look out the window again. *Puff.*

He turned to face her directly now. "There. That thing. You did it again."

Her face clouded. "You're crazy. I did not."

"Yes, you did." He imitated her again. "That was it."

"I did?"

"Oh, yes. You did."

She tilted her head. "I didn't even know I did it."

"Oh, you did it."

"Okay, okay, I believe you." She turned to the window again.

"Well," he said.

"Well, what?"

He sighed. "What did that mean? I mean, even if you didn't know you were doing it, you were thinking something."

She studied his face for a moment. "What's with you? You don't say a word all the way up here and all of a sudden you're Mr. Chatty about the puff thing."

"Hey, you started the conversation."

"By asking you about your date last night."

"Yeah."

"And you said, if I may quote you, 'Nope' in response to my question to you."

"Well, I wasn't thinking about it."

She arched an eyebrow. "Well, how did it go?"

He turned back to watch Fizer and his father.

"Don't make me puff again," she said, her face completely serious.

He turned and looked at her again. For a long moment they stared at each other. Finally, he gave an embarrassed laugh.

"Not good," he said. He told about the surprise visit by Lucky and company outside the restaurant, excluding a few details about his romantic embrace with Rosie in the alley.

"Ahh," she said.

"Yeah," he said. "Not your typical date."

"Tough to have a major crime figure break up your hot date."

"Hot date?" He made a *hmmphh* noise and turned away.

"Aha, you did your own noise."

"I did not."

"Oh, yes, you did."

"You are looney."

She turned to a hulking guard leaning against the wall nearby. "You heard him. He did that grunt thing, didn't he?"

The guard's face was stone behind his sunglasses. "Yup. 'Cept more like a snort." He paused. "Like a bull snorts. Through the nose. A little softer maybe."

Forte looked back and forth between them. "This is the craziest conversation I've ever had."

"Hey, you started it, talking about my puffing." Jackie's eyes sparkled with mischief.

"Yup, I heard it. You started it," the guard said.

Forte stood up and pointed to the Beals. "Isn't their time about up?"

The guard glanced at the wall clock protected by its grid cover. "Yup."

"Give me five minutes with Teddy Beal."

The guard nodded.

Forte walked over and traded places with Fizer, who sat with Jackie on the other side of the room.

"Teddy," he said. "You know they're after him."

Theodore Beal was not much taller than his son. His thinning hair had grown out enough to be gathered into a pony tail. His glasses rested on the tip of his nose and he peered over the top of the lavender-tinted lenses at Forte.

"Yeah, I figured they were. They've come after me here a couple of times, too." He rolled up the sleeve of his denim workshirt. Three parallel razor cuts were carved into his forearm, leaving black beads of hardened blood behind as the cuts scabbed over. "Who did Marchetti send first?"

"Lucky Battier."

Beal displayed no overt reaction to that news, except for the widening of his nostrils. "Lucky, huh?" He turned to look out the window.

Forte was quiet. He shifted on the hard bench of the picnic table, still feeling the bruise in the small of his back.

"You got three more years in here, Teddy. You know you won't make it unless you give back Marchetti's money."

Beal leaned away from table top and crossed his arms over his chest. "Marchetti's money? He stole that money, a nickel bag at a time, one cheap screw at a time."

"Yeah, and you think you're Robin Hood, robbing from the biggest hood in New Orleans? You were in on it, too, Teddy."

Beal's arms tensed. A crimson trickle seeped from one of the razor cuts on his arm. "I tried to get out."

Forte took a slow, deep breath. He believed him, but what could be done about that now? "Listen, you could cooperate with the D.A. The Feds could put Fizer in Witness Protection."

Teddy Beal snorted. "And Lucky Battier would find him so fast...No thanks."

Forte laid his hands on the hard plastic table top, palms up. "So what's going to happen, Teddy? You know we can't keep Fizer forever. His court appearance is next week, and after that he goes to a foster home. Marchetti will wipe out everyone in that house if he has to. You want to carry that on your mind, too?"

"Not my problem."

Forte locked eyes with the smaller man for a long moment. From the corner of his eye, he caught the movement of the guard approaching the table.

"Think it over, Teddy. You can make this all better."

Beal remained silent but didn't look away.

The guard rapped on the table. "Time's up."

* * *

"You don't think it's that simple," Jackie said, "just handing over the money in exchange for his son's safety?"

Forte checked the rearview mirror to make sure Fizer was still wearing the earphones for his portable CD player. The music on the player was loud enough for Forte to hear the lyrics of "Weathered" by Creed. The boy was slumped on the bench seat of the van, his eyes closed.

Forte shook his head. "If he can, Marchetti will kill Teddy Beal, and probably the boy, too, even if he gets his money back. Teddy's alive now only because they think he might break down and make Fizer tell them where the money is."

"So, they will keep coming, Lucky Battier and his pals."

"Yep."

In the rearview mirror he watched as a green van pulled out and passed the two cars that were behind the van. Seconds later, another vehicle passed, this one a fullsize black sedan with tinted windows. The two vehicles stayed about a hundred yards behind him, carefully matching his speed.

"Don't be obvious, but it looks like we've got company," Forte said. He checked the mirror again. Fizer was still on the earphones. Forte picked up the radio handset. "This is Lead Man for Cleanup Man. You see the van and the black car coming up behind me? Over." Immediately, Nomad's voice came over the radio. "I've got them in my sights. I'm three cars behind them. They passed me a coupla minutes ago. Over."

Forte kept his speed steady and watched the van behind him. It was keeping its distance for the moment. He spoke into the handset again. "Looks like they're not eager to pass me. You think it's our friend from the city?"

"We have to assume it is," came back Nomad's voice. "Got a plan?"

The two-lane highway wound its way through more of small-town south Louisiana countryside. Ahead was the turnoff for Highway 22 which connected with Interstate 55 about 10 miles away. From there, it was a straight shot into the city. They could outdistance the vehicles or dart off another exit ramp if needed.

"I'm taking a left on 22 about a mile ahead. Follow me and stay alert."

"I'm all over it," said Nomad's crackling radio voice.

Forte glanced over at Jackie in the passenger seat. She was sitting with her hands folded calmly over her nine-millimeter Glock pistol in her lap. Her eyes were riveted on the outside rearview mirror.

"Hang tight, Jackie. Could be nothing."

He slowed and signaled for the left turn. Through the rearview mirror he saw the pair of vehicles slowing to match his speed. He took the turn and watched. The others followed him.

"Then again, it could be something."

He noticed a white car parked on the shoulder of the road ahead. It pulled out in front of Forte's van but made no attempt to slow him down. Forte could count five passengers in it. The barrel of a shotgun poked into view briefly, then withdrew.

Forte snatched up the radio. "We've got another one ahead of us now, a late model white Chrysler New Yorker. Five guys inside, with guns. Stand by." He clicked off the handpiece but held it ready as he watched the vehicles tailing him. They had cut their distance in half but remained at a steady speed. He clicked the radio on again. "Looks like they're waiting for the traffic to thin out. Watch for their moves. They've got plenty of firepower, I bet."

"Watchin' and waitin'," said Nomad. His voice was low and flat, devoid of emotion, sounding almost bored. It was his most dangerous tone, one that Forte had heard several times on lethal missions with the SEALS. And once or twice since then.

In the rearview mirror, Fizer's expression had changed. The headphones were off. His body was leaning forward, straining against the seat belt. His eyes were wide with fear.

"What's up?" he asked, his voice cracking.

Forte looked over at Jackie, who twisted in her seat to face the boy. "Stay calm and listen to me, please," she said. Her voice was so relaxed she might as well have been asking the boy his favorite subject in school. "I want you to slowly slump sideways in the seat as much as you can without unbuckling." She kept eye contact with him as he obeyed her. "Now, just stay down and wait for a few minutes. If we have to leave the van, keep your eyes on me and follow me, staying as close as you can. Got it?"

Fizer nodded.

"We will protect you," Jackie said.

Chapter 19

"Did my Dad send you after me?" Exxie asked the man who had suddenly appeared at her shoulder.

Thomas Penderby blinked at the question and took a step backward. "Why, no, Exxie." The man took off his rimless spectacles and polished them with a handkerchief. His eyes were mere slits in the bright sunshine of midday. "I just saw you standing here alone and wondered if you needed help."

Exxie pivoted back and forth, searching the plaza to make sure her father was nowhere in sight. She cursed under her breath. "Don't lie to me. Did my dad send you?"

The man fumbled with his eyeglasses as he hooked the earpieces over his ears. "No, I swear to you, he didn't." He paused. "Why? Does he not know where you are?"

Satisfied her father was not close by, she turned on the man and poked him hard in the chest with her finger. Her finger bent backward and she yelped. "That's none of your business, Penderby." She put her finger in her mouth. "Ow. You almost sprained my hand." She stared at him for a moment, taking in the hangdog expression. "Hey, you're not nearly as soft as you look." She watched as his face reddened. "Oh, lighten up, it's a compliment."

Penderby stood up straighter and smoothed the front of his yellow knit shirt, then hitched up his black slacks. "Well, I do work out several times a week." He carefully folded the handkerchief and put it in his back pocket. "I own my own Stairmaster."

Exxie had resumed searching the crowd again for her date. *Where is he? He sounded so hot in the chat room.* She silently chided herself for the momentary lapse in her coolness, even if was only in her thoughts. *Control. Control belongs to me.*

"Huh? Oh, yeah, your own Stairmaster. That's cool, Penderby." She had always considered her father's right-hand man a prissy preppy. Maybe she had been wrong. She turned and looked at him again. "Those things are expensive, aren't they?"

The man tried to slip one hand in his pants pocket and missed it twice before hitting the mark. He struck a pose that he must've assumed was casual and cool. "Well, yes. Your father pays me well enough to afford it."

The girl raised her hand to flip her blonde locks away from her neck for a respite from the heat. At the movement, Penderby flinched. Exxie laughed. "Relax, Penderby. What is your first name anyway?"

"Thomas."

"Not Tom or Tommy?"

"No, just Thomas."

Inside the stadium, the horn blasted to sound the end of the first quarter. Exxie took one long last look around the plaza.

"Well, Thomas," she said. "You want to give me a ride somewhere? It looks like my friend stood me up. Imagine that." She smiled and put her hand on the man's upper arm. "Wow. You've got a muscle there." She stepped closer to him, close enough to see the sheen of sweat on his neck.

His face flushed again as he cleared his throat. "I'd be happy to drop you off wherever you need to go."

Exxie linked arms with the man and gave him her most alluring smile. "Lead me to your car."

* * *

123

The traffic on the interstate coming into downtown slowed to a crawl as cars full of college kids and weekend partiers veered toward the exits that would take them to Canal and, eventually, the Quarter.

Cray barely noticed the cars around the Jeep. His driving was calm now, especially when compared to the hurtling pace at which he had driven to the nursing home. *No need to hurry now.*

The truth that his daughter would not come out of the coma had darted through the shadowy places of his mind during the months since the attack. He had not allowed that terrible reality to take up permanent residence in his consciousness. The nightmares, however, had battered him from the early days. Jenny, running and screaming, her arms outstretched to him, almost there, almost touching his fingers as he reached out to protect her, to draw her close. Then the dark figure snatching her back into the blackness filled with cackling evil.

That nightmare was over for him, he knew now. For those on his special list, the bad dreams were just beginning. Starting with his next selection, one who had moved quickly to the top of the list.

And now, there would be no restraint, he realized. He had long since given up any concern for his own safety, his life an empty shell with a single purpose of ridding the world of the child destroyers. But he had been overly careful in the planning and execution of his missions, knowing that his daughter needed him, even if she did not know it.

Now she was gone.

And his target of the hour was next.

Cray had paid little attention to the man's name on his list during his initial research. He had ordered the priority of his victims by their previous crimes and by the brevity of the sentences they had served. The courts in America had become notoriously soft on sexual predators, believing that a few months of rehabilitation was enough to "cure" them. Even when the bastards struck again, they were sometimes coddled by the system, giving them a third chance to destroy lives.

The man had never spent a night in jail, Cray's research had shown. Even after three different complaints had been filed against him for molesting underage girls and boys, he had walked free thanks to high-priced lawyers and a judicial system that favored the rights of wrongdoers over those of the innocent.

What particularly drew Cray's attention was his quarry's skill at using the Internet to lure his victims. He seemed to have unlimited access to porn websites of unimaginable depravity and would gradually expose his new, young friends to deeper and deeper cesspools of lurid experiences until they had gone too far. Then he would strike. And wipe them out. *Just as Jenny had been wiped out.*

A horn blared behind him and Cray jumped. He had stopped on the highway, his knuckles white on the steering wheel. He breathed fiercely through his nose and gently pushed the accelerator down and slowly made his way down the Canal Street exit ramp with a dozen other vehicles.

Once off I-10, he carefully joined the flow of traffic circling the SuperDome. He knew that his quarry could be long gone from the area by now, but it was worth the drive by to check it out. He knew where the man lived; he had spent many hours during the past month casing the residence and making checklists of his routines. He would not be hard to track down.

From inside the stadium came a blast of noise that ricocheted off the concrete towers. The Saints obviously had made a big play— maybe Deuce had broken for a long run—and the hometown crowd made sure to savor any small successes of their team.

Cray slowed the Jeep to a crawl and scanned the crowd in the plaza of the stadium, searching for any sign of the man in the yellow shirt. Maybe something had come up, forcing the man to break his date with the girl. He signaled to turn. He would make the block and then park the Jeep in order to walk the plaza for a closer inspection. *Maybe they went into the stadium.*

Only one way to find out.

* * *

Exxie could sense Penderby peeking at her as they walked down the side street to his car. "What?" she barked.

The man jerked. "What?"

"You keep looking at me. Stop it."

Penderby swallowed. "You just seem...upset. Are you okay?"

"Yeah, yeah, I'm fine. It's his loss anyway."

"His loss? Who...oh, the friend you were meeting here."

Exxie kept walking, but glanced at the man next to her. She had seen the man plenty of times in her life. He was the type who made himself indispensable by never turning down any assignment her father threw at him. Exxie had witnessed her father trashing the man to his face in a spasm of drunken laughter in front of others. Penderby always smiled and said nothing. She had thought him a wimp for letting her dad push him around. But he was one of the few who had never made a pass at her, even when he'd had a private opportunity to do so. His loyalty extended even to her, apparently.

"He better have a good excuse is all I'm gonna say," she said. When the man turned to peek at her again, she stuck out her tongue at him, then laughed.

He chuckled nervously and pushed his eyeglasses up on his nose.

"You ever think about getting contacts?" she asked.

"I tried to wear them. Twice. They were just too darn uncomfortable."

"You should try again. Those glasses are super geeky."

He colored again.

"Oh, c'mon, it's nothing personal. You'd just look better without them. I can tell." She put her arm through his again.

"Well, maybe I will check it out again."

At the next corner, a yellow Corvette pulled out and sped away. It reminded her of her father's car.

"Hey," she said. "This thing here today, the fact that you saw me here, it's just between us, right? Do not tell my parents I saw you here, got it?"

Penderby slowed his pace slightly and frowned at the girl. "Were you planning something that would get you in trouble, Exxie? You know I can't keep something from him if it might potentially hurt you...."

She cut him off. "No, it's nothing bad, I promise. I just...I didn't tell the complete truth about what I was up to, that's all." She smiled at him again. "You know how protective they are of me." *If only*, she thought. They barely know I'm there even when I'm right under their noses.

He searched her face, then kept walking toward his car. "All right. It's just between us then." He pointed. "There's my car. The silver sports utility vehicle."

She whistled. "Damn, Penderby. You been bagging me, with a cool ride like that. Tinted windows and everything." She ran her hand over the rear fender and admired her reflection in the window. The view of the inside of the truck was completely obstructed. "And it's just called an S-U-V, if you want to sound...not so uptight."

He nodded as he hit the remote to unlock the truck. "An S-U-V. Got it." He opened the door for her. "Because I certainly want to be cool."

She hopped into the passenger seat and watched the man walk around in front of the car to let himself in.

Once in, he carefully clicked his seatbelt into place and checked the adjustment of the outside mirrors.

The inside of the truck was shaded from the glare of the outside sun by the darkly tinted windows.

He waited while Exxie put on her seatbelt. "Let's roll," she said, waiting for Penderby to start up the truck. "C'mon, what's the holdup...."

She barely saw the white of the oncoming chloroform-soaked handkerchief before it was clamped over her mouth and nostrils.

Penderby's grip on her head allowed her to thrash only once before she slumped over in her seat, unconscious.

* * *

Inside the SuperDome, the bands marched across the field blaring away to signal halftime. A band of smokers gathered near the ticket gate that Cray had been staking out earlier. He watched the idiots commit ultra-slow suicide for a few minutes then let his gaze again sweep over the plaza.

He pondered for a moment whether he should go through the gate and mill around, hoping to see his target somewhere among the crowds. Too many people, he decided. He'd never find the man, even with the girl in his company.

He wasn't overly concerned at missing their actual meeting and following the man back to his house. He knew exactly where he lived. He'd just drive there, knock on the door, and say hello.

Cray smiled. Immediately, he put his hand to his face and let his fingertips trace the contours of the smile on his lips. Such a long time since he had smiled.

He walked across the plaza and back to his Jeep, cranked it up and eased back out into traffic.

Chapter 20

If you can't pick your fight, pick the site for your fight. Forte watched the rearview mirrors of the van as he remembered a favorite saying of one of his SEAL trainers. Behind him, the pair of vehicles had cut the gap to a mere thirty yards. The black car kept edging over the center line behind the enemy van to keep an eye on Forte's van.

The white car ahead had kept a steady 50 miles an hour. Now, as traffic had nearly vanished on this two-lane road, it was slowing even more.

A quarter-mile ahead, Forte saw the sign for a roadside restaurant he'd visited before—*A Taste of Bavaria.*

He snatched up the radio handset again. "We're pulling into the restaurant ahead. Pull around and lay down some covering fire for us." His words snapped out hard. He glanced back at Fizer lying across the bench seat behind him. The boy's mouth was pressed tight but his eyes were open and alert.

"Gotcha covered, bossman," came Nomad's response on the radio.

Beside him, Jackie leaned forward and pulled two pistol-grip Remington 870 pump shotguns from their hideouts beneath the seat. She turned and unlocked the sliding side door next to the boy.

Forte kept his eyes on the road and called back to the boy. "Fizer, look at me and listen very closely. When we stop at the restaurant, you follow Jackie through the front doors and keep low. Just stay with her. Understand?"

"I understand."

Forte gripped the wheel and kept his speed steady as the driveway for the restaurant appeared through the roadside trees. "Okay, passengers, hold on to your butts."

Without tapping the brakes, he jerked the steering hard right. The force of the turn slammed him into the driver's door and the shriek of tires against pavement tore through the air. Then, they reached the gravel. The van lost all traction and spun full circle toward the front porch of the restaurant, barely missing a pickup truck, the only vehicle in the parking lot. *Blammm.* They hit the protective circle of stumps that had been sunk into the ground around the porch to define the parking spaces. The van tilted onto its right wheels and teetered, then crashed back to a shuddering stop.

"Out! Out!" Forte yelled and heard the sliding door ripping open.

He flung open the driver's door and leaped out on to the gravel, pumping a double-ought buckshot shell into the gun's chamber. Squealing of tires came from the road at the end of the driveway. He could see nothing through the cloud of dust from his skidding stop.

He thumbed off the safety of the shotgun. And waited.

The black car lunged through the fog of dirt and roared straight at him.

He raised the shotgun and blew out the windshield.

The car veered left and crashed through the trees next to the parking lot. It slammed sideways into a huge oak tree. A shower of Spanish moss drifted down over the car as its occupants struggled to escape its mangled doors.

Forte turned and ran into the restaurant.

Outside, gravel rattled against the front windows as the the white van and the car slid into the lot.

Once inside, Forte broke out a pane of the front window and sent two quick blasts from his shotgun out through the dust. He ducked low just before a half-dozen rounds from shotguns and handguns outside smashed out the rest of the window panes.

From behind him in the kitchen came muffled screams.

Eerily, the chords of a Handel symphony floated through the restaurant from hidden speakers.

Jackie called out from behind the front counter with a cash register on one end. "Everyone's fine. All employees are in the walk-in freezer now. Fizer's with me, under this counter." Next to the counter, the glass panels of a pastry display lay shattered. Shards of glass were stuck in the strudels and Bavarian creams in the display case.

Outside, a barrage of gunshots slammed into the vehicles, these coming from the trees on the other side of the parking lot. Nomad had opened fire on the attackers. They returned fire and this time the rattle of an automatic rifle was mixed with the reports of the other weapons.

Not good, thought Forte. That kind of firepower could quickly wipe out a group of people with automatic pistols or even shotguns, not matter how well they shot.

"You dial 9-1-1 yet?" he yelled behind him.

"Yes," came back Jackie's reply.

It would take a while for the sheriff's deputies from this parish to respond to the call. Even when they did, they wouldn't be prepared for this type of onslaught. But they would bring more guns with them. *If we can hold out long enough.*

The distant gunfire died away. Nomad was either reloading or moving to a new location from which to attack or both.

Forte stooped and began to move toward the counter where Jackie and Fizer were hidden. A round of gunfire sent him to the floor. Immediately, Jackie sprang up and scattered a clip from her Glock through the open window. Forte crawled through the broken glass, staying below the line of sight from outside.

"Thanks," he said. Jackie knelt on one knee and slapped another clip into her Glock nine. Under the counter beneath the cash register, Fizer sat in a tight ball, his arms wrapped around his knees, drawing them under his chin. His eyes seemed less afraid now.

"You okay?" Forte asked.

The boy gave an attempt at a smile. "Not quite like the video games, huh?"

Forte chuckled softly, reached out and slapped the boy on the knee. "Not quite."

To Jackie he said, "Everyone in the freezer?"

"Yes. They'll be okay for a while."

He peeked around the edge of the counter. From another section of the woods came the sound of gunshots; Nomad had opened fire again. No bullets were flying toward the inside of the restaurant now.

"There's a walkway to the left that leads to a larger dining room." He pointed with the barrel of his shotgun. "If we can make it to there, we can head through the woods to some guest cabins." He had chatted with the owner a few months earlier about the cabins they were renovating. "Follow me." He crawled toward the corridor and raised himself into a crouch once he'd reached it. The other two followed quickly.

The entrance of the walkway was solid wall for a mere six feet, then the sides became windows and skylights, creating a glass tunnel for a dozen feet. Forte poked his head out beyond the edge of the wall next to the window and quickly drew back. Nothing but trees and shrubbery were visible through the windows of the walkway.

He motioned for the other two to follow him.

He stepped out into the unprotected area of the walkway.

A man with a rifle stepped around the corner just four feet away.

"Down!" screamed Forte.

He watched as the barrel of the rifle swung toward him.

Forte's 12-gauge was already in position. He pulled the trigger. The blast knocked the man flat on his back, as if he'd been snatched from behind by a gigantic rope.

Forte stopped, watching. No blood had soaked through the man's shirt. Through the now glass-less opening of the window came a groan from the figure lying prone in the bushes. "They're wearing bulletproof vests," he said aloud. He took out his Glock and shot the man in the upper right arm close to the shoulder.

They sprinted toward the dining room.

Outside, the intensity of the gun battle had increased. Another automatic rifle joined the previous one, making a continuous string of sharp rattattats punctuated by the deeper booms of the shotguns. Branches rattled down on the parked cars as they were clipped from their trees by the bullets. *Nomad must be shuttling fast from one side to the other.* Ka-bloom! A gas tank exploded on one of the vehicles. Forte smiled. He had remembered his SEAL buddy practicing that manuever on junked cars for hours on end, blasting the rear ends of the cars until they became their own bombs.

He paused. *Unless it's our van.*

He motioned Jackie and Fizer to come close. "That far exit of the dining room leads out onto a path that winds toward the cabins. We're going out but cutting back through the woods directly behind the restaurant and circling back to the cabins. Fizer, you stay with Jackie if we get separated. Understand?"

"I got it."

The trio stayed lower than the table tops as they crept through the room toward the exit. Halfway there, Forte signaled to stop. He watched the windows of the room for any sign of movement. Seeing none, he waved them to continue.

At the door of the exit, he peeled up a tiny corner of the gingham curtain over the window in the door. No attackers were lying in wait for them.

The gunfire erupted again, this time from the opposite end of the restaurant from where they now crouched. *Perfect.*

"Let's go. Stay close and stay low," Forte whispered. He cracked open the door carefully, took another quick look around and went out. Fizer followed and Jackie brought up the lead, the pistol-grip shotgun held at waist level.

A bricked patio outside the back door held four tables for outside diners. Man-high bushes stood guard around the patio with an open gate in the hedge. They darted toward the gate. The path to the cabins was bordered with skull-sized stones and paved with pine bark that crackled under their feet. Once clear of the building, they dashed through the thick underbrush that hugged the restaurant from behind.

On the other side of the building, the gun battle heated up abruptly, sounding like someone had dropped a match into a box of mixed fireworks. *Just keep them busy for a few more minutes, Nomad.*

They moved slowly through the woods, toward the closest cabin. To their left, the rock-bordered path serpentined as it came and went from their view. No one was on it.

Forte could feel Fizer's hand lightly touch his back as they crept along carefully avoiding any branches that would crack under foot. In between the gunfire, every snapped twig beneath their footsteps seemed deafening.

The guns stopped firing. Forte held up a hand. The group stopped, listening. From a speaker mounted on the outside of the restaurant came the sounds of Mozart's *Marriage of Figaro*. The smell of gunpowder lay heavy in the air now.

The roof of the cabin was visible now, a hundred feet away.

Not far to go. He moved ahead, the other two following closely.

The guns had not started up again. Was Nomad out of ammo?

He paused next to a thick pine tree, listening.

Braaap. A coughing noise came from forty feet away just as a bullet slammed into the trunk near his head. "Down!" Forte hissed. The three of them scrambled to the other side of the big tree. Someone with a silencer had glided through the woods away from the unmuffled firefight. *Someone sneaky....*

"It coulda been your head, podnuh," Lucky Battier said, his voice low. He sounded as if he were standing next to them.

Forte raised the shotgun but hesitated. Had Battier signaled for the others to surround them?

A splattering of gunfire broke the silence, still on the other side of the building. It stopped. Forte listened. No sound of people rushing through the woods.

He scanned the underbrush around him. Nothing. Behind him he sensed the figures of the other two, crouched and waiting. He turned and curled a finger at Jackie to come close. Putting his mouth against her ear, he whispered. "Take him to the cabin. I'll cover you." The smell of her shampoo seemed unworldly in the midst of the aromas of dust and burnt gunpowder. He pulled back and looked into her eyes for assent. Her face was calm.

Far-off gunfire sounded again. The woman and boy scampered away, bent double.

Forte watched for any movement from the direction he had heard Lucky's voice. The wind had stopped. Nothing.

He backed toward the cabin, the shotgun barrel level. He stopped, waiting, watching. He turned to take another step.

And everything exploded.

Bullets cut through the air above him, sending a shower of bark and pine cones down. To his left a shotgun blasted. A figure darted to his right about 20 feet away. He whirled and sent three blasts through the woods as quickly as he could pump. He barreled through the trees now toward the cabin.

Ahead, he could hear Jackie's pistol snapping shots.

He reached the cabin and dove around the corner just as a storm of bullets slammed into the side of the log structure. He pointed his Glock behind him and scattered four shots back through the trees. The window above his head shattered as a shotgun blast came from a clump of trees to his right. *Either he is the worst shot in the world or he's deliberately missing me.* The rear of the cabin was a dozen feet away. He dived for the back porch and scuttled into the crawl space under the worn floor boards.

Fizer was huddled there in the dirt. On the other side of the porch, Jackie was firing away.

The shooting had stopped on the other side of the building. *They're closing in on us.*

"You okay?" he asked the boy, who nodded.

In the trees, a pair of figures rushed through the underbrush. He sent a shotgun blast after them.

"We've got to get inside," he yelled to Jackie.

A fusillade of machine gun rounds ripped along the top of the porch above his head.

Forte reloaded his scattergun and popped another clip into his Glock.

About 50 yards out from the cabin, a shotgun war started up. *Nomad.*

Suddenly the attackers closest to the cabin turned and began firing out in the underbrush.

Forte leapt out from underneath the porch and emptied the Glock into the bushes where he had last seen movement.

In the distance, sirens broke through hot summer air. The county cops had arrived faster than he had estimated. *Thank goodness.* He had used his last clip for the Glock.

From the parking lot came the sounds of engines cranking up.

A few more shotgun rounds boomed from close to the restaurant but were directed toward the fleeing cars.

Forte slowly straightened up and swept the woods around the cabin for any other attackers left behind.

Gravel spun against the trees out front, then the squeal of tires on pavement as the attackers fled.

Across the porch, Jackie brushed the dirt and leaves from her hair.

"The cavalry has arrived," she said.

Forte fingered a bloody spot on his T-shirt where a fragment of glass had cut him.

"Let's get Fizer and move around to the front."

He bent down to look below the porch. "C'mon, we've had enough fun for...."

The boy was gone.

Chapter 21

Exxie watched the little girl watch the juggler. The man was perched on a ten-foot-high unicycle which he caused to mock-sway and fake-tilt for the tourists bunched around him. With each awkward, teetering turn of the sprocket, the man on the high seat drew oohs and ahhhs from the crowd. None were more captivated than the five-year-old blonde girl, her blue eyes sparkling with laughter then flying open when the jokester nearly plunged to the pavement of Jackson Square in front of the cathedral.

Exxie took note as the unicyclist finally balanced himself enough to call for three items: a bowling pin, a machete, and an apple. One by one the items were tossed up to him. And he began to juggle them. She had seen it before, dozens of times as a child. Her attention was drawn to the child's rapt enjoyment of the moment.

"Ooohhh, he's...he's juggin' the big knife, daddy. Look, look, lookee." Her voice rose higher as she tugged at the man's pants leg next to her. He bent and scooped her up, the little girl pointing at the man on the bike and waving and waving and calling out to him.

Exxie sighed. What was it about the girl that drew her?

The juggler went faster. Machete, bowling pin, apple. Machete, bowling pin, apple. Machete, bowling pin, apple. Machete, bowling pin...*chomp*. He bit the apple and flung it up again into the rotation of the juggling act, keeping the three items going, then taking another bite, then another, then...the act was over. Applause and tips came from the tourists who had driven miles to see such outdoor fun in this famous square. The crowd dispersed and wandered away, past General Jackson tipping his hat on his rearing steed, on to other sights in the Quarter.

The father and child slowly turned and now their faces could be seen.

Exxie gasped.

The small girl with the golden hair smiled at her.

It was her face. Her own face looking back at her.

It was five-year-old Exxie.

Older Exxie looked at the girl, transfixed. It didn't seem too strange. She was fascinated by the sweetness in the girl's face. Had she been that innocent and trusting?

The little girl smiled and older Exxie smiled back for the longest time.

Then she looked at the man. But it wasn't her father.

"What are you doing here...why are you with the little girl...what are...what are you going to do to her...No, No, NO, NOOOOOOO!" she screamed and flung her head back but no sound would come out. She felt the blood rushing to her temples, throbbing, the pain, the light....

And the man cackled. Louder and louder and...

Exxie's eyes snapped open.

Penderby was laughing as he leaned against the wall of a room she had never seen before. The laugh was high-pitched and sounded more like the cackle of a witch than that of a grown man.

"Bad dream, little miss rich bitch?" he said.

Exxie bore into the man with her eyes and let loose a stream of invective reserved for the worst of those who had earned her ire. The curses died and dwindled to mere mumbles against the duct tape over her mouth. She thrashed and tried to kick, but her arms and legs were taped to a heavy wooden chair in the middle of the room.

Penderby stopped laughing and watched her for five seconds or so, then strode across the room and slapped her hard.

Exxie's head snapped back and the chair tipped over, slamming her to the hardwood floor. The back of her head bounced on the wood and her vision filled with dark spots, then cleared.

The man reached down and easily picked up the chair-bound girl, slamming her upright again. He leaned close and put his face in front of hers, staring into her eyes from a half-foot away.

Looking into those pitiless eyes, she felt fear overtake her anger for the first time.

He was studying her now. When he spoke, the softness of his voice cut away her courage more than if he had screamed at her.

"You really thought you were in charge, didn't you? You have no idea what it's like to be in total control, do you?" His face drew near, so close she could feel his breath on her cheek, smell the mint of his mouth. His face brushed against hers and she jerked back.

Suddenly, she slammed her forehead toward him. *I'll smash you, you bastard.*

But he had stepped back.

Another slap sent the chair crashing to the floor again.

This time he left her there.

Exxie lay on her side, her back to the man. His footsteps on the wooden floor sounded close to her head.

He stepped over her and walked over to a leather sofa stylishly arranged across the corner of the room. He sat and watched her.

"I'm going to enjoy this, Exxie Graham, even more than I thought I would."

Exxie heard a snorting noise and realized it was her. Her breath was pouring out of her nostrils like a frightened animal. *Stop it, stop it,* she told herself. She forced her breathing to slow down. Slower, slower. That's better.

Penderby crossed one leg over the other and brushed a speck of lint off his knee. No hint of the nervous mannerisms he had shown earlier remained with the man. He was relaxed and confident now. *Like MuchoMan.*

Exxie had never seen him like this before. The after-effect of the knockout drug made her wonder if she was imagining him like this. She rolled her cheek against the floor and felt the bruises already forming. *No, this was real.*

She closed her eyes and breathed deeper, slower. *Must think. What's happening to me here?*

* * *

Cray drove twice past the house, noticing that the garage door was down. He always kept the garage door closed when he drove the silver SUV home. *You perverted bastard, you're going to pay.*

He had driven past the man's house dozens of times in his van, at all hours. He knew every part of Penderby's routine. It hadn't taken long; the man was extremely predictable. Up at 5:30 for a three-mile run, work out on the Nautilus machine, punch a heavy bag, then the speed bag and practice the footwork, black coffee and bran cereal, and drive down to the VillaCom offices by 7:30 a.m. After a day of doing whatever flunky work he did at the office, he was back home by 6:30 p.m. Back out by 8 p.m. on Tuesdays and Thursdays for his martial arts classes. Monday evenings were for grocery shopping. Wednesday nights he did laundry.

The weekends were for his extracurricular activities.

Cray would be quite satisfied to put a stop to Penderby's routine.

He drove to a small park a quarter mile from the house and parked the Jeep in the shade. He sat for a moment and watched the people milling about the area, kids playing on slides and monkey bars, watched by their mothers and a few weekend dads. Everything seemed normal here. He had no reason to suspect that the police were closing in on him yet. But it never hurts to notice what is going on around you, a drill instructor had told him early in basic training—right before he had been jumped by two other soldiers in an impromptu ambush.

Cray got out of the Jeep and began his stretching exercises, bending low and gripping his legs, holding that pose for 30 seconds, then stretching out the legs, just as anyone should before they embark on a nice jog in muggy New Orleans on the last Saturday in August. Already the sweat was beading up on his forehead. He paid it no mind. The stretching continued and it wasn't all for show. A cramp in the midst of this operation could prove disastrous. No, he wanted to be loose and ready. Completely ready.

He began the jog slowly, winding his way through the park on the new trail the city had built in this neighborhood in an attempt to draw residents back within the city limits. Or at least to stem the hemorrhage of urban flight it had experienced during the past couple of decades. Walkers were out in force today, some strolling along in the heat while others power-strode along, arms churning. A few runners weaved past the walkers. One college boy sprinted past Cray but he kept his pace. No time for a race today, sonny.

His breathing was easy. This run was a pittance compared to the five-mile run he had logged every morning for the past year. After the attack on Jenny, he had nearly run himself into the ground in an attempt to make himself sleep at night. After the first month, he'd found that he enjoyed the process, the routine of it. Even the pain of it. It reminded him he was alive and that he had a purpose, a mission to complete. He was strong, as strong as he'd ever been in his life, he felt, including his time in the Rangers.

Back then, he'd been so competitive that he felt he had to best every other person in his squad in every aspect of training: hand-to-hand combat, marksmanship, even getting his bunk so neat it looked as if it were cast in a mold. And he had bested everyone around him. That's why he was recommended for Ranger training. And there he had excelled, too, but he was not the absolute best in everything. Except for sniper training. There he'd been the base champion and had, in fact, beaten the long-standing record for the longest sniper hit in history. Or course, there was no plaque given to him to that effect, but his commander had made sure he knew the truth about it.

Today, however, he would not be relying on the long shot. His sniper rifle was safely hidden back at his place in the secret gun cabinet. Today, he would be using his bare hands. The compact nine-millimeter in the holster in the small of his back was just for insurance.

He kept jogging, once more around the park. Then he veered off toward Penderby's neighborhood.

Once away from the park, he saw no one in the yards outside the houses. A sweltering August afternoon such as this demanded that one have a reason to be outside. Reasons like kids screaming for the playground or a swimming pool in which to splash. Everyone was inside, enjoying the air conditioning.

Cray loped along until he came to the street that ran parallel to Penderby's, behind his house. He began counting the houses as he passed them. *One, two, three, four, five....* There it was, the brick house with the columns. As usual, the boat was gone from its concrete pad next to the garage. The family was at the lake.

Without looking around, Cray turned and ran along the hedge that blocked the view of the neighbor. He sprinted now, through the side yard of the house, vaulting the fence without slowing. Ahead was the fence that separated the back yard from Penderby's. He never slowed down.

And it happened just as it had a hundred times in his mind.

He leaped the back fence and ran full speed toward the back door. Up the steps of the deck and across it in three huge bounds, flinging open the storm door, and ramming the door with his shoulder knocking it loose from the lock and hearing it blam against the kitchen counter, and tumbling across the floor just in case he was expected and now up again running to the back bedroom where they would surely be.

He hit the bedroom door and splintered it open, his face flushed with excitement knowing he would witness the last look of astonishment that Mr. Slimeball Penderby would ever display on this earth.

He dived into the bedroom, tumbled and rolled, springing instantly into combat stance. The room was empty.

Grabbing the closet doorknob, he flung the door open. Waiting a beat for any response, he swept the clothes off the hanging bar inside the closet. No one hiding here.

He stopped. And listened. Silently, he sprinted from room to room, checking out every space.

No one was in the house.

* * *

Penderby stood in the kitchen sipping orange juice as he watched a heron circle above the cypress trees. The bird glided lower and lower until it lit on a gnarled root at the edge of the swamp. It stood motionless for a moment, making sure no other animal predators were close enough to attack. Then it picked its way across the exposed roots of the trees, searching the water for food.

A dozen yards away an alligator watched the lanky bird with the only visible part of his body, his eyes barely penetrating the surface of the swamp.

Penderby watched the gator as it waited patiently for the heron to come closer. He had seen the alligator many times on his trips to the swamp and had even thrown some scraps out for the huge reptile.

He loved the old cabin, even though he had not visited here in months. No one knew about it, not even his closest workmates at VillaCom. Of course, he had known that someday he would have to give it up. Even though the stilt-supported structure was accessible only by canoe or swamp boat, it could be found eventually. If the stakes were high enough.

Penderby felt a small chill of pleasure run down his spine.

Outside, the heron stabbed its beak into the water and came up with the fish. The bird, feeling the victor, tilted its head and gobbled it down.

Suddenly the water erupted next to the bird. The alligator lunged, jaws gaping, snapping.

The heron sprang into the air, wings thrashing. The jaws of the hunter barely missed the tail feathers of the bird, which lifted above the water, then above the trees.

The man at the window raised his glass and tipped it toward the animal. "Better luck next time, old pal."

He turned from the window. The girl lay where she had fallen, still strapped to the chair. He watched the rise and fall of her chest as she tried to calm her breathing.

He stepped toward her—

His pager went off.

Brow furrowed, he unclipped it from his belt and held it up. Only two people knew this number—the security company in charge of the burglary system at his regular residence and....

It was the security company.

He stepped into the bedroom, unzipped a backpack and pulled out a cellphone, one of several dozen. He punched in the number, waited. "I'm responding to your page. Yes, this is Thomas Penderby...a break-in...nothing taken...yes, thank you."

He pushed the End button on the phone.

The girl was lying still now, listening.

He stepped over her, went to the front door. On the front porch of the cabin, he flung the cellphone out over the water. It skipped once across the water and landed near the cypress roots where the heron had fled.

He stood for a moment, thinking. A mosquito buzzed close to his face and he slapped it away. He spun and walked back through the cabin.

In the bedroom, he flipped open a laptop computer and punched the power button. As he waited for it to boot up, he pulled out another cellphone and switched it on. From a sidepocket of the backpack, he took out a small cable and plugged it into the phone.

He clicked the other end of the cable into a slot in the wireless modem card in the laptop.

A few taps on the mousepad and he was logged on to the Internet. He pulled up the web browser, entered a password-protected web page, and waited for the page to load.

He clicked on a link to view the video capture log. The log showed that the remote cameras in his house had indeed recorded the break-in at his house, automatically sending the digital video clips to this web page.

He clicked the "PLAY" button on the screen of the laptop.

The playback was jerky because the video was captured at a rate of five frames per second as opposed to the usual 30 frames per second that made for smooth video playback. He could plainly see the intruder, however.

The man had hit the back door at a run, apparently, and never slowed down.

No rifling through drawers or searching for items to steal. The man, clad in running shorts, sneakers, and T-shirt, had come straight to Penderby's bedroom at the end of a hallway in the back of the house.

Penderby watched as the man flung himself into the room. He was obviously ready to attack.

Something was wrong here. The intruder wasn't looking to steal anything. He's after me, Penderby realized. How could they have come after me so quickly?

He logged off and walked back to the den where Exxie lay. She came alive again, thrashing against the tape restraints.

Penderby slapped her, hard. She lay still, her eyes trained on him fiercely above the gray tape over her mouth. He reached down and ripped it off her face.

She screamed curses at him now. Another slap silenced her.

He stood over her. "The only sound you are allowed to make will be to answer my questions."

She shook the hair from her face. "You sick...." The force of the next slap bounced her head against the wooden floor.

Penderby waited a moment. "Nod once if you understand me."

The girl nodded.

"Here's your question. Who else knew you were going to the football game?"

Exxie glared at him hard, her eyes still filled with hatred. She spat blood at him from her split lip.

He slapped her again, this time in anger.

The girl started sobbing now.

He grabbed her by the hair and pulled her face back toward him. "Who else?" he whispered.

Exxie opened her eyes now. The anger was gone now, replaced by fear.

"Nobody. Nobody knew." She broke down into tears.

Penderby watched her for a moment, then released her hair.

He strode back into the bedroom and reached into the backpack again. He brought out two items: a roll of duct tape and a cell phone. After snatching off a foot-long length of the tape, he roughly put it over Exxie's mouth to gag her again.

He stood and watched the girl for a moment. Then he punched a number into the cell phone and waited for an answer.

Chapter 22

Magazine Street shoots straight away from downtown and takes on more personalities than a she-male cabaret performer at one of the cheap clubs in the Quarter. The street loses its neat curbs and office buildings as it gets past RiverWalk and the renewal projects that drew the big investors in the eighties and nineties. It becomes dangerous for a mile or so as it crosses the war zone of burnt out warehouses and drums filled with scrapwood fires circled by the homeless. Up near Felicity, the funky shops begin, starting with a litter of cat and dog grooming establishments, then blending into craft shops, antique places, eateries, and bars. Further down, it hugs the backside of Audubon Park and the storefronts get funkier as the college kids from Tulane and Loyola pedal their bikes across Magazine to their flats and walkups.

Forte took the last deep drag from Checkers Number Three for the day and ground it out in the ceramic pelican's open bill. Through the window of the bar, the shadows of dusk were just beginning to stretch toward the private gym across the street. It had been a half-hour since Lucky Battier and a pair of bodyguards pulled up in a black Lincoln and let themselves in the side door of the unlabeled building. Another guard stayed behind to watch the side entrance.

He had guessed right. And Nomad had confirmed the location by tailing Battier and company for the past two hours.

Not much security, Forte thought. A lot of gall or stupidity. Or both.

He checked his watch. Almost time.

It had taken all his willpower to refrain from breaking down Marchetti's front door and shooting people, one by one, until he found someone who would tell where they had hidden Fizer Beal. He knew from past experience that that tactic rarely worked, and he had undoubtedly used up more risks than his cat Boo had lives. Besides, he only had two people on his attack team this afternoon.

Patience would have to do its work.

Earlier, when they discovered Fizer was gone, he had left Jackie behind to tell the restaurant owner that they would be talking to the FBI later about the shooting incident. All the paperwork could be filled out then. He and Nomad had raced down Highway 22 towards I-55 to catch Battier and the attackers. Hasty calls had gone out to local cops for assistance but the shot-up cars and van they were chasing seemed to just melt into the countryside.

So, they waited a few hours for Battier to pick up his routine. He didn't let them down.

Three blocks away, Nomad sat on a mountain bike, drinking a soda with his ball cap turned backwards on his head. Three college guys were gathered around him, listening to some outlandish tale of mercenary exploits that, if truth be told, were authentic. Through the window of the bar, Forte watched as Nomad glanced at his watch, then quickly wrapped up his story.

On the next corner past the gym, a thirty-something woman wearing a peasant skirt and tank top pushed a baby stroller along the sidewalk. She stopped every few steps and cooed into the deeply scooped bottom of the stroller. Forte watched as the woman peered over the top of her sunshades at her watch. *Nice routine, Jackie*, he mused.

He got up from the table, left a ten for his waiter, and walked out the door.

Nomad was waving behind him one last time before standing on the pedals of the bike. It picked up speed.

Jackie approached with the stroller, almost to the corner of the gym now.

Both members of his team watched him walk out of the eatery. He nodded.

Jackie pushed the stroller even with the guard at the door. She flashed a brilliant smile at the man. He grinned back.

Nomad swerved around the corner of the gym.

The guard's head jerked toward the bicyclist.

Jackie's hand plunged into the stroller. Out came a stun gun. One zap and the man went down, writhing on the sidewalk.

Forte sprinted past a middle-aged couple who gasped and stepped back under the awning of the restaurant.

Jackie reached again into the stroller and snatched up two H&K submachine guns. She tossed one to Nomad as he leaped off his bike.

Forte was at the door of the gym now, his Glock drawn. Nomad stood next to the wall and flashed a silent count with his fingers. *Three, two, one....*

They banged the door open and fanned into the open room.

Battier stood in the middle of a boxing ring, squared against one of the bodyguards. Both men wore headguards, boxing gloves, and footpads. They spun toward the entrance and crouched slightly, then slowly straightened.

The other bodyguard dropped the soft drink bottle he was gulping and made a motion toward his holster.

Jackie tapped the trigger of her H&K once and sent a three-round burst over the man's head. He froze and slowly put his hands over his head.

Forte nodded and his two team members walked the perimeter of the inside of the building, carefully peering over a counter in the corner of the room. They checked out the locker room and came out.

"All clear," Nomad called out.

In the ring, Battier had regained his composure somewhat. He strolled over to the elastic ropes and spread his arms out over them. An Elvis ballad oozed out of the frazzled stereo speakers bolted to the steel girder ceiling of the gym. Two man-high fans were pointed toward the ring, sending cross-blasts of warm air swirling through the metal building.

"Talking about the canary coming to the cat," he said.

Forte took five long strides, leapt through the ropes into the ring, and knocked Lucky down with one punch. The sparring partner moved toward Forte, but Nomad released a burst from his H&K. One of the stereo speakers crashed to the concrete floor.

"Where's the boy?" Forte asked softly.

Lucky wiped the back of a glove across his mouth and examined the smear of red. He lay on the mat and exposed a bloody grin.

Forte kicked him in the ribs. Lucky groaned and quickly rolled away, then sprang into a standing position. The smile was gone now. The gangster began unlacing his boxing gloves. He turned to the sparring partner. "Get out of the ring." The man climbed out under the watchful gaze of Nomad and Jackie.

Lucky flung off the gloves, took off the head protector and the footpads. He squared off against Forte.

"You don't know where he is, do you?" the gangster asked.

Forte backed away and handed his gun to Jackie through the ropes. He turned and silently faced the gangster again.

Lucky spit blood out of the ring. "You think we have him, and you're going to come in here and beat the information out of me. Is that it?" He was bouncing on the balls of his feet now. "If your people promised not to shoot me, I would invite you to try and beat it out of me right now." He spit on Forte's shirt.

Forte snapped a jab that missed Lucky's head. Two returning jabs, a left and a right, hit him so quickly he took a step backward.

Jackie moved toward the ring. "Al, I don't think...."

Forte waved her away. He turned and started circling his opponent. "So, you didn't come after him today?" He feinted a punch, then sent a quick kick into the other man's ribs. Lucky partially deflected the kick and countered with a kick that numbed Forte's lower back.

Lucky danced away to dodge a roundhouse kick. His eyes sparkled now, circling, moving in and out, faking a punch, looking for weaknesses.

"Oh, we came for the boy," he said. *Whap, whap.* Two jabs bounced off Forte's forearms. "We just didn't leave with him."

"Liar." Forte waited for the next punch, catching and holding Lucky's hand and sending an elbow into the hoodlum's jaw. Battier stumbled and moved away, wary now.

Forte's cellphone in his pocket went off. Battier's leg shot straight out, a lightning kick to the chest. Forte felt the breath whoosh out of him, sending him to one knee on the pad. He watched as a drop of sweat fell from his nose to the mat, dropping in slow motion. Then everything sped up again.

Lucky's second kick was hurried, too eager to put the downed man out for the count. Forte caught his leg and twisted hard, sending Battier crashing to the mat. Forte tried punching the man, but he was too close to put power behind the hit. The two men grappled and rolled across the mat until they rested against one of the corner posts.

Forte, on top, stared into Battier's eyes inches away. The man's gaze was calm, almost amused. His voice seemed strained however as they remained locked in a stalemate. "Think about it, podnuh. Would I be playing patty-cake here with you tonight if I had Fizer Beal locked up somewhere?" He paused and sucked in another lungful of air. "Alvin, there's more going on here than meets the eye."

Forte's phone rang again. He could feel it digging into his hip. He rolled free of Battier.

The two men sat on the mat of the boxing ring, gulping air and watching for another move from their opponent.

Slowly, Forte rose to one knee again, then stood. He moved to the opposite side of the ring, and pulled out the phone to check the caller ID. One call was from the FBI office, presumably from Rosie Dent.

The second call was from the home of Exxie Graham.

As he peered at the phone's display, it rang again, its electronic tones strikingly discordant with the next offering from Elvis coming from the remaining speaker in the ceiling joists.

The Grahams were calling again.

Forte turned off the phone without answering.

Battier had sat up, his back against the corner post and his legs splayed out in front of him. "Not a bad little scrap, Mistuh FOH-TAY. 'Course, in a few more minutes, I woulda whipped your ass in front of your little friends." He rolled his head toward Nomad, whose face was impassive.

Forte stood stock-still and focused on the man seated on the mat. He touched a finger to his lip and brought away a crimson droplet. Was he telling the truth about not having Fizer? And if so, where was the boy?

It had always been easier for him to take action than to deal with failure or disappointment. Or fear. On the football field, he was an emotionless missile spearing running backs like Battier. In the SEALs, he had volunteered for the worst missions and had never looked back. IceMan, they'd called him. Even when his wife had been murdered in the gang prank, he had immediately tracked the boy down. The action had come easily; within an hour he'd found the 14-year-old and had him against the wall of his rat-infested slum apartment, a .45 automatic against his head, the boy's eyes wide with fear as the grandmother and younger sister pleaded, whimpering in the corner. So close, he'd come so close to pulling that trigger.

The action he could handle. It was the despair he could never face. That drove him to the liquor. Then the drugs. And the black hole with nothing but more despair, more loneliness, a hole so big he couldn't find the edges, couldn't feel the handholds to pull himself out. He'd needed help then.

He needed it now.

As sirens drew closer to the gym, Forte signaled to the two other members of his team. They walked out of the building and faded into the crowd.

Chapter 23

Fizer Beal laughed at all the right times, his guffaws blending in with the rest of the crowd as they watched the Peabody Brothers perform their street tap dance and comedy routine on the corner of Bourbon and Toulouse. The three brothers had to be in their late twenties to late thirties now and were famous in the Quarter for their performances. Tourists who had taken in their act in the past spied them from blocks away and hurriedly gathered others to swarm around "the boys," they called them. "Come watch these boys," they'd yell to their buddies.

Someone observing the Brothers' audience this day would see a skinny boy with spiked hair and scruffy clothes enjoying the show. They might notice the dirt stains on the boy's shirt and on the knees of his baggy jeans. But isn't that how they all dressed these days, proudly wearing the grimiest garb they could find? The slight cuts and scrapes on the boy's arms and necks looked as if he'd been rushing pell-mell through the brambles somewhere, going so fast he failed to dodge the low-lying branches and thorns hidden in the woods as he went.

But he wasn't staying put long enough for that close an examination.

Fizer laughed again along with the crowd. His eyes, however, weren't smiling, and they definitely were not trained on the Brothers' flailing limbs as they wound up their final dance. He was looking past the edge of the audience, looking for a special type of person.

A person who was looking for him.

The Peabody Brothers finished and took their bows as the applause exploded in the dusk. As the tourists surged forward and dropped their folding money into the rumpled, felt fedora placed upside down in the middle of the dirty intersection, Fizer casually walked away.

He increased his pace to match that of a group of five teens—two boys and three girls—who were walking along the middle of Bourbon. Walking to the rear and left of the group, he would appear—to an outside observer—to be part of the group. If any of the teenagers glanced in his direction, however, he looked away or up at one of the balconies where the gawkers were already gathering even though the most raucous of the Quarter's antics would not happen for hours.

He had milled about the Quarter for years, more recently with his pals who reveled in talking the college girls into buying them Hurricanes and bringing them outside Pat O'Brien's. The clowns. He blinked and felt a salty sting in his eyes as he remembered. He shook his head violently. *No time for that now; gotta keep going.*

Ahead, a man walked across the intersection with a small boy on his shoulders. Fizer slowed his pace, keeping the man and child in view. The tot had his arms wrapped around the man's head and was kicking his legs, yelling something. As Fizer drew closer he could hear the boy's admonitions now. "Go, big horsey! Go, go big big horsey!" The man jogged in place, bouncing the toddler on his shoulders and bringing down a shower of giggles.

Fizer realized he had stopped moving. *Go horsey, giddap go go go.* His father bouncing him as they strolled the Quarter, his mother doubled up with laughter as her tiny son gripped his father's ears and dug his heels in, spurring the horsey on to go go go. A few years later, he had drawn a first-grade picture of his memory and had brought it up to his father's study to show him. The door was cracked, and he peeked through before entering. The look on the man's face arrested him. He had been living the memory of that wonderful family day in the sunshine and could almost feel the smile on his father's face. But the man at the desk was crying silently. Six-year-old Fizer had watched the teardrops fall on to a sheet of paper on the desk. The man had crumpled the paper in his fist and tossed it in the trash can, then wiped his nose on his sleeve.

He had never shown his dad the picture.

Sure, there had been smiles and laughter after that. But never like that special day, it seemed to Fizer. And the smiles shined less and the laughter faded over the years until his mother died. Then they were gone. Forever. His father had never seemed as big as he had that horsey-ride day on Bourbon.

Fizer blinked away a tear. The man and boy were gone now.

Keep moving. Gotta keep going.

He caught up with the crowd as it flowed along Bourbon. From the corner of his eye, he caught sight of a man in a black T-shirt. He casually turned and looked into the window of a bar, watching the man's reflection. He breathed a sigh of relief. It wasn't Forte, the one who had been protecting him.

It wasn't that he didn't appreciate the man's help or the safety he had felt at The Refuge. In fact, he actually was sorry he had to put Forte and Jackie in the position of feeling as if they had lost him. He knew they would be on the lookout for him, once they found he had not been captured by Mr. Marchetti's men.

And he couldn't be captured until he had completed his dad's mission.

When his father spelled out the plan earlier that morning at the prison, it had been all he could do to keep a look of astonishment off his face. Could he pull it off? He had whispered his concern to Teddy Beal three times: *Are you sure I can do this? Are you positive this will work? How can I pull this off?*

The first part of the plan had been his escape. His dad couldn't possibly have known about the attack on the van carrying Fizer or that they would pull into the restaurant parking lot surrounded by woods. Just look for the first good opening to get away, his father had whispered to him. He had been closely guarded by Jackie during the first part of the attack. When they finally reached the cabin and hid under the porch, however, the gun battle had heated up, drawing Jackie away. He had waited until her attention was diverted for a few seconds, then crawled away from the cabin. He had cautiously slipped away from the area, then had broken into a run through the woods, ignoring the slaps of the tree branches and the roots that sent him sprawling three different times. He could tell from the sound of the shooting that no one was chasing him. And if they didn't immediately know he was gone, his protectors would believe that Marchetti's men had taken him, just as they had said they would.

Two miles through the thick undergrowth, he finally came to a barbed-wire fence surrounding a horse pasture. Past that, he'd found a mud-covered four-wheeler with the keys in the ignition parked behind a tool shed. Searching the shed, he had come up with a pair of heavy-duty wire cutters. He had grabbed them and sped away on the all-terrain vehicle. Four fences later he came across a gravel road that dumped him onto another two-lane country avenue. Weaving through the back-roads took him to a country store where he ditched the four-wheeler and begged for a ride into town from a couple of LSU students heading for a party in the Big Easy on a Saturday afternoon.

The college students had dropped him off at Jackson Square. He had taken his time meandering through the Quarter to his destination.

And now he was almost there.

He followed the small group of teens along Bourbon Street but turned left on St. Peter at the next corner. Another left on Dauphine and he was a block away. He slowed and studied the sidewalk as if searching for money that might have accidentally dribbled out of some tourist's pocket. The streetlamps were just now blinking on as the sun slid behind the old buildings on the narrow street. Fizer imperceptibly checked up and down the street to see if anyone seemed to be watching for him. An old woman in a purple beret led a golden retriever down the sidewalk on the opposite side of the street. Ahead of Fizer, a Japanese couple had stopped to read the plaque describing one of the houses that had made it onto the historical register. No one seemed to be taking the slightest interest in the stained boy with the spiked hair.

He shuffled along the sidewalk in the 500 block of Dauphine, looking at his feet, searching for the sign. He stopped. There it was. Scratched into the sidewalk were the initials F.B. He turned to glance behind him. No one was after him.

He was standing next to a narrow gate blocking an alley between two of the centuries-old houses that dotted the Quarter. He looked both ways again, then scaled the gate and dropped to the ground on the other side. He listened for a beat, then scurried down the dark alleyway. At the back edge of the building to his right he paused and peeked around the corner. A spacious courtyard spread out behind the building, which, like many old buildings in the Quarter, had been converted into an apartment. The backs of two other apartments overlooked the courtyard on two sides. A fence ran along the other side. Fizer got a running start and easily scaled the fence, dropping to the ground on the other side and scampering to a covered porch that blocked the view of any prying eyes.

He waited for the sound of people shouting or the noise of pursuing feet. Nothing.

He let his breath out slowly, realizing he had been holding it as he listened. He turned and walked along the porch to a shutter that had been fitted with a clasp and held tight with a combination lock. Tilting the lock to catch the last of the fading light in the courtyard, he twirled the knob of the lock and tried the combination his father had given him. Two revolutions right to number 52, one turn left to 7, a half-turn right again to number 14. He tugged on the lock. It came open.

He carefully pried open the shutters and prepared to go into the house.

BANG! Something hit the tin roof covering the porch. He dropped the lock and accidentally kicked it, sending it banging across the ancient wooden porch. He whirled toward the sound at the corner of the porch overhang.

The porch roof creaked once. The head of a tabby cat poked down from the roof and looked at him.

Fizer stared at the cat and leaned back against the building. He could feel his heart pounding through the thin T-shirt. He listened for a moment longer, then picked up the lock from the floor of the porch and crawled through the open window. Once inside, he pulled the shutters closed and found the new latch that had been installed there. He looped the combination lock through the latch and clicked it shut.

He stopped for a full minute, counting off the seconds silently to himself as he listened for any movements inside the old apartment. Nothing. The air had that stuffy smell of a place that had been shut up for a while.

He moved cautiously through the kitchen, opening the drawers that traditionally held cutlery. He found the hammer, then the pry bar. A door opened into a hallway that ran the length of the dwelling. Letting his fingertips graze the wall in the semi-darkness, he followed the hall, pausing to listen every few steps. The small flat had two bedrooms, a bathroom and a den. He entered every room, opened every closet door and leapt back in case someone was lying in wait. By the time he was satisfied no one else was in the apartment, his T-shirt was soaked with sweat. Late August was no time to be closed up in a place with no air conditioners, at least in New Orleans. He had no choice. He pulled off the T-shirt, wrung out his sweat, and draped it over the footboard of the bed in the second bedroom.

Across the dusty bedspread lay a pattern of parallel streaks of light as the louvres of the shuttered windows let in light from the street lamp outside the window. It wasn't quite enough to read by, but enough to reveal the contents of the room: a scarred wooden straight-back chair, a heavy oak chifforobe in one corner, and a bed in the center of the room. Fizer tossed the hammer and prybar on the bedspread and dragged the bed away from the center of the room and pushed it against the wall.

He walked up to the tall chifforobe and pushed against it, grunting. His dad had told him it was heavy but it could be moved. With all his strength he heaved against the piece of furniture, tugging and thrusting an inch or two at time. The progress was excruciatingly slow but it was moving. First this side, then the other, and finally it was repositioned away from the corner.

With one last push, Fizer uncovered the space where the wooden behemoth had hunkered. He slumped to the floor, gasping. The air in the old apartment burned his lungs; Fizer imagined the decay and mold and dust he was inhaling. After a few minutes, he was ready. *More work to do.*

He picked up the tools from the bed, then knelt on the warped hardwood floor, stooped and rapped on the floor lightly with his knuckles. It felt solid. He scooted across the age-worn floorboards on his knees to another spot a few feet away. Bending low and listening, he knocked again. *Tap tap tap.* Still solid. His father had said it would sound hollow when he found the right spot. *Where was it? Had he heard his father right?*

He repositioned himself and found another spot on the floor to rap. His put his ear an inch away from the board. *Tap tap TAP.*

Hollow. He tapped again.

This was it.

Fizer sprawled and put his left ear next to the wooden floor. In the faint light of the streetlamp he could see no seams in the floor. Was this it?

He sat up and took a deep breath, held it, then blew it out slowly. *Patience.*

Lying on the floor again, he closed his eyes and let his fingertips travel lightly along the floorboards. Up one board and down the other, he felt for any crack in the boards, any irregularity in the pattern. A century of footsteps had etched tiny imperfections in the floor that could only be detected by touching the wood. Inch by inch Fizer's fingers explored the surface of the antique floor until...*there*...the crack where two boards butted together seemed a little too uniform.

He snatched up the tools and put the prybar at the crack. Tapping gently with the hammer, he sank the tip of the bar into the indentation. He stopped and listened. From outside the flat came the typical sounds of the Quarter, the laughter of tourists and staccato horn beeps from the taxis punctuating the music from the bars and street players. Fizer would have fretted if the sounds weren't there. He went back to work.

He tapped twice more, then pulled against the lever of the prybar. The edge of the board resisted then...*POP*...it came free. Quickly Fizer ran the prybar under the edge of the board, lifting the edge of the wood until he came to the next seam and the board came loose.

He set down the tools and lay down next to the black gap in the floor. He took another deep breath. He put his hand into the hole and felt around. *Nothing.* He lay flat on the floor and let his hand grope deeper in the darkness beneath the floor. "No rats, please, no rats," he muttered aloud.

He shifted so that he could feel in the opposite direction under the floor. Trying not to imagine what could be lying in wait for his hand as he groped in the blackness. Just when he thought he had made a mistake, he felt something. *The bag. It's here, just like Dad said.* He ran his hand over the waterproof nylon duffel bag, then withdrew his hand. He picked up the prybar and began prying up the boards surrounding the opening he had made.

In five minutes, he had pulled away enough of the boards to see the edges of the oversized bag. It was bigger than he had first imagined, and packed full. He lay flat on the floor, reached down and tugged on the handle of the black bag. It did not budge. On his hands and knees he grabbed the bag with both hands and strained, trying to heave it upward from the hole. It lifted maybe an inch. He finally fell backward onto the floor, gasping. *Heavier than I thought it would be; it must weigh a hundred pounds.*

Fizer leaned against the wall, his legs splayed in front of him, staring at the dust-covered bag, his breath rushing in and out of his lungs from the exertion of pulling up the boards and trying to extricate the bag. Finally he scooted himself close to the hole again and pulled the metal zipper open.

The contents were wrapped in heavy plastic, the edges of which were duct-taped together to make a watertight seal. In the semidarkness, he felt for the edges of the tape and pulled the plastic covering free. He paused and took a deep breath, then put his hand into the bag.

His hand closed first on a heavy-duty flashlight with a sealed package of D-cell batteries. Fizer clicked it on and shone it around the dingy apartment, seeing for the first time the cobwebs strung from every corner and dappling the furniture. He turned it off, wanting to avoid attention from outside the flat. He reached in again and pulled out another, smaller, flashlight, a portable radio, and an envelope.

He clicked on the little light and looked at the envelope. In his father's careful handwriting were the words "To F.B.".

He took the letter and scooted behind the chifforobe to help block the light from the window. There, he laid the envelope on the floor and steadied the light on it, looking at the writing on its face for a long moment. Bending low, he traced the writing with a fingertip.

He breathed deeply, exhaled slowly, then picked up the envelope, tore it open. It contained a single page. He unfolded the paper and flattened it on the floor.

He read it quickly, then reread it, absorbing its message as he bent close with the flashlight held next to his head.

The words seemed more blurry the third time through. Fizer watched as a splotch of wetness stained the paper.

Finally, he straightened and wiped a hand roughly over his eyes. He picked up the letter, folded it, and put it in the back pocket of his jeans.

He stood and stepped over to the bag again. He turned on the radio and tuned it to a station. A song by Creed was playing. He set the radio on the floor and reached into the duffel bag again.

The first bundle of hundred-dollar bills he examined was carefully wrapped; he could tell they were used bills. He counted them. A hundred bills in the stack.

He reached into the bag and began making two piles of the money.

Chapter 24

The black cat was in stalking mode, moving a half-inch at a time through the clutter of the balcony three stories above the French Quarter. Yellow eyes half-open, ears perked, tail-tip twitching, Boo steadily circled the round, rattan lounge chair toward a pair of pigeons busily cooing into the dusk.

Pop. A firecracker sounded a block away. The birds stopped bobbing their heads. Boo froze. Five seconds passed. *Coo coo coo coo coo.* The pigeons on the wrought-iron rail of the balcony rejoined their conversation. Boo resumed his hunt, displaying all the instinctive concentration and prowess of a leopard in the Amazon tracking some oversized, hapless rodent.

The cat was beneath the birds now, his hind quarters slightly rocking back and forth as he gathered his legs under him for the spring, his head lowered with only his eyes directly pointed at the hated intruders of his domain. Another tail twitch. Then another. Then...he leapt, his body uncoiling and launching his fury straight up to the rail. And past it.

The pigeons launched into flight at the first movement from below. Instead of flying straight out from the balcony, one bird went left, the other right.

Boo immediately batted at the pigeon to his left. His claws raked through the tail feathers but only managed to knock two of them loose. The birds flew away. Boo's momentum carried him up and over the rail and, for a moment, seemed to destine him for a thirty-foot fall to the street below. He twisted, however, and performed the physics-foiling acrobatic moves possessed only by felines. He dropped harmlessly to the edge of the wooden balcony floor that extended six inches past the wrought-iron rail.

The cat sat for a moment. Then he yawned and licked his left paw.

Forte leaned against the door that led into his apartment from the balcony, watching the scene play out. He raised his Bugs Bunny mug and drained the last of his coffee. "I know how you feel, buddy."

From behind him in the apartment, the voice of FBI agent Rosalind Dent pulled him from the Boo show.

"If it's all right with you, Mr. Forte, we'd like to ask you a few questions." Her voice was calm but sharpened with just enough edge to get attention. *Mr. Forte*. "That is, if you are finished watching your cat chase birds."

Forte turned and walked back into the den of his apartment. He set his coffee mug on a side table and slumped into an overstuffed black leather chair.

The FBI agent jerked her chin toward another man in a gray suit. "This is Agent Dennis Bradbury from the New Orleans office of the Bureau. And you remember Ms. Taye Jarreaux from the D.A.'s office." A slim, caramel-skinned woman in a black skirt and jacket gave a neutral smile. Next to this group stood Jackie Shaw, who leaned against the wall by the door dressed in jeans and a crimson T-shirt with the words "Sister Deadeye" emblazoned in white across the front. In the kitchen that opened off the den, Verna Griffey scooped coffee into the filter of the coffee maker.

Without looking away from her coffee-making, Verna spoke. "Al, you gonna sit there and pout or you gonna invite your guests to have a seat?"

Jackie covered her mouth with her hand.

Forte waved his hand at the sofa and chairs in the den. Everyone sat down except Verna, who remained in the kitchen.

Rosie Dent opened a leather-covered notebook with the gold-embossed words "Rosalind Dent, FBI" on the cover. She referred to notes on the legal pad and began talking. "Here's what we know, so far." Next to her on the sofa, Agent Bradbury took out a cassette recorder, placed it on the rough-hewn coffee table, and turned it on. Rosie continued.

"Today at approximately 1:30 p.m. a small band of attackers shot up a restaurant about an hour north of New Orleans. Their intent, it seems, was to either capture or murder one Fizer Beal, age 14, the main witness in the upcoming racketeering trial against the Marchetti crime organization. Fizer, who had been in the custody of personnel from Forte Security after having been placed in the protection of The Refuge by the District Attorney's office, disappeared during the ensuing gun battle between the attackers and representatives of Forte Security, which included Alvin Forte...." She looked up at Forte, who had his eyes closed with his head against the back of the chair. "...Jacqueline Shaw, and Michael Jones, a.k.a. "Nomad", whose association with Forte Security seems to be..." Dent looked at a spot on the ceiling as she searched for the right words. "...rather informal and intermittent. Would that describe his relationship with your company, Mr. Forte?"

Al shrugged, keeping his eyes shut.

Agent Dent continued. "At the same time of the boy's disappearance, the attackers at the restaurant fled in two vehicles. Before local law enforcement arrived at the scene of the shootout, both Forte and Jones left the scene, apparently in pursuit of the attackers. Ms. Shaw stayed behind to brief the authorities."

Dent looked up from her notes again and locked eyes with Jackie Shaw, who maintained the same calm expression she had worn from the start of the meeting. The FBI agent was the first to blink. She looked down at the pad and continued reading from her notes.

"At approximately 5:30 p.m. today, shots were fired at a gym in New Orleans. Witnesses said two men and a woman forced their way into the gym and a few minutes later several short bursts of gunfire were heard. New Orleans police arrived at that scene and questioned Luke Battier, a local businessman..." From the kitchen came a snorting sound. "...and two others at the gym who were working out at the time. Battier declined to identify the people who came in and disrupted his workout. In fact, he went so far as to say that he wouldn't press charges even though two of the lights in the gym had been shot out and other equipment destroyed. The description of one of the people by witnesses in the restaurant sounded quite familiar, however. An athletic, serious-looking man with short black hair and yellow eyes."

The clink of cups and saucers interrupted the meeting. Verna carried a tray of cups and passed out coffee to everyone present, not bothering to ask if anyone wanted it. "Sugar and cream on the tray here," she said, pointing a thick finger that was almost as black as the undiluted coffee. She straightened and placed her hands on her hips as she looked over the group in the den. "If you ask me—which you didn't of course but I'm gonna tell you anyway—you'd be a whole lot closer to getting that boy back if you were out there lookin' for him 'stead of sitting 'round here talking about what evvaboddy already knows."

No one said a word for a moment. Agent Dent broke the silence. "Thank you for your observations, Mrs. Griffey. And for the coffee."

Verna peered down at the agent from her six-foot height. She smoothed the chef's apron with which she had covered her size-18 yellow Chanel suit, turned and walked back to the kitchen.

The two FBI agents and the assistant district attorney all sipped their coffee then set down the mugs, as if on cue. Taye Jarreaux opened her own leather-covered notebook and sat with pen poised above the page. She spoke up now.

"In addition to the threat of harm against Fizer Beal, we have to consider the implications of losing the key witness against the Marchetti organization. We need to know everything you know," said the woman, her voice pitched low and almost musical.

Al Forte opened his eyes. "We'll get him back."

"You're the ones who lost him to begin with."

"It wasn't quite that simple."

"Oh? One second he was with you, and the next, he vanished. Isn't that right?"

"Yes, but at the time, there were bullets flying every...."

"But the D.A.'s office trusted you to protect the boy until the trial."

Forte said nothing, his eyes half-shut as he studied the lawyer.

Agent Bradbury broke in. "When you visited the prison, did Theodore Beal give you any indication the boy would try to escape for some reason?"

Forte shook his head.

Bradbury looked at Jackie Shaw, who remained mute, then spoke to Forte again.

"You believed that Battier's men took him, didn't you?"

"Of course."

"And what did Mr. Battier tell you about that when you visited him?"

No response from Forte.

Rosalind Dent held up her hand to silence the other agent.

"Al, you think Battier's men have the boy?" She stared hard at Forte.

Forte squeezed his eyes again and rubbed his forehead. "I thought he did, of course. They've made no secret about wanting to get to him. You heard Lucky, last night, in the alley...."

Jackie spoke up. "The alley?"

A cough came from the kitchen, then the clinking of dishes.

The FBI agent ignored the interruption. Her expression remained hard, but a flush passed over her cheeks. "I heard him. But when you confronted him today, what did he tell you?"

"He didn't say, but it was the first place to go. You know that."

"He said nothing?"

Forte glanced at Jackie, who seemed amused at the conversation. "He laughed."

Agent Dent cocked her head. "Laughed?"

"Yeah. It was like he was finding out that Fizer was gone for the first time. He thought it was funny, apparently, that the boy was gone and that we thought Lucky's guys had him."

Taye Jarreaux broke in. "He may have been just playing you. Making you think he didn't have him. I mean, if he DID have him, he wouldn't just come out and admit it to you."

Forte picked up his coffee mug and drank from it, holding it to his lips for a few seconds. He carefully placed the mug on the table and remained silent.

From outside on the balcony came the sounds of pigeons cooing again. Boo, asleep on the back of Forte's chair, reacted with a single tail twitch.

Rosalind Dent stared hard at Forte for a moment longer. Finally she stood up and motioned to her entourage. "Meet me at the car, please." They gathered their briefcases and left. "May I speak to you privately, Mr. Forte?" Without waiting for an answer, she stepped out onto the landing for the stairs leading to the ground floor. Forte followed her.

"What aren't you telling us, Al?" The words came out in a hiss.

"That's it. That's the whole story. We had the boy, we were attacked, the boy was gone."

The FBI agent's eyes narrowed. "And what are you going to do next?"

"What do you mean?"

"You know what I mean. Al Forte ignores everyone else, all the efforts made by all authorized law enforcement agencies and stages his own personal posse to catch the bad guys." Her voice was rising now.

Forte leaned back against the door and pinched the bridge of his nose between thumb and index finger. He opened his eyes to find the agent glaring at him. He grinned.

"Listen, Rosie...."

The agent stabbed at the air an inch from his nose with her finger. "Don't you 'Rosie' me. I promise you, Al, if you go off and do anything to jeopardize our recovery efforts, I will do everything in my power to have you...."

"Agent Dent, are you teed off at me about last night?"

She stopped, her mouth still open. A tint of red played across her cheekbones. Recovering quickly, she closed her mouth and snorted. "That has nothing to do with anything, Al. I was just feeling the drinks...."

Forte studied her face for a moment. "I wanted to talk to you about that. But we were interrupted."

The agent held up a hand. "Nothing to talk about really." She took a deep breath and tucked her briefcase under her arm. "Remember, don't do anything stupid about trying to get Fizer Beal back." She spun and went down the stairs.

Forte watched her go, then stepped back into the apartment.

Jackie was sitting with her legs curled under her in the overstuffed chair in the corner. Boo lay on his back in her lap as she stroked his neck.

Forte picked up his coffee mug and drained it. "He usually doesn't let anyone do that. 'Cept me."

"Guess I've joined the Boo club." She looked up from the cat. "What was all that about?"

"All what?"

Jackie arched an eyebrow and said nothing.

"Oh, she just wanted to warn me about going off half-baked, interfering with their investigation blah blah blah...."

"And you assured her you wouldn't."

Forte peered at her. He never could tell when she was kidding unless she made it obvious. "No, I didn't assure her of anything."

A tiny glint appeared in Jackie's eyes. "And what was that remark about the alley?"

"What alley?"

"Agent Dent, she said something about hearing Lucky Battier say something in the alley." She looked down at Boo and tugged at his ears. "Exactly what were you doing in the alley, again?"

"Well, it was nothing, really. We had just stepped out for some air and...."

"Oh, you don't have to tell me. I was just curious."

Forte felt his face flush. *This is crazy. What does it matter?*

Jackie stood up suddenly and handed the cat to his owner.

"I'll be downstairs at The Refuge." Her voice was low now. She brushed past him, leaving a waft of wisteria in the air.

Forte opened his mouth but no words came out. The door clicked shut behind her.

He looked down at his cat, who was watching him through slit eyes.

"Boo, do I know how to handle women or what?"

"Rowwww," said Boo in his best tortured Satchmo impersonation.

"Yeah, I know. Or what."

Chapter 25

Micah Cray jogged back toward the park where his car waited, forcing himself to stay calm and keep his pace relatively slow.

Back at Penderby's house the alarms pierced the neighborhood calm with their *whoop whoop whoop* sounds. Cray had slowly retreated, knowing that the security cops wouldn't arrive on the scene for at least ten minutes. He had retraced his steps, out the back door, over the back neighbor's fence, to the street leading out of the neighborhood.

As he passed a house, a woman holding a baby stepped out to her front yard. Her attention was focused on the alarms blaring the next street over. She never looked in Cray's direction.

He kept up his leisurely pace. Ahead he could see the park. The corner of his Jeep peeked through the bushes bordering the parking spaces next to the playground. *Almost there; go slow, go slow, relax now.* Ahead was one more street to cross. Behind him the house alarms were fading.

Abruptly a police siren squawked nearby. Cray jerked slightly then slowed his pace. A police car charged through the intersection in front of him. The two cops in the car paid no heed to him.

He continued across the street and into the park, passing the monkey bars and bright yellow swingset. He turned and jogged through the tennis courts to the parking lot beyond. Finally, he reached the Jeep. He forced himself to pause and take a towel from the back seat. He mopped his brow. The action of wicking his sweat away hid the searching looks he sent in every direction to determine if anyone was watching him too closely.

A couple of mothers sat on a bench watching their kids play in the sandbox. They glanced in the direction of the house alarms a couple of times, then went back to their chatting. Like the others, they failed to notice him.

Cray threw the towel into the Jeep and climbed into the driver's seat. He started it up and drove out of the parking lot, carefully watching for police approaching the area. He steered the vehicle slowly away from the park, took a left then a right as he meandered for nearly a mile. Then he pulled over to the curb in a nearly abandoned area.

Slowly he clenched his fists and raised them above his head. He slammed them against the steering wheel. The Jeep shuddered with the pounding of his hardened palms. A moan welled up from deep in his throat and spilled out of his mouth, changing to an animal sound of pain, a howling mass of hurt and grief. "No! No! Nooooohhhhh!" He screamed into the bright afternoon sunshine, the hot tears burning trails of misery on his cheeks. He dropped his head against the steering wheel and sobbed.

She was gone. She was gone for good now. Before, I only thought she was gone but now.... She's been taken from me forever now. I'll never see her again, even in her sleep, her hair resting on the pillow as she sleeps.

It seemed the weeping would never stop, but in a few moments the tears dried. He sat still with his head still resting against the wheel, his breathing still heavy.

He felt someone watching him. He opened his eyes, feeling the eyelids become unstuck after the weeping. He sat up and looked to his left.

Next to his car stood a boy of about four, his forehead smudged with mud, a one-armed GI Joe clutched under his arm. The boy was studying him with some curiosity.

Cray looked back at the boy for a moment, then wiped a hand across his eyes.

The boy switched the doll under the other arm, then reached out and ran a pudgy hand over the fender of the Jeep. He looked up at Cray again. "Mistuh, you hurt?"

Cray stared at the boy for a long beat. In the distance another police siren made its way to Penderby's house. "No," he said, his voice hoarse.

The boy cocked his head and thought for a minute. "Yeah," he said, "I say that when I get hurt, too."

When I get hurt, too. Cray squeezed shut his eyes again, then opened them. He noticed a bruise on the boy's jaw, barely visible under the dirt on his face. "You should go home now, where it is safe."

The boy's mouth changed just enough to look like a smile, but one that belonged on a much older face, a face that had seen enough pain to fake a smile when necessary.

"Okey doke," the boy said. He switched the doll to the other armpit again and walked away on the cracked sidewalk.

Cray turned and watched him go.

Behind him, two blocks away, a van with the words "Kramer Security" sped through the intersection, an orange light flashing from the front dash.

Cray stared at the van for a moment. He turned the ignition key and started the Jeep again.

* * *

Penderby stood on the porch watching the light fade out over the swamp. A faint breeze carried the heavy scent of something rotting past the cabin. He sprayed more industrial strength bug spray over the back of his neck. The giant mosquitoes were buzzing now at sunset, swarming up around the twisted cypress trees that surrounded the cabin like ancient monsters who stood guard out of sheer habit.

The bull alligator had abandoned its lazy sunning routine where it had draped itself over the tree roots earlier. Somewhere in the muddy swamp water it waited, watching the cabin, Penderby knew. He smiled. "Ok, Greedy Gut, I'll get you something." He went back into the cabin, took a whole chicken out of the big ice chest in the corner, and walked over to where Exxie lay on the floor. He knelt and put a finger to the blood smeared on her face. At the touch, Exxie jerked awake and screamed. Penderby pulled his hand back to slap her, but she fell silent again. In the dim light, her eyes were lit with terror. *Good, she needs to be afraid. Very afraid.*

He wiped the blood on the raw chicken and carried it out to the porch where he set it on the weatherworn planks. Then he went back inside, picked up the girl, chair and all, and brought her out to the porch where he carefully placed her near the door. He leaned close and whispered, "Be very still. This is the evening entertainment."

Nothing was moving in the black water. Penderby held up the chicken and waited, watching the surface of the swamp around him. Only the upper branches of the trees caught any light from the sunset now. The birds had withdrawn and only the buzzing of the mosquitoes broke the silence. He watched and waited a moment longer, then tossed the bird about 10 feet out from the porch.

As it splashed, a surge of motion erupted from underneath the porch. Penderby reflexively jumped back toward the door, then watched as the alligator snapped up the chicken and gulped it down. Was it his imagination or did the huge predator pluck the chicken out of the air even before it hit the water? Almost immediately, the surface of the swamp became calm as the creature submerged.

Penderby leaned against the wall next to the door, as far from the water's edge as he could get. He realized his fingers were gripping the uneven boards of the cabin wall. Next to him, Exxie had slammed the chair back against the wall, her eyes wide with horror above the tape that gagged her. Penderby turned back to the swamp and kept watching. After a moment, two bumps a foot apart appeared in the water 50 feet out from the porch. The gator was watching the cabin for another treat.

Good boy. You know what you want, don't you?

He lifted the girl in her chair and brought her back inside the cabin. He set her down in the center of the room and went to the ice chest for more orange juice. After taking a long swallow of his drink, he sat on the dusty sofa.

Exxie stared at him, her eyes still dilated from shock.

Penderby smiled and took another sip of his juice. "Did you enjoy the show?"

The girl closed her eyes but made no sound.

The man nodded as if she had answered. "I thought it would break the monotony a bit. I'm sure you noticed that our little vacation getaway is lacking in many of the accoutrements to which you've become accustomed during your short life."

A small moan came from behind the tape on the girl's mouth.

Penderby rose and walked over to the girl. He stopped and leaned close to her ear. "Anything for a little excitement, eh, Exxie?" He straightened and slowly paced away from her, then back again.

Her shoulders began shaking, then the sobbing started.

He stopped next to her again. "You want to tell me something, young lady?" He ripped the tape away from her face.

She gasped and gradually quieted her crying. When she spoke, her voice was hoarse. "Why...why are you doing this?"

He sat on the sofa again and studied her. "What difference does it make? Do you think you can stop it?"

Her eyes brimmed again. "I'm sorry...." Her voice cracked and she sobbed again.

Penderby pulled the roll of duct tape out of the duffel bag and retaped her mouth.

He put his face next to hers and screamed. "Sorry!!!"

Exxie's head snapped back with the sound.

"Sorry for what? For treating everyone around you like trash?" He kicked the chair over.

"Sorry for making your parents suffer with worry that you'd be lost to them forever?" He threw the half-full cup of juice at her.

"Or sorry for making me feel like an inferior as I waited on your every spoiled demand over the past two years? Is that what you are sorry for, Exxie?!!"

A high-pitched keening came from the prone girl.

Penderby glared at her for a moment, his breathing raspy now. He knelt beside her and pulled her head up by her hair. She jerked once, then became very still. Her crying waned until it had died away to a barely audible whimper.

"Here's something for you to think about. Are you listening?" His voice was calm now. "That thing out there, that monster in the water...." He paused and put his face to her ear and whispered. "He has had a little taste of your blood now."

She moaned louder again, low in her throat. He released her hair and she slumped to the floor.

He stood up and looked down at her.

"Do you think he'll forget the taste of it?"

* * *

The Kramer Security van pulled into the Penderby driveway just as a New Orleans policeman came around the corner from the back yard. The alarm still drowned out all other noises as it whoop-whooped its belated warning.

The cop leaned close to the Kramer rent-a-cop, who was nervously adjusting the bill of his Kramer cap as he looked at the house. The cop yelled in his ear. "Tell me you can shut this off."

The Kramer man nodded, still watching the house. "No problem." He walked around to the back door, lifted the cover to the security alarm panel, and punched in a series of numbers. The sirens stopped. Everything was eerily silent for a moment. Then a bird chirped in the trees a few houses away.

The rent-a-cop took a single step back on the porch, bowed, and swept his hand toward the broken back door. "The burglars are probably long gone, but you can go in first." He patted his hip. "No gun."

The cop glanced at the man and let his eyes travel down to the embroidered "Kramer Security" patch on the polyester shirt pocket. *Probably a real good reason they don't let you carry a weapon.* He brushed past him and went into the house. Inside the back door, he stopped and listened. It had the kind of quiet worn by an empty house, as opposed to the forced silence of a house where someone was hiding. He'd been in enough houses of both types to have an uncanny sense of which was which. Still, he carefully walked through the kitchen, his sidearm drawn and pointed toward the ceiling.

At each doorway off the hall, the cop went in low and swept his gun from side to side. Finally, he covered the house and all the closets. He called out to the security guard. "It's clear. Nobody home."

The Kramer man came in, still skittish, judging by the way he peeked into every room as he came down the hall. Finally, he stood next to the cop in the back bedroom. He looked around and sniffed. "Looks like no damage was done."

The cop glanced around the bedroom, taking in the computer and the tidiness of the desktop. He turned back to the rent-a-cop and was amused to see a hint of grim determination on the man's face. *He thinks he is dealing with big-time crime now.* "Looks like they didn't stop to take anything with them. The sirens probably scared the crap out of them." The Kramer man's expression of casual boredom had clicked back into place.

"Yeah," he said, "that happens on about half the robbery attempts for our customers. The real pros stick around and take what they came after. The amateurs panic." He lifted his hand to cover a yawn but let it drop as his mouth gaped open.

The cop shrugged. *As if I don't know that.* The guy was fading quick. "Will your customer want to file a report?"

"Nah. We'll take care of resetting the alarm. Thanks for showing up."

"Just doing the job. You'll lock up then."

"Sure. No prob."

The cop went out through the back door. In a moment, the police car started up and revved away.

The Kramer man yawned again and watched the policeman drive off. Then he strolled throughout the house again, checking in each room, looking in all the corners. He scratched his head as if he were musing about something.

Finally he stopped in the main bedroom and peered up at the cooling vent, then looked away. He put up a hand to feel the flow of cold air from the vent. He walked over to another corner of the bedroom and dragged a chair over to the vent. Standing in the chair, he took a multi-tool out of his pocket and unscrewed the vent cover. He reached up into the opening and yanked. In his hand was a tiny video camera. He had torn it loose from its metal mounting bracket.

Abruptly he stepped down from the chair and strode the length of the hallway. Once in the kitchen, he dropped the camera onto the Spanish tile floor and stomped it twice with his boot. With the toe of his boot, he scattered the plastic and metal scrap pieces of the dead electronic snooper. Satisfied, he walked back down the hallway and stepped into the bathroom.

He pulled off his cap and ran a hand over his hair, raking through the cropped bristles with his fingers. Then he cupped some cold water from the faucet and splashed it on his face.

He looked in the mirror and examined the gaunt features of Micah Cray.

Not much time left, Cray mused. The security guard he had captured would eventually wake up and make enough motion under the tarp in his Jeep to attract somebody's attention.

He forced himself to take a deep, slow breath and let it out slowly. Then another, and another. He sat at the kitchen table and closed his eyes. *Think think think.* He knew that Penderby would never leave any clues as to where his hideaway was. He could have done a title search for any other properties registered in the man's name, but there was no time for that now. Besides, it probably wouldn't be registered in Penderby's name anyway.

Who could lead me to him? Who could possibly be involved with him? Friends? He seemed to have none. Coworkers maybe? No one seemed to spend any time with Penderby. Except his boss. *His boss.*

Cray squeezed his eyes tighter and concentrated. If he could get close to the Grahams, he had a chance of finding Penderby.

Maybe his only chance.

Hopefully, this won't take long.

Chapter 26

Teddy Beal lay on his bunk and blocked out the Saturday night chatter in the cell block. Four men were playing cards at the table near the barred windows while the rest of the dozen or so inmates crowded around the television screaming at the two contestants in a boxing match. Teddy heard none of it. He was thinking about his son.

He had wondered before the visit this morning how he would feel once Fizer walked away from the visitation room where they had talked. Would he feel crushed, letting his despair break through the comforting numbness he had surrounded his mind with in the months since he had come to the prison? Would he be totally defeated by the realization that this visit was different from all the others?

None of those feelings had come over him. In fact, he lay on the bunk trying to determine exactly how he felt at the moment. A word popped into his mind. *Satisfied.* That was it. He felt satisfied that he had done everything he could do now. It was up to his son. Fizer would carry it through.

"Maybe that's why it feels funny now, to all of a sudden be satisfied," he murmured aloud. He glanced toward the card table and the TV crowd. No one was watching him.

He rolled off the bunk, stripped off his clothes, and wrapped a towel around him. Without another look around the room, he walked toward the shower stalls.

After adjusting the temperature of the water, he stepped under the stinging needles of the shower. He closed his eyes and let the hot water flow over him. When he opened them again, three men were standing at the door of the communal bathroom. The largest of the three, a man one who just been transferred to this cell block, carefully closed the door.

Teddy reached over and turned off the water, then backed into the corner and dabbed the water from his eyes again.

The new man took three steps closer to Beal, circling to his left while another of the men sidled to his right. The smallest of the trio stayed at the entrance and pushed his shoe against the bottom of the metal door.

The big man stopped. When he smiled, Teddy could see that two of his teeth on the left side were much whiter than the others, showing that he had recent crowns put in. The man spoke and his voice was surprisingly soft.

"Teddy, you know what we want, don't you."

The chill of the wet tile on his back was comforting to Teddy and he wondered why. *I can feel something at least,* he thought. *Maybe that's it. After years of skimming over life like a coma patient, now I can feel again. Now that it's almost over.*

"Sure," he said aloud. "I know exactly what you want." His voice sounded different. It echoed off the hard shower walls with a resonance he never knew it had before. "But you won't get it." He smiled and realized it wasn't for show. He was glad this moment had come.

The new man's eyebrows rose slightly—the only movement Teddy saw before he felt the hard slap of the man's hand on his jaw. His head bounced against the tile wall. He shook his head and willed the stars to clear. After five seconds, the big man's face came into focus again.

He was grinning but with no real humor. His breath reeked of death.

"Wrong answer, Teddy." He jerked his chin toward the other thug without taking his eyes off Beal. "Let's try again."

The other man moved toward Teddy, who remained slumped against the shower wall. When the man was close, Beal kicked him between the legs. Before the man hit the wet floor screaming, Teddy felt his legs sweeping from under him. The floor rushed toward him and his head banged hard. Then blackness.

SLAP! The sharpness of the big man's blows brought him back to consciousness. Then the deep, dull ache of a concussion displaced every other sensation. He moaned and lifted a hand to his left ear. When he brought his fingers to his face, they were slick with redness.

"Bad move, boy," the leader said. He was standing about six feet away, his feet spread and his arms folded across his chest. On his right forearm was a crude tattoo of a spider with blood dripping from its fangs. He cut his eyes toward the man Teddy had kicked. Without hesitation, the man kicked Beal three times in the ribs with the toe of his heavy boot.

Teddy groaned and rolled on to his uninjured right side. The water on the chipped tiles of the shower stall felt icy now. Suddenly he felt himself being lifted and leaned against the wall again.

There was a bump against the bathroom door but the prisoner there kept his boot against the door.

After a moment of silence, there was the sound of footsteps shuffling away from the bathroom.

The leader lifted Teddy's chin and looked into his face. "Time's running out, Beal. Mr. Marchetti says you can live and the boy can live. Just give him his money." He paused. "Does the boy know where it is?"

Teddy could feel a trickle of wet coming from his ear now. He knew it wasn't water.

Naked and racked with pain, he focused on the man by the door. Gradually, the features of the lookout's face became sharp. An expression of fear and disgust was trained on Teddy. The man was mouthing something. What was he trying to say? Teddy blinked and tried to focus more.

Tell. Tell them or you will die.

The two holding up Teddy glanced at the man at the door. He stopped the silent warning.

The big man leaned close to Teddy's good ear. "You know," he whispered, "that Marchetti will find the boy anyway. And he won't be in such a good mood then."

Teddy jerked his head toward the man. For a split second, their eyes were inches apart. The big man's bloodshot orbs opened wide and his head jerked back slightly at the look on Teddy's face.

Beal opened his mouth to speak; no sound came out. He ran his tongue over his lips and tried again. "Listen," he said, his voice barely audible, "give Marchetti a message from me, will you?"

The big man glanced at his partner and leaned close again to the injured man.

"Tell him," Beal began, then moaned as one of his broken ribs shifted, stabbing his side with pain. He gasped, then began again. "Tell him...that the money...will be put to good use."

Then he smiled.

The leader studied his bruised face for a beat, then shook his head slowly. "You had your chance, Teddy."

The first punch bounced his head against the tile wall, but the other man kept him from slipping to the floor again.

Whap. Whap. Whap. The punches kept coming.

And Teddy kept smiling as the darkness settled over him.

* * *

Fizer Beal put the last stack of hundred-dollar bills into the second of the two piles he had made on the floor of the dusty apartment. Each wrapper held 100 bills. He had made two piles of 500 bundles. He added it up in his head. *Hundred-dollar bills, a hundred* *in each bundle...that's...$10,000. So, ten bundles would be...$100,000...and a hundred would be...an even million. And five hundred bundles would be...five million.*

He leaned against the wall. His T-shirt was soaked again from the effort of counting the money in the stifling apartment.

He gazed at the two piles of bills.

Ten million dollars.

"Wow," he said aloud.

After a few minutes' rest, he pulled two other smaller gym bags from the hole and began filling them with one of the piles he had made. He made sure each bag had the same amount, then carefully pushed them to the corner of the room.

He straightened up, took a few deep breaths, then began refilling the original duffel bag with the other stack of bills, tossing them into the gaping, zippered hole of the black bag. Finally, he zipped it up and began replacing the boards he had pulled up.

He stepped back and shone the flashlight over the floor. Then he walked over and pushed the big, wooden chifforobe over the excavation site.

Shining the flashlight around the room again, he located the radio he'd found in the bag. Walking over to the corner, he slumped down next to the two gym bags of money. He set the radio on the floor and clicked it on.

A tune from the latest boy band was just finishing. The news came on.

Fizer closed his eyes and listened. *Maybe I can sleep for a few minutes before...*His head drooped lower, lower....

The news announcer's words seeped into his consciousness: "...not known which inmates were responsible for the murder..."

Fizer's eyes opened. *No, not like that....*

The news blared on. "...was originally scheduled to testify against the Marchetti crime organization for a series of allegations including racketeering, prostitution, murder...."

No no no, I just saw him. Fizer realized he was on his knees now, staring down at the radio.

"...but prison officials vow to investigate the murder of Theodore Beal."

"Unnnnhhhh," Fizer moaned as he slumped forward in the dust. He kicked the radio across the room, silencing it against the wall.

"No no, daddy, Nooohhhhh!" The boy sobbed louder now, his tears making a muddy pool on the floorboards. "Why...why...." The anguish poured out, his grief undiluted. He remembered his father's face now clearly at the visitation room in the prison. It seemed so long ago now. *It was only this morning.* His father had leaned forward, his voice calmer than he'd heard it in years.

Quickly, Teddy Beal had whispered the instructions to his son, confident that Fizer would be able to escape and make his way back to the French Quarter. He had made him repeat the exact location of the apartment where he now sat, the combination of the lock, the details of where the money would be....

The letter. Fizer sat up and dragged the back of his hand across his mud-smeared face. He pulled the sheet of paper from his back pocket, unfolded it and reread it.

Dear Fizer,

If you are reading this then you are as smart and resourceful as I always knew you could be. I'm proud of you, my son.

This letter will tell you what to do. There are things you must do which are hard things. But, Fizer, you must do them. I know you can.

Son, when you look back on this, there will be many sad things to remember. Don't ignore the sadness, but don't keep beating yourself up with it. Remember those times we had, you and your mother and me, all of us together as a family. Those were good times, weren't they? I smile as I write this, thinking about those fine days. They make these hard days a little easier to bear.

My boy, after you get through this, promise me that you won't repeat the mistakes I've made. I've made my peace with the Lord, by His grace, and I know I'll be in a better place one day. As for my life here on this earth, knowing that you are safe makes me rest easier.

Now, here's what I want you to do....

Fizer reviewed the rest of the note, then carefully reread the last line his father had written. *I know you won't want to, but burn this letter when you are through reading it. It is important that you do it, for your own good.*

Fizer swallowed hard now, feeling the terrible tightness in his throat. He hadn't wanted to burn the letter and now even less so. *It is important that you do it, for your own good.*

He rummaged in the duffel bag again and came out with a cigarette lighter. He clicked it on and held up the sheet of paper. *For your own good.* He touched the flame to the paper and watched as it turned to brown, then charred, black ashes.

Outside, a car beeped twice as it rushed past the apartments. Had the traffic stopped before he turned on the radio...or had he simply not heard it? Fizer sat with his back against the bedroom wall. The staleness of the air in the old flat seemed unbearable now. He had to get out of here.

I've got to keep going, keep moving, got to finish this.

He got up and walked back through the apartment. In the only other bedroom he opened the closet door and reached up to a shelf. After groping a few seconds, he felt it. The phone was exactly where his dad said it would be. He pulled it down and ran his hand over the wall until he felt the phone jack his father had installed a year earlier. He plugged in the phone and listened. The dial tone was there.

Fizer hung up the phone and listened to the street noises filtering through the windows.

Everyone is walking around as if my life hadn't completely crashed, he thought.

He swallowed again to try and wash away the hurting in his throat.

Then he picked up the phone and punched in Al Forte's number.

Chapter 27

The bar on St. Anne's was never meant to be a biker bar. After the bikers took a fancy to it, however, the typical tourist trade seemed to dwindle away.

Forte and Jackie Shaw walked in silence along St. Anne's. Two huge riders stood guard outside the front door of the bar, one with a red beard and the other with a black, braided beard. The guards took in the approaching figures from behind their sunshades—worn despite the darkness of the night. Then they noticed Forte and quickly began studying the beer bottles clutched in their fists.

"Gentlemen," Forte said.

"Howdy there, Al," said the one with the red beard. Braided Beard tilted his chin upward in salutation and lifted the beer bottle slightly as they passed.

Jackie glanced at Forte. "Pals of yours?"

Forte kept watching the streets and alleys ahead as they walked. "Acquaintances," he said. "Never can tell who might be of help at a certain time." He looked down at Jackie to see she was watching him closely. "As they say, it's not what you know but who you know."

She nodded and tried to follow his gaze as he kept searching the streetscape around them. "You never stop looking for trouble, do you?"

"Not looking for it. Just making sure it doesn't sneak up on me."

At that moment, Forte's cell phone rang. He pulled it out of his pocket and read the Caller ID screen. He turned off the phone's ringer and put it back in his pocket. After a dozen more steps, he felt Jackie's gaze on his face.

"It was the Grahams," he said. "Again."

"How many times have they called you?"

He shrugged. "Four or five times."

"And you're not going to talk to them again?"

He felt the pace slowing. "I did what I could."

"That was then. This is now." Jackie's voice sounded different now.

He let out his breath slowly. Manny's church was still several blocks away. Ahead, the crowds had thinned as they skirted around Jackson Square, away from the river. Here the Quarter was a little less touristy and more residential, if any of the dwellings in the historic neighborhood could be deemed that, in a normal sense. A tattered clown in grimy jeans whizzed past on a bicycle, a five-gallon bucket looped around his neck. His Saturday's work in the Square, the most profitable of the week, had come to a close. Forte knew that a bundle of cash was hidden somewhere in the clown's ragtag outfit. Also hidden would be a handgun of some variety, just in case an enterprising mugger strayed from the tourist trade and decided to pick off one of the locals.

"Yo, Al," the clown muttered and was gone.

Forte had time to tilt his head at the clown before he sped past. He turned to look at Jackie as they walked.

"I knew from the start that Exxie Graham had not been abducted. She's trouble and her parents have done nothing but encourage it. I did what they asked. I found Exxie and brought her back and got kicked in the shin for it." His eyes strayed to the side streets as he talked. "With some people, saving them from their mistakes only leads to more and bigger mistakes."

Jackie was silent as they walked; Forte sensed she had more to say.

"What?" he asked.

"What what?"

"I know you're not going to leave it at that."

"Does it matter what I say?"

He slowed the pace again. *Does it matter?* "Why are you being so...so...."

"Being so what...so nosy...so intrusive...what word are you searching for....?"

"How about...pushy?"

He immediately felt the heat of her stare.

"How long have you known me, Al Forte?" Her voice was softer now.

"A year or so. Since you were hired at The Refuge."

"And how well would you say I know you?"

How well does she know me? "I'd say you know me pretty well. I try not to pull any punches when it comes to who I am, where I've been."

"Yes, the big picture is pretty well defined for you. But there is part of you that you seem determined to hold inside. Maybe you hide it from yourself even; I don't know."

He stopped and looked at her. "What are you talking about?"

She was standing with her fists on her hips, facing him, leaning forward slightly. "You've got your program for sobriety down pat. How many years is it now?"

"More than three years." He sensed people steering clear of them as they made their way through the Quarter.

"And that's great. But there's part of you..." Jackie's eyes were shining now "...part of you that seems...almost seems...afraid."

Forte almost smiled. "Afraid? I'd be a macho idiot if I claimed I wasn't afraid every day of my life. In case you haven't noticed, this is a dangerous planet we live on."

Jackie closed her eyes and shook her head impatiently. "No, no. That's not what I'm talking about. The physical stuff you're ready for; you're a tough man, really." She reached out and put her palm

190

flat on his chest. "This is what I'm talking about. Your heart." She kept her hand there. "It's behind a fortress with walls so thick that nothing will penetrate if you don't do something about it."

He felt her hand through the black T-shirt, part of him wanting to slap it away and another part wanting to hold it there. *My heart. Is it still there? Wasn't it blown away years ago?* A knife of pain slashed across his memory. The days after the funeral, the phone calls unanswered, the cards and letters unopened, the desolate aching inside him every time he thought of Ruth, the beginning of the drowning of sorrow those weeks and months of darkness.

A sudden surge of anger flashed inside him. "With everything else that's going on with Fizer being gone—why are we even talking about this?"

Jackie didn't back away or remove her hand. "Al, there will always be something that keeps us from talking about this."

He glared at her for half a minute before he felt the heat leave his face. Her eyes were calm now, but they remained locked on his. Finally, he looked away. When he spoke, his voice sounded tired. "And why do you think we need to talk about it, Jackie?"

In the flicker of the streetlamp on the corner, her eyes sparkled. "Because I care about you. And don't ask me what that means right now. I just know that you need someone to trust sometimes, not with the battles we are forced to fight out here in the world but with your heart. Every so often, you let your heart peek out from behind the wall but it dashes back inside." She took a deep breath and let it out. "Al, you've helped so many people, so many children set free, even as you struggled to put your life back together. I think you deserve to be set free yourself. Forever."

He kept his gaze locked on hers and felt the rest of the anger and fear melt away. *To set my heart free forever.* Was he holding his own heart captive? A dozen thoughts and excuses collided in his mind. What was wrong with protecting himself, for keeping that part of himself that could truly care about someone guarded so that nothing could ever push him over the edge again? But that self-protection, was it really freedom? Did the walls he'd built to keep out the hurt also keep him from really being free, from really caring about someone...again?

He realized his eyes had not focused for a second as the thoughts flooded his mind. He saw that Jackie was still trained on his face. An odd thought hit him: *She is pretty brave—and caring—to confront me like this; it couldn't be easy.*

"Listen," he said, "I appreciate what you're saying to me. I won't deny that there is truth in it." He put a hand on her shoulder. "I promise you I will think about it. When we get through this with Fizer, maybe we can talk again. Deal?"

She locked eyes with his for a beat, then gave a small nod. "I've said as much as I feel comfortable saying right now. I won't bring it up again until you do. That's the deal." She held out her right hand.

He took it and squeezed it. And held it for a moment.

Finally, they resumed their stroll toward Manny's church.

A few blocks later they wended their way through the construction barriers that lined the street where the church met. This section of the Quarter had lain in disarray for years as would-be investors and developers waited for the right tax incentives to come along. Now the buildings that sandwiched the two-story structure where Manny worked and lived were being restored gradually and brought into the twenty-first century.

Music poured out of the open double doors of the church building, providing a pleasant contrast to the street noises of taxies honking and the revelry of conventioneers enjoying the pleasant evening countenance of New Orleans. It was this fun-loving face the city showed to her guests for a weekend or so, the face that hid the dirty complexion under the surface that only the Quarter's residents, or the occasional tourist-victim of a mugging, knew about.

Through the doors, Forte could see the worshippers: hookers and strippers dressed more modestly than their jobs required but still a far cry from the attire usually seen in church, a few artists and performers who had finished their work on the square, a couple of street people sitting in the metal folding chairs with their feet propped on their precious five-gallon buckets stuffed with their worldly possessions, several Yuppie-types he recognized from AA meetings. They all were singing along to the praise choruses with gusto.

Manny sat on the front row of chairs, singing along with the two musicians at the front of the gathering. A large, yellow Lab-mix dog lay at the old man's feet. The dog, named J.D. after Manny's favorite beverage in his past life, apparently was making an attempt to sleep through the entire worship service.

Jackie paused at the door of the church. "You coming in this time?"

Forte took out a cigarette pack and shook out his last Checkers for the day. "I'll wait for you here." He lit the cigarette and stepped inside the doorway, leaned against the back wall, and took a deep drag.

While he watched Jackie take a seat, his cell phone rang. He looked at the Caller ID and did not recognize the number. He stepped out of the back door to the sidewalk and answered it. "Al," he said.

"This is Fizer Beal," came the voice through the phone.

Despite the heat, Forte felt a chill on the back of his neck. He immediately looked up and down the street. Small groups of revelers meandered through the closest intersection of the narrow streets. A woman seemed to be window-shopping two blocks away.

"Where are you, Fizer?"

"I'm okay. Don't worry."

"Are you alone?"

"Yes."

"Did Battier's men find you?"

"No. I had to get away. I'll tell you all about it later."

"Fizer, tell me where you are and I'll come for you right now. If they catch up with you...."

"Stop it. I'll be okay." The boy's voice had an added ring of authority since he had heard it last. "Listen. I'll meet you tonight at The Refuge at midnight." A pause. "That's three hours from now. Will you meet me?"

Forte felt his anger rising. "Fizer, you've got to get to a safe place quicker than that...."

"Will you meet me then?" Fizer was insistent now.

Forte scanned the area around him again, searching for anything out of place, any sign of danger. The night seemed heavier now, a blanket of humidity even worse than the usual mugginess. He pinched the bridge of his nose and brought away sweat from his forehead. "Yes. I'll be there."

"Good." Another pause on the line. "Thanks, Al, I appreciate you looking out for me." The line went dead.

Immediately, Forte stuffed the phone in his pocket and began walking back toward The Refuge. He would keep his promise, but there was more to be done in the meantime.

Within two blocks, he knew he was being followed.

He kept his pace consistent but stopped once to tie his shoe, checking his peripheral vision enough to note a figure darting into a recessed doorway a block behind him.

In the next intersection, he abruptly darted down the street to his left. At the first alleyway he slipped into the shadows and waited. He had seen no other signs of others tracking him; maybe it was a single attacker. *Doesn't seem like Lucky's style, but who knows.* He pulled the Glock nine out of his waistband holster, crouched and waited.

The clacking of footsteps approached the opening of the alley, slowed, then almost stopped. A figure appeared, moving cautiously, searching the darkness of the alley.

Forte lunged and swept the feet from under the attacker, who was totally caught off guard and crashed to the grimy brick floor of the alley. A small scream of fright pierced the air.

A woman? Forte instinctively had put a knee in the abdomen of the fallen figure and had the gun pointed at the person's head.

Another whimper, then, "Don't...don't hurt me...it's me..."

He recognized the voice. Quickly, he stood up and held a hand out to the fallen figure.

"Mrs. Graham," he said, "what are you doing here?"

Chapter 28

On the wrought-iron bench under the dim streetlight, Cheryl Graham looked nothing like the woman he had seen the previous day. Gone was the glamorous air and the aura of everything's-in-control-in-my-domain. She seemed smaller now, somehow. Dressed in casual khaki shorts and a black cotton knit top, her arms and legs were smeared with grit where she had fallen in the alley. Small abrasions decorated her forearms and knees. Her hair had sprung free from its ponytail clip and hung over her eyes as she slumped on the bench.

"We've been calling you," she said, her head still bowed.

"Yes, I know," Forte said. He stood next to the bench where he had deposited her. He continued to scan the surrounding buildings. Mosquitoes flitted around the streetlamps, and tourists continued to stroll through the Quarter on their way to their next highlight in the Big Easy.

After a moment of silence, he realized she was looking up at him now.

"Why didn't you answer your phone?" He voice was hoarse, as if she had been crying.

"I was a little busy today. And you may remember that my last words with your husband weren't exactly friendly."

She brushed the hair from her eyes. Anger flashed in them now. "But you had to know that if we kept calling, it was serious."

"You could have left a message."

"We did. I did." Her voice weakened again, on the verge of tears. "It's Exxie...."

"I figured."

"No, no, it's not the same thing, not this time. Please listen to me." Her voice trembled now. A single tear rolled down her cheek.

The angry words were in his mouth, ready to spill out and teach this rich woman what real pain was like. Words designed to show her that wealth and power don't always get their way, that sometimes rich, spoiled people have to suffer along with the rest of the world.

As quickly as it came to the surface, Forte's self-righteous fury floated away. After all, hadn't he overinflated his value many times in his past? Didn't he do that still? *Just do what you can do and don't worry about protecting yourself,* an old-timer in recovery had repeated to him many times in his first year after rehab. *If you think you're worth more than someone else, you'll always be protecting your turf.* He had chosen to forevermore protect someone else's turf now. It was part of what got him through each day clean and sober. And, after all, he had enough money from the parents and grandparents of the children he had rescued that he never had to worry about where the next dollar came from. *I guess it's easier to not care about having money if you know it's there for you.*

He sighed and focused again on Cheryl Graham. "What has happened with Exxie now?"

The woman before him, a brokenhearted mother now instead of the *nouveau riche* matron he had seen the day before, leaned forward. "She's gone but it's not the same. She really has been taken. Please, you must help us."

"Why didn't your husband come talk to me?"

"He was going to, he really was, but...he had to go...to the bank...."

"The bank?"

Her face was strained, but Forte could not tell if it was from lack of her usual evening dose of wine or from something else. The strain seemed real.

Forte sat next to her on the bench. "Tell me what's happened."

Cheryl folded her hands in her lap and swallowed. "My husband...my husband's company...VillaCom...you know about it..."

"Yes." He pushed down his impatience and waited.

"Some of his business partners have been...." She sobbed once and recovered. "Oh I hate this...." She blew out her breath and steadied herself. "I will just tell you this straight out. He has been given a lot of money in exchange for allowing VillaCom's Internet servers to host some porn websites." She paused. "A lot of porn sites. Making a lot of money."

He waited.

She continued. "None of the stockholders or the board of directors have known anything about it. But when Bryce wanted to cancel the contract and dump the porn sites, the people behind them threatened to tell his board. When he decided he'd tell them himself, they made more threats. Against us, against our family. They've taken Exxie." She broke down now.

Forte patted her shoulder and waited. *And you wouldn't even answer their phone calls.*

When the crying ebbed, Forte asked, "And your husband has gone to the bank?"

Cheryl wiped the back of her hand across her eyes. "They said they would do...awful things to her unless he paid them twice what they said he owed them, plus reinstating the websites."

"And who are these people?" *As if I couldn't guess.*

The woman could not hide the fear in her eyes.

Forte squeezed her arm. "Cheryl, I can't help you if I don't know everything."

She nodded. "I know. It's Marchetti's group."

An image of Lucky Battier flashed across his mind—Lucky grinning at him from behind the boxing ring ropes. How much more trouble could the man cause?

He realized Cheryl Graham was staring intently at him again. When she spoke, her voice was barely audible. "Will you help us, Mr. Forte?"

He had heard the question dozens of times. Yet every time he heard it, the sheer despair of the question rocked him. *Why would you put your hope in me,* he wanted to ask every time. Then the answer always came to him: because this is what you do, this is what you're made to do; you may have screwed up in a thousand other ways in your life, but you can do this; you've done it before and you'll do it again. Or you'll die trying.

Or someone else will die.

In front of Cheryl Graham or any other mother or father or sister-brother-aunt-grandfather that ever asked the question, Forte's face never betrayed self-doubt.

"Yes, I will, Mrs. Graham."

The woman collapsed into his arms, sobbing. He held her for a moment then gently retracted from her grasp. "We need to go over a few more details.

"First, do you know exactly who has her?"

"Yes. It's Thomas Penderby, my husband's so-called assistant." Her voice hissed now. "You met him yesterday."

"Right, he brought me to your house. How long have you known him?"

"About five years or so. Marchetti's people insisted that Bryce hire the man after they became partners with VillaCom." She paused a beat. "Penderby has been in trouble in the past. He's a pedophile. But he somehow has kept his name off any of the sex offender registries." The fear was back in her eyes.

He let the information sink in. "How much money do they want?"

"Five million now, for Exxie's release. More to be paid later, on an ongoing basis."

"A wire transfer?"

"Yes, to an offshore account for some unnamed consulting service. We make the call to transfer the money, then we get her back safe. That's what we worked out."

Forte frowned.

The woman leaned forward. "What? What is it?"

He shook his head. "Nothing, really. I just don't trust Marchetti's group." He caught the look of alarm on the mother's face. "But hopefully we won't have to worry about the transfer at all. What time did they set to meet your husband with Exxie?"

"At 3:30 a.m. The money transfer will happen before that."

He checked his watch. A little less than four hours until the transfer. And in the middle of everything, he had to meet Fizer at The Refuge. "Should be an interesting night," he said aloud.

"I hope that means in a good way." Cheryl's voice was calmer now. "You know we will pay whatever fee your company charges. But I want to thank you for doing this. I promise you, things will change in our household."

Forte stood up and held out a hand to help the woman up from the bench. "Let's get through this night first and see what it looks like."

* * *

In the shadows of the alley across from the bench, a rat scurried from behind a rusted trash bin. The rat slowed its pace and nosed among the food wrappings and leftovers that had spilled from the overstuffed receptacle. After a moment, it darted into the darkness of the alley, slowing only slightly as it went over the black-rubber-soled shoe of the man standing behind the trash bin.

Micah Cray felt the rat run over his foot but didn't flinch. He had endured much worse. The stench of the alley, the 90-degree heat even at 9:30 p.m., the drenching humidity that seemed to squeeze greasy sweat from the very air around him—all of these were mere inconveniences at this point.

He almost felt something that reminded him of a pleasant emotion from his other life. What was it? Was it *joy*? Maybe that was stretching it. But compared to the crushing sadness he'd felt earlier when he thought he had completely lost the trail of that pervert Penderby, this was something wonderful.

He was back on track to find Penderby.

Chapter 29

The strains of an Irish fiddle floated out over the rail of the third-story balcony of the rambling house. The music came through the French doors from inside the house, a CD player somewhere close by. Sprawled in a rattan chair in the corner of the balcony, Lucky Battier sat perfectly still and might have been mistaken for asleep if not for the occasional wave of his hand in time to the music. A near-full glass of wine sat on the table next to the gangster's chair.

The house was obviously out of place in the Irish Channel neighborhood. Its owner had bought four lots and immediately leveled the disheveled cottages that once housed the working class of New Orleans, the dockworkers and trolley drivers and doormen of the city's gloried past. After years of neglect, the neighborhoods of the Channel had been targeted by the young and cool climbers for renovation and renewal, mostly for investment purposes.

Battier's house was obviously built without a thought toward recouping any of his development costs. Plopped down in the midst of one-story structures that realtor ads described as "cute" and "adorable," Battier's home sat in the exact center of the four-lot plot. A horde of Spanish Oaks surrounded the house on every side, obliterating a clear view of the house from passers-by.

From where Forte sat in the lot across the street, he could easily watch the balcony where Battier lounged. He shifted in the shadows of the overgrown bushes and listened to the Irish music. *What was the name of that tune?* He remembered his grandmother playing it on the old record player at the liquor store where she worked. Forte closed his eyes for a few seconds and saw the old wooden countertop with the phonograph next to the cash register.

He remembered the tune and opened his eyes. "Shule Aroon," he whispered. *Strange that he'd be playing that song after all these years.*

Battier remained in the chair on the balcony.

Forte checked his watch. A half-hour before he was to meet Fizer back at The Refuge. Forte wanted to keep an eye on Lucky until the minutes before the meeting, to make sure the boy was safe from the people who wanted to track him down.

He had already located the two guards who seemed to move at random through the grounds surrounding the Battier house. Both men were dressed in gray-mottled camouflage that blended in almost perfectly with the darkness of the shadowy yard. Forte had had trouble seeing the men for a few minutes when he had first set up across the street. Only after seeing the movement of one guard when he was backlit from the lights of the house had he been able to pick them out. They were very good at their jobs, Forte could tell. Now he sat and tracked them while keeping tabs on Battier on the balcony.

He check his watch again. Twenty more minutes until Fizer was safe again. Forte felt his caution ebbing slightly. Better safe than sorry.

He heard the vehicle approaching the house before he saw it. A black Ford Expedition powered around the corner two blocks away and accelerated toward Battier's house. It turned into the driveway, slowed and glided to a stop at the house.

Forte tensed and watched.

The driver of the big SUV got out and opened the right passenger door. A slight figure got out. His hands were tied behind his back.

It was Fizer.

Forte involuntarily started up but caught himself. He looked up at the balcony.

Battier was gone from the rattan chair.

When he glanced back at the Expedition, the driver and Fizer were standing at the side entrance of the house as if they were waiting for someone.

The left passenger door of the truck opened and a man got out. He was older, from the way he moved.

Forte concentrated on the man. *Turn this way, just turn a little....*

The old man paused at the door and looked out toward the street, just enough so that the light from inside the house showed his features.

It was Marchetti, the boss of the criminal operation that employed Battier.

All three people walked into the house and closed the door.

Forte realized he was holding his breath. He let it out slowly. With a slow deliberate motion he bent his face and wiped the sweat from his face on the arm of his black T-shirt.

It's now or never time. He let his breath out slowly again and forced himself to think. Somehow they got to Fizer, and now they were going to force him to tell them where the money his father had stolen was hidden. *Think, think, think calmly.* That meant that Forte had some time before anything happened to Fizer. But was there enough time to call the FBI or the NOPD for help?

Forte was scanning the yard across the street to locate the two sentinels when the side door of the house opened again. The driver opened the back door of the Expedition and hauled out a large duffel bag. The man, tall with a weightlifter's build, seemed to heft the duffel bag without much strain, but anyone observing closely would know the bag was fairly heavy. The driver carried it into the house and closed the door.

Forte closed his eyes and wiped away sweat again. *The money was in the bag.* He knew he had less time now. No time for backup. Time to focus. In the darkness next to him lay a black nylon bag. He picked it up and unzipped it. Two weapons were inside: a sawed-off Remington 12-gauge with a collapsible stock, and an H&K submachine gun. He paused, then slung the shotgun over his back and put away the H&K. If he needed more firepower than the Glock nine-millimeter pistol in the waistband holster at the small of his back, he would need the lethal close-range blast of the shotgun. It would also minimize the danger of stray bullets to innocent neighbors.

He watched as one of the guards walked from the back yard around to the driveway and stood next to the Expedition. The man took out a cigarette and lit it. Apparently they were relaxing now that the package had been delivered. Forte waited and watched. Within seconds the other guard appeared in the shadows at the other end of the house.

No time like the present, Forte told himself. He punched the timer on his watch, then backed out of the bushes in the vacant lot and began doubling back through the neighborhood.

* * *

"He said this was all his daddy said to bring us," Lucky Battier said.

Fizer Beal huddled at one end of an oversized leather sofa in the center of a book-lined study. Battier was standing at an open window staring out at the darkness with his still-full wineglass in his hand.

The big duffel bag lay open atop a polished wooden desktop in a study. The bundles of cash peeked out of the opening. The only other item on the desk was a bowl of apples.

The old man sat in a leather armchair across the room, his legs crossed. A quarter-inch of brandy colored the bottom of the glass in his hand. He glanced at the hulking figure of his driver standing behind his chair. The driver took the tumbler and immediately refilled it from a bar in the corner of the room.

"Count it," Mr. Marchetti said softly.

The driver set the glass of brandy on a small table next to his boss's chair and began making stacks of the bundles of hundreds on the table.

The Irish music CD had switched to another old tune, "Endearing Young Charms."

"That's what I hate about Irish music," said Marchetti. "It sounds sad even when it's trying to be happy." He took a swallow of the brandy. "Why do you listen to that crap, Lucky? And why is it so damn hot in here?"

Battier said nothing for a moment, still gazing through the window. The muted static from a portable radio on the table broke the silence as the guards in the yard outside reported in to each other. Lucky reached out and closed the window, then turned and walked over to the radio and turned the volume off. "Mr. Marchetti, you know some of our best friends have been Irish." He raised his own wine glass and sipped. The old man grunted and drank from the brandy snifter again.

Fizer sat very still on the sofa. Through slitted eyes he studied the ancient gangster drinking brandy. He still looks like a lizard, the boy thought. He remembered him from gatherings his parents had dragged him to years past. The parties had been full of noise and hugging and cheek-pinching. When Mr. Marchetti arrived on the scene, it seemed to Fizer that the very air in the room changed somehow. Big men, who had been swaggering about seconds earlier, were transformed into the meekest of servants. Except for his father. He had wondered why his father seemed so cool toward his boss.

Now he knew.

The driver finished making stacks from the money bundles. "Five million exactly," he said. He returned to his place behind the boss's chair and grasped his hands behind his back.

No one said anything for a moment. Battier stood at the window, his back to the room. Mr. Marchetti remained in his chair, eyes closed, making tiny circles with the brandy snifter to make the amber liquid swirl. From the other room lilted the next Irish song on the CD. Fizer could not name the song, but he found himself thinking of his father and their last meeting at the prison. "Fizer, everything will be okay if you'll just follow the directions in the letter exactly. Even if you don't understand them. Just do it." His dad's eyes had been clearer than in any other visit to the prison, as free from pain and as joyful as those times when he was a young boy. Fizer felt the tightness in his throat gradually relax. His dad knew how things would end, even before he had entered the prison. *I hope you were right, Daddy*

Finally, Marchetti carefully set his glass on the table. He bent his head slightly and rubbed his temples with the thumb and forefinger of his left hand. Then he murmured a single word. "Lucky."

Fizer felt the sting of Battier's slap before he even noticed the man had stepped away from the window. The blow was not hard, but the suddenness of it brought tears to his eyes. The blurred image of Lucky's face floated inches away from his own.

"Wait, I can..." the boy managed to blurt before the look on the gangster's face stopped him. Battier held up a finger to keep him silent. He straightened and took another sip of wine.

The other two men in the room had not moved.

When Mr. Marchetti spoke, his voice seemed less alive than Fizer had ever heard it. The syllables and words and sentences rasped into the air in the room like sheets of sandpaper being plucked from between pieces of lumber.

"Come here, boy."

Fizer glanced at Battier, who jerked his head toward his boss and said, "Move." He found himself standing in front of Marchetti. Though the man's voice was still soft, the nearness of him was oppressive.

"There are those in this business who would hesitate to deal with a child in the manner this situation warrants," the old man said, his eyes still closed as he rubbed his temples. He let his hand drop to the arm of the chair and looked at Fizer from a distance of a couple of feet. A mirthless grin formed on his face, making the boy grimace despite his resolve to show no fear. He would rather have endured a barrage of angry threats than to have witnessed the old man's smile. He dropped his gaze to the Persian rug.

"I believe, however, that we all choose the consequences by our decisions, at whatever age we find ourselves." Marchetti let his head swivel on his leathery neck as he looked at the money on the table, then back at Fizer. "This is not all the money that was taken from me. You have made an unwise decision by not bringing the entire amount. Let me tell you now the outcome of our visit here tonight.

"You will eventually beg us to take the rest of the money. You will beg for your life, just as your mother did." He paused as he watched the boy flinch from that news. "But you will cooperate. Make no mistake about it."

Chapter 30

Forte crouched amidst azalea bushes near the corner of the house opposite the driveway. Twenty feet away, guard number one leaned against the wall as he smoked a cigarette and gazed out at the street.

It had taken ten minutes of agonizing caution to reach the rear of the house but Forte had dared not move more suddenly. He had made sure the guard near the car had stayed there—his only chance was to deal with them one at a time. He slowly circled back to the other guard.

Both men seemed overly familiar with the house. They were probably Battier's regular sentries but weren't regularly called on for weekend duty like this, Forte surmised. Once the car had arrived, their watchfulness seemed perfunctory.

Forte took his eyes off the guard for a moment and watched the shadows dance across the window of the third-story room above. He fixed the location of the room in his mind as much as possible. Once inside he would have to get to that room rapidly.

The guard blew a sloppy smoke-ring and yawned.

Forte silently launched himself out of the azalea bed.

The guard began to spin toward the sound, his radio transmitter in hand.

Forte punched him in the throat. The man dropped the radio and gasped, his hands flying toward his face. Forte swung the buttplate of the shotgun stock against the side of his head. The guard dropped with a thud and lay still.

Forte knelt and felt for the man's pulse on his neck. He was still alive but unconscious. He jumped up and ran around the back of the house.

No sleeping dogs here—good. He stayed close to the house, winding through the shrubbery below the light that poured from the windows on the back of the house. He stopped once and listened. No sudden noises. Good. The Irish music still played somewhere but was barely audible from where he crouched now. He crept forward again, knowing that what little time he had to reach Fizer was ticking away.

A window slammed shut above him. He threw himself against the wall of the house and waited. Instead of looking up, he watched the corner of the house where guard number one was stationed.

Almost immediately, the orange tip of a cigarette appeared at the corner. The guard's head poked around the corner. The man was backlit from the lights at the side of the house; the outline of a compact submachine gun was clear. He splayed the beam of his flashlight over the back yard then along the back wall of the house. Forte froze and closed his eyes so that no light would reflect. When he opened them, the guard was peering up at a window above that had closed. He withdrew around the corner.

Forte counted to ten then advanced again. He paused at the back door but continued past it. Entering the house there would've meant he had to watch his back every second. He knew there were only two guards outside; he had to immobilize them both.

At the corner, he stooped, peeked around the edge of the building, and pulled back.

Guard number one was leaning against the car now, lighting another cigarette.

Forte judged the distance to the man to be about 35 feet. Brick-pavers covered the drive, making it more difficult to conceal the sound of his footsteps.

He knew he had no choice but to take his chances.

He stepped around the corner and began walking toward the car.

The guard's head swiveled back and forth listlessly as he watched the street in front of the house. The haze of cigarette smoke was caught in the light from the house before it dissipated into the darkness.

Forte reached into his pocket and brought out a quarter. He was within ten feet now, still moving slowly.

The guard began to turn toward him, not in alarm but almost as an afterthought.

Forte tossed the quarter through the night, then darted toward the guard.

The quarter hit the driveway in front of the car. The guard spun toward it, bringing up the submachine gun.

Forte hit him with the shotgun stock and the man went down, bounced once against the fender of the car, then fell to the brick surface and lay still.

Forte crouched behind the front of the car and watched the house as he counted. *One-Mississippi, Two-Mississippi, Three-Mississippi, Four-Mississippi....*

No sounds of someone rushing to check out the noise.

He checked the timer on his watch. Nearly twenty minutes had passed since they took Fizer inside.

From the balcony above, the Irish music was still playing. Forte sprinted toward the side door of the house and went inside.

* * *

Fizer felt the bony hand of Mr. Marchetti close around his arm. The grip, surprisingly strong, pulled him closer until his face was less than a foot away from the old man's. He wanted to turn and look at Lucky Battier again, but the gray eyes of the lizard in front of him seemed to prevent him from averting his gaze. The man's breath stank, as if decades of festering evil had rotted away the inside of the creature before him. Marchetti leaned forward and whispered to him.

211

"If you knew what was ahead for you, you'd be crying already." The man coughed twice without turning his face away. Fizer squeezed his eyes shut against the spittle from the lizard's twisted mouth. The rasping voice continued. "But it's too late for crying. There's only time for telling."

Marchetti released the boy's arm.

Battier stepped forward and dragged Fizer toward a straight-back wooden captain's chair next to the desk. "Sit," he said.

Fizer locked eyes with the man for a beat, then lowered himself into the chair.

Battier opened a drawer on the desk and pulled out a briefcase. He placed it on the desktop, flipped the latches and opened the case, the top blocking the boy's view. Lucky reached in and brought out a roll of duct tape.

He quickly snatched off two foot-long lengths of the tape and turned back to Fizer.

"Wait, you said if I brought the money...." Fizer's words pitched higher as he frantically tried to talk.

Battier back-handed him hard, then slapped the tape over the boy's mouth. He then taped his arms and legs to the chair.

From across the room came a cackling laugh from Marchetti. "Their tune always changes when they get to this point."

Fizer shook away the hair that had fallen over his eyes. The ringing in his ears from Lucky's slap faded, and the music returned. *What were they playing now?* A single violin started up a mournful melody and was joined by what sounded like a flute. Suddenly he thought of his father's face at their final visit. The sadness of the music slid away from his mind now and along with it any fear.

Battier saw the change in the boy's face and smiled. He bent over the briefcase and brought out three items: a cheese slicer, a bottle of rubbing alcohol and a tourniquet.

Fizer's feet involuntarily twitched against the restraints on his legs. When they did, his shoes made a whisking sound on the floor. He looked down. His chair had been placed in the middle of a plastic tarp used to catch paint splatter. As he lifted his head he noticed the dark stains on the scratched-up seat of the chair. He looked up again at Battier.

"You know, we once tried to scrub that old dried blood off that chair," he said, the amused look still playing on his face. He reached over and took an apple from the bowl on the desk. "But we could never get it all out." He took the cheese slicer and made a deliberate pass over the fruit. A paper thin layer of peel curled through the blade of the slicer and fell to the wooden surface.

"Do I really have to explain how this is going to work?" Lucky's voice was lilting, and for a moment Fizer imagined that he was actually talking in time to the Irish jig that was playing.

"The trick is to take off just the right amount of skin so that the blood won't spurt too much. You see, when that happens the effect of the alcohol is diluted."

Fizer's eyes focused on the driver's face. His expression was still blank, but all the color was drained out of it now.

Battier spoke to the driver. "Are you okay? Because I need for you to come give me a hand."

The tall man looked down at his boss for direction. Marchetti nodded. The man took his place next to the chair where Fizer was bound.

Battier handed him the bottle of alcohol. The driver grimaced.

Battier grinned at the man. "You've never had this kind of fun before, huh?"

Battier took the cheese slicer and lowered it to the boy's forearm just past the point where the duct tape bound the wrist.

A drop of sweat fell from the driver's face and made a louder noise on the plastic drop cloth than it warranted.

Lucky looked up again and saw that the man's eyes were closed. He placed the slicer on Fizer's arm.

At that moment, the door behind Mr. Marchetti exploded.

Chapter 31

Forte stood at the door with the shotgun in one hand and the nine-millimeter pistol in the other. The pistol was pointed at Battier. The shotgun was leveled at Marchetti's head five feet away.

The old man stayed perfectly still, the brandy snifter in his hand.

The driver was caught in a half-crouch as he stared at Forte. His hand was poised in front of his chest, inches away from the shoulder holster holding his handgun.

As if by magic, a .45-caliber automatic had sprung to Lucky's hand. He held the muzzle of the gun to Fizer's head. He seemed completely relaxed as he smiled at Forte across the room.

No one said a word for a long moment.

Finally Lucky spoke.

"Podnuh, I was wondering when you might show up here."

In the half-second it took him to kick open the door and step inside, Forte had taken in the entire room and was satisfied with the fact that Fizer wasn't hurt. He held Lucky's insolent gaze steadily without speaking.

"Ain't this what they call a 'Mexican Standoff,' where neither side can make a move without causing their own destruction?" Lucky's lip curled slightly, his speech lapsing into the thick N'awlins accent that Forte remembered from their days on the football field.

Forte kept his eyes locked on Lucky's. "Except this ain't a movie, Lucky." He could see beads of perspiration forming on the back of Marchetti's neck from where he stood. "And then there's the fact that I have two guns and you have only one."

Lucky nodded. "This is true. And you think that you can keep me from killing the boy here as long as you threaten to shoot my boss. That about sum up things, my friend?"

Marchetti interrupted, his voice barely audible above the music now. "Lucky, quit yapping and shoot this do-gooder junkie." He cursed softly, his voice trailing away in a bored mumble.

Forte kept his eyes locked on Battier's while the old man spoke, watching the younger criminal's eyes as he talked. The amused glint was still there. *Is the man truly crazy?* He knew that he had little chance of blasting Lucky with the shotgun without also hurting, maybe killing, the boy. And he knew that Battier was too fast to allow Forte to switch the handgun from targeting Marchetti. But what choice did he have here?

Battier spoke again. "But this is where Mr. Big-Stuff Navy SEAL done figured out things all wrong. 'Cuz you know what? You can shoot that dried-up old fart all night long and it won't make a bit o' difference to me."

The driver twitched his eyes toward Battier.

Lucky sighed. "Guess I don't blame you for not believin' me. Go on, shoot him. It'll make me happy."

Marchetti chuckled, his voice crackling. The sweat beads on his neck had begun to trickle toward his collar.

Forte kept both guns steady, though the strain of holding the pistol-grip shotgun was beginning to burn in the muscles of his forearm.

Lucky shrugged. "Okey dokey, Mr. Pokey." He spoke to Fizer now. "Close your eyes, boy, and keep them shut."

Fizer obeyed, his eyes squeezed together, shoulders hunched forward.

Forte's finger tightened on the trigger of the automatic pistol. He'd have to aim high, away from Fizer.

The music in the next room stopped.

Battier pointed his gun toward Marchetti.

The force of the blast from Battier's .45 knocked Marchetti backward, his chair plummeting to the floor.

Marchetti's driver-bodyguard whirled, his hand plunging toward the pistol in his shoulder holster. Both Battier and Forte shot him, sending his body careening against the bookshelf behind him.

Both Marchetti and the driver lay where they had fallen.

Almost instantly, Lucky's gun was again pointed at Fizer's head. He had crouched behind the boy's chair, his head close to Fizer's.

Forte stood now with both guns pointed at the gangster.

The smell of burnt gunpowder and a haze of smoke covered the room now.

Battier spoke again, this time with no hint of humor in his voice.

"Al, I could kill you right now, just like the others. But I'm going to let you hear something from little Fizer here. Then you can decide how you want to play this thing out." He reached around the boy's face and jerked off the duct tape.

Fizer screamed and cursed. He looked across the room at Forte. "Sorry," he said.

Battier poked him in the shoulder with his gun. "Go ahead. Tell him."

Forte waited, the sight of his pistol trained on the bit of Lucky's forehead he could see behind the boy.

Fizer grimaced. "My ears are ringing." He closed his eyes, then opened them. "He did what I told him to do, what my dad had arranged with him a year ago." He swallowed and Forte could see tears in the boy's eyes now. "Mr. Marchetti killed my mother, and my dad only took the money to pay him back for that." He sobbed once, then cleared his throat. "Now it's done."

Forte kept his guns leveled at Lucky. "That's right, it's done. But why should I let you walk out of here with that money?"

Only one of Lucky's eyes was visible from behind the boy. But it twinkled. When he spoke, his voice contained none of the thick

Cajun accent. "Very good question, Alvin my compadre. Here's your answer.

"First, I will shoot the boy if I have to. Now I don't want to do that, mind you. He's been through a lot of crap that he doesn't deserve, for sure. But I'll do it if you force me. Second, even if you don't force me to shoot him but you keep those guns on me, I'll load up this money and back out of here all the way to the car and we'll be gone."

Battier paused and turned so that Forte could see most of his face now. He was grinning. The gangster insolence came back into his voice. "But the last reason is the most best of 'em all. You see, if you don't let me go, you won't get to find out exactly where that girl is before she is killed."

Fizer jerked his head toward the man. "What are you...."

"Hush, Fizer," Forte said. He stared at Lucky. "Tell it. What girl are you talking about?"

Lucky made a clucking noise with his tongue. "Don't talk down to me, son. We both know what girl I'm talking about. The one that pervert Penderby is holding out in a shack in the swamp. Marchetti had it all set up to get money from her daddy, but as soon as the money is transferred, Penderby will kill her."

Forte let the man's words sink in. "How can I trust you that this is the truth?"

"You can't, Al. You just have to make your choice here. I'm a bad man, I ain't never denied that. But that don't mean I'm all bad all the time. Penderby is a sicko and no girl deserves to go through what she will as soon as that money is transferred." He shifted slightly and for a moment left himself open to a head shot. Forte waited, finger on trigger. Lucky continued. "Think about it, buddy. You think it would've been so easy for you to get in this house?" He pointed to the radio. "It's turned off, right. Why do you think that is? You think I'd really have Fizer brought here to my house, knowing you were looking for him too?" Lucky's eyebrows were arched. He still seemed amused at the scene being played out.

Forte said nothing. But he slowly lowered his weapons. "Tell me how to find the girl."

Lucky stood up and put his pistol in its holster. He stretched and pointed toward a cabinet with rows of small drawers. "In one of those 20 drawers is a map with Penderby's location. As soon as Fizer here stuffs all the money back in that bag and I'm standing at the door ready to go, I'll tell you which drawer it is. Pretty simple."

Forte looked down at Marchetti's body. The old man seemed shriveled and pitiful in death. None of the great fear he had spread among his friends and enemies was evident in the dapper figure on the carpet with the crimson stain spreading across his white shirt. Where is he now, Forte thought, then immediately caught himself. Why would he even wonder such a thing? At one time, he had dismissed the thought of an afterlife as foolishness. Since Ruth's death, he pondered the possibility from time to time. He mentally shook himself. He had too much to think about here and now. For the time being, he'd leave pondering the hereafter to Manny Leard and his church members.

"It's a deal, but you know you got worse problems than me now."

Lucky smirked. "Makes life interesting, podnuh." He took out a knife, flipped it open, and cut the tape to free Fizer. Within minutes, the money was reloaded into the duffel bag and zipped up. Lucky picked up the bag and slung it over his shoulder. He backed toward the door of the study, his pistol held at his side.

Forte watched and waited, his hand resting on the shotgun.

Battier paused at the door. "The map is in the drawer labeled 'L' for Lucky, of course. You shoulda guessed that one." He started through the door, then turned back. "One more thing. If I were y'all, I wouldn't be hanging around here in the study for too long. Things could heat up here real soon." He vanished into the darkness of the house.

Forte yanked open the drawer of the cabinet and rummaged through some blank paper until he found an envelope. He tore it open and pulled out a copy of a hand-drawn map. At the bottom of the page was written a cell phone number.

He grabbed Fizer by the arm. "Don't stop until we're away from the house."

They sprinted down the stairs and out of the side door. The SUV was gone. The guard lay where he'd been cold-cocked on the driveway. They ran past the prone figure and kept moving until they were across the street in the overgrown lot.

Just as they were turning to look back at the house, three explosions erupted on both sides of the study. Almost immediately, flames appeared in the windows of the house and began lapping their way out to the balcony where Lucky had been sitting just an hour earlier.

Forte looked up and down the street. Battier was already long gone.

He turned back to look at Fizer. The boy lay in the weeds watching the fire across the street.

Forte held out his hand. "Come on. This place will get real busy soon; we don't have time to do much explaining right now."

Fizer looked up at the man. Tears shone in his eyes. He took the proffered hand and stood up. Forte put an arm around his shoulder but said nothing for a moment.

"We'll have time to sort things out later," he said finally. "Right now, I've got to go see a man about a boat."

Chapter 32

A fat moon glowered down through the moss-draped branches at the canoe silently slipping through the swamp. Thousands of cypress roots rested just beneath the shallow surface of the inky water, each waiting to betray the canoe's location if the aluminum boat bumped against it. The slender boat indeed nudged a root every few seconds, but its lightweight rubber bumpers dampened the noise, blending the craft's journey with the swamp sounds of the night.

Forte felt a tap on his right shoulder and immediately he steered the craft to the right. He peeked over his shoulder at Larue perched on the back seat of the canoe, his head sweeping back and forth to pick out the landmarks to guide them to the cabin. In his hands he held a hickory cane with an alligator head carved into the handle.

The wizened barber had shown no surprise when Forte appeared at his house in the middle of the night. Forte had known the vicinity of the cabin when he perused the map, but he also knew that only someone totally familiar with the swamp would be able to take him to it. He remembered the long afternoons fishing with Larue, drifting through the swamp for hours in silence. Those were the days before his sports activities had claimed most of his idle time. He'd never wondered before now if the old man had missed those times in the years that followed.

This night, Larue had sat at his kitchen table and listened to the plan without interrupting or asking any questions. He held out a leathery hand and took the map, studying it for a full minute before looking up. "I know da place. I done fished close by there 'bout 'leven or ten times maybe."

Forte studied the man's calm features and thought of the years he'd spent in his house. *There are all kinds of toughness,* he mused. "And you can take me to it, tonight, in the dark?"

Larue didn't exactly smile but came close. "Ain't I done tole you I know where it's at?"

Gliding through the moonlit water now only a few hundred yards from their destination, Forte smiled at his question earlier. There had been no wrong turns, no backtracking. The tiny outboard motor lying in the back had propelled them through the twisting channels to get this far. Now they were totally under paddle-power, progressing more slowly but steadily advancing in silence.

Up to this point they had seen a few other canoes as the Cajun trappers and night fishers and frog giggers came out to catch their food for the next day or so. Other shacks on stilts had been spaced far apart along their watery path, squatting in the moonlight among the cypress stumps, windows black. They had seen no other boats or shacks for a while now as they drew closer to their destination.

Forte approached a denser patch of trees and undergrowth to his left now. He felt the tip of Larue's cane slide down his backbone. That meant "slow down here."

He dipped the paddle into the water perpendicular to the left side of the canoe, then repeated the manuever on the right side of the small craft. They slowed as they approached the clump of trees and brush that blocked the view to the left. He could see now that the trees actually framed a small sandbar in the swamp.

Another vertical stroke along his back. Then two soft taps in the small of his back. *Slow more, and stop here.* Again he dipped and back-thrust slightly on both sides of the canoe. The bow of the craft edged past the group of trees.

Forte leaned forward and peered left along the natural, watery path through the swamps.

Fifty yards away, Penderby's cabin looked over a natural lagoon. A half-dozen huge cypress trees loomed over the shack on three sides. One lantern flickered inside the cabin, giving off a pale yellow light that scarcely competed with the moon.

Forte back-paddled softly, drawing the canoe behind the trees again.

A branch crackled nearby. Forte put his hand on the Glock and peered through the underbrush, waiting and watching. He pointed his gun toward the trees and slowly counted to ten. Behind him there was no sound from Larue.

On the sandbar, a pair of eyes appeared on a log. The eyes were about a foot apart. The log suddenly slid into the water. *Gator. Big gator. This might make things trickier.* Forte heard a barely audible sigh behind him. *But it's been done before.*

He slapped at a mosquito on his neck and felt the bug squish beneath his hand.

His watch read 1:25 a.m. Almost time for the transfer.

He reached for his snorkel mask and dipped it into the water, keeping an eye out for the alligator.

There was a coughing sound to his left but before he could turn to look he felt a sting on his neck. *Bigger than a mosquito.*

As he reached to brush away the bug, he heard a splash behind him.

He turned and saw that Larue was gone.

He smiled at the thought of Larue falling out of the canoe. Then the thought: *Why do I think this is funny?*

He reached for his neck again where he had been stung. His fingers closed on feathers.

He frowned. *Feathers?! What the...*Then he felt the dart. He tried to pull it out. His hand wouldn't obey him.

Then the man in the moon stopped smiling. And began laughing.

Alone on his back in the bottom of the boat, Forte grinned back at the foolish moon.

Then darkness.

* * *

Thomas Penderby looked at his watch. It was time for the phone call from the Grahams. Once the money was transferred, the fun would begin.

He heard the splash out in the lagoon. Exxie stirred from her slumber on the floor, still tied to the chair. She mumbled something, then resumed the rhythmic breathing of a sleeper.

Penderby stepped to the door of the cabin, took a flashlight from a nail, and opened the door to the porch. He stepped out cautiously and shone the light across the black span of water in front of the cabin. The water was calm.

Thirty feet out from the porch, a pair of eyes blinked open.

"My friend, my monster," Penderby said aloud. "You want another appetizer before the main course?"

He went back into the cabin, pulled another chicken out of the cooler, and started back to the porch. As he passed the girl on the floor, he stopped, held out the chicken and let its juices drop on her. She whimpered but lay still.

Back on the porch, he estimated where he had seen the alligator and heaved the chicken in that direction. The bird entered the water with a splash. Immediately the monster thrashed toward the spot. Under the light of the flashlight, the creature's huge jaws flashed open then snapped shut on the chicken. And it was gone.

Behind him the phone bleeped. Penderby jumped, his focus on the water in front of him. He quickly moved back inside, feeling his adrenalin pumping now.

"Have you transferred the money?" he barked into the phone.

A pause, then Bryce Graham's voice. "It's ready to go. I want to hear my daughter's voice."

Penderby cursed into the phone. "She's fine right now, Graham, but you only have one more minute before she won't be if I don't confirm the money has been transferred."

Graham's voice was firmer now. "As soon as I hear her, it will happen."

Penderby held up the phone and fought back the raging impulse to fling it out into the night. He breathed deeply, in and out, slower, slower, talking himself out of his anger now. *Delay it, put it aside, for now, let it build later, let it build.*

He put the phone to his mouth again. "All right, hold on for a minute." He put his hand over the phone and stepped over to the girl on the floor. With the point of his boot, he dug into her ribs. She grunted and struggled against the ropes as she awoke.

Penderby knelt and brought the chair up from the floor, setting it upright. He bent his face to Exxie's ear and whispered, "Tell your father everything is fine or I will kill you now, then I'll go and kill both your parents." His voice rasped with the wrath rising inside him. He held the phone to her face.

"Daddy?" She sobbed then recovered. "I'm okay now, just bring me home...."

Penderby snatched away the phone. Graham was crying on the other end.

"Shut up that crap," Penderby snapped. "Do the transfer now."

Graham stopped crying. "If you hurt her...."

"Do it. Now."

Over the phone came the sound of breath being sucked in, then out. "Hold on."

Penderby waited, listening to the creaking of the cabin as the water moved against it. The gator must be swimming close now, he thought. *Only a few more minutes, my monster.*

He looked at the girl's face, upturned toward his, her eyes full of terror but searching for hope. There will be no hope for you this night, he mused. *Or ever.* He covered her face with a chloroform-soaked handkerchief and watched her jerk twice before her head lolled against her shoulder.

He stepped out onto the porch but left the flashlight hanging on the nail by the door.

The moon bathed his face with soft light. He felt the euphoria beginning to rise inside him now.

"Okay" came Bryce's voice over the phone. "It's done."

"And the confirmation code?"

The man read it to him.

Penderby began to relax. "Good. Be outside the food court exit at RiverWalk in exactly one hour."

Graham's voice blurted. "Don't hurt her, Thomas, or I will...."

Penderby clicked off the phone. He flung it out over the water. It splashed and immediately the alligator's jaws snapped shut on it.

"You idiot, Graham. She's gone now," he said to the sky.

"Nope," said the man behind him.

Penderby started to spin toward the voice but an iron grip clamped over his mouth, a handkerchief smothering him. He struggled briefly, then slumped to the floor, unconscious.

A tall figure lowered the man to the wooden boards of the porch. He then stood up and peered out across the water.

"No, she's not gone," said Micah Cray. "But you are."

Chapter 33

A wiry brown hand came out of the water and gripped the side of the canoe. A man's head followed the hand, eyes searching the surrounding darkness. Larue waited a full five minutes, completely immobile in the water except for the steady swiveling of his head, back and forth.

The moon illuminated just enough of the area to make the trees and undergrowth on the sandbar seem sinister. His eyes barely above water level, Larue scanned the outcropping for any movement. Nothing seemed out of sorts now. The frogs had even resumed their croaking calls and replies across the lagoon.

Satisfied that no one was close by, he tugged on the canoe and trudged through the muddy bottom of shallow water until the narrow craft rested on the sandbar.

Suddenly a splash sounded somewhere between the sandbar and the cabin. Larue stopped in the water, crouched next to the canoe. Through the bushes of the sandbar he could see two men, one short and one tall, struggling briefly on the porch of the cabin. The tall man then lowered the other one to the floor of the cabin and stood on the porch looking out over the water.

Larue could not see from this distance whether the man was looking at him. He felt the slime of the swamp on his skin, in his hair; he wanted to rake a hand over his scalp and scrape away any slugs that might've hidden in his hair. But he kept still and waited.

The man on the porch bent over and grabbed the fallen man by his feet. Backing toward the screen door of the cabin, he flung it open and dragged the man inside.

Only then did Larue let out his breath. He turned to examine his boy in the boat.

When he'd heard the coughing noise earlier, he had known immediately that the sound didn't belong to anything natural in the swamp. Decades of examining almost every square foot of the swamp had tuned his ear to the blend of noises to be sampled here. He had started to turn toward the sound when he saw Forte reach for his neck. He saw the dart immediately, decided instantly that the next dart would be for him, and without hesitation launched himself over the side of the canoe. He had swum underwater away from the sandbar and had clung to a log only fifteen feet from the boat. He waited with his head barely above the surface, his face masked by the leaves of water lilies.

After a moment, another canoe came alongside theirs. A tall man with a fishing cap and several fishing poles in the canoe reached in and poked Forte in the ribs. As he did so, he watched the surrounding waters, presumably for Larue. After a full minute of watching, the man back-paddled and disappeared around the other side of the sandbar.

Larue had waited. He had seen the man in the cabin throw the chicken out to the alligator. *Big Gator, him.* He paused for another full minute before swimming back to the canoe. He knew they were too far to draw the attention of Mr. Big Gator as the creature awaited its next snack.

Now Larue bent over the edge of the canoe and felt along Forte's neck for the tiny dart. He had heard the sound of the dart and watched it strike the boy's neck. *The boy. He might go off saving the world, but he still be the boy to me.* His mind flashed an image of Forte at age 13, standing at his grandmother's graveside, having lost his parents in a car wreck six years earlier. Then again, the boy standing in the entryway of Larue's home, a cracked leather suitcase hanging from his left hand as he examined the old chandelier above. Larue was never sure if the boy ever realized how much light he brought back into the old house those empty years since the cancer had stolen his wife from him.

The old man blinked the water from his eyes and focused on the present again.

He crouched, half out of the water, groping for the dart along Forte's arms and shoulders while watching the cabin through the underbrush. He could see movement inside the shack but couldn't tell what was happening.

Finally, he found the dart dangling from Forte's neck and pulled it out.

Forte moaned but remained sedated in the boat. Larue brushed away a mosquito, then cupped some water and splashed it over Forte's face. The man snorted as water ran into his nose but he did not awaken. Larue watched to see if the noise drew any reaction. Nothing. He continued to gently slap Forte's face and pour water over his head. "Wake up, cher. There's more trouble here than them crawfish got eggs."

* * *

Cray stood above the man lying on the cabin floor. He didn't consider him a human being, just a despicable piece of wickedness who deserved only to be wiped from existence. Like the unredeemably evil creature who had taken his girl from him. His daughter's face floated in front of him. A red curtain of rage blotted out the image. He fought back the urge to take out his knife and slit the man's throat on the spot. "No, you worthless piece of crap, you won't have it that easy."

He found the duct tape on the table and quickly bound the man's hands and feet.

A whimper behind him drew him back to the girl tied to the chair. Her mass of tangled blonde hair covered her face. He knelt and put a hand on her head for a moment. Then he cut the tape away that bound her to the chair. In the semidarkness of the cabin he picked her up and laid her on the threadbare sofa against the wall. She didn't stir but her breathing was steady. He would come back for her in a few minutes.

"As soon as I finish my business," he said aloud.

He turned and walked past Penderby's prone figure, out onto the porch again. Somewhere out across the murky lagoon, Forte would be coming out of his sedated state soon. As for the old man in the canoe, he had apparently lost his balance and had fallen into the water after being struck by the second dart. Cray felt a momentary pang of guilt over the old man's demise. He shrugged it off. It was just a quirky twist in the journey for Cray. As for Forte, he would be too groggy to act quickly for a few minutes after reviving, but at that point he might decide to get in the way of what Cray had in mind for the pervert he had tracked down.

Cray had been on autopilot during the past few hours as he tracked Forte.

The chase had been trickier than Cray had expected. There had been the boring wait at the house in the Irish Channel as Forte conducted his business about the boy, whatever that was about. Cray had followed in the man's footsteps, watched him expertly take out the two guards and enter the house. He had waited a minute and followed him in, listening from the hallway. When the gunshots went off, Cray had almost burst into the room firing. But he had waited. His reward was hearing of the map that led to Penderby. From that point, a stolen canoe with a small outboard motor and a few fishing poles had kept him close enough to the man.

He almost enjoyed the midnight jaunt through the swamp.

He had been genuinely sorry that he had to tranquilize Forte and the old man. There had been no way around it though; Forte's reputed capabilities meant he could possibly prevent Cray from reaching Penderby.

That was not acceptable.

Cray felt a sadness come over him, unexpectedly. He looked up at the moon as it floated, magnified, above the twisted cypress trees guarding the shack. All these months he had visited his daughter, murmuring to her and stroking her fine hair. Though she would never again have spoken to him, she at least offered her father one more chance, each visit, to touch her face, feel her blood pulsing in her temples, brush her locks. He felt embarrassed now at his selfishness. What kind of life was that for her? She was better off now, having left this evil planet.

A surge of weariness washed over him. He stretched and shook his shoulders. *Time to finish this.*

He spun, walked back into the cabin, and paused. He had seen Penderby fling the chicken out into the darkness. He spied the ice chest. He stepped past the man on the floor and took out the last chicken. He flipped open his knife, sliced away the plastic wrapping from the bird, then held it over Penderby, letting the juices drip over his head then down his body. The man on the floor moaned and began to roll over.

Cray walked to the back door of the cabin and stood on the small back stoop. He found where he had tied the rope that led to his canoe among the cypress roots behind the shack. Hand over hand he pulled the boat up to the cabin. He reached into the bottom of the boat and found his rope.

The girl's voice startled him. "Who...who are you?" Her voice sounded drugged. He walked past her toward the man on the floor.

Cray knelt next to the man and spoke to the girl over his shoulder. "Tonight I'm your savior. But I have one more thing to take care of. Just sit there, relax, and enjoy the show."

He quickly looped the rope around Penderby's feet and double-knotted it. He stood and dragged the man toward the porch. Penderby moaned louder now and began to awaken. "What...who...." His head banged over the threshold of the door. He cursed loudly now.

Cray knelt and slapped the man hard. With his left hand, he jerked the man by his collar to within inches of his face. "I am the nightmare you deserve, Penderby. You and all like you." He held the knife in his right hand and for a split second considered plunging it into the pervert.

Instead he lowered the man to the floor of the porch. He grabbed Penderby's hair and made three slits in his forehead. Penderby screamed and thrashed, causing a handful of hair to come out in Cray's hand.

Cray slapped him again. "Shut up. Those cuts won't kill you." He smiled and the other man stopped thrashing.

Cray threw the other end of the rope over the crossbeam supporting the roof of the porch. He wrapped the rope twice around his forearm and pulled back toward the door of the cabin. Penderby rose feet-first until he was hanging upside down at the front edge of the porch.

The swamp was completely quiet now as if every creature stopped to see the spectacle on the cabin porch.

Cray lowered the rope a few inches until Penderby's head barely touched the surface of the swamp. He tied off the rope on the porch post.

A sharp noise broke the silence over the lagoon. *Someone's being slapped.*

Cray listened for a moment, then quickly picked up the chicken and tore one of the legs off. He tossed it into the lagoon twenty feet from the porch.

Immediately, a huge form surged through the water, jaws snapping up the morsel.

Penderby screamed even louder now. "No, you can't...."

Cray tore off the other chicken leg and flung it about ten feet out. The water churned again. He could see the monster now in the moonlight.

Penderby twisted vainly on the rope.

A drop of blood dripped from his head into the water.

"Please, please, whoever you are...there's money...." The man's voice cracked. He sobbed incoherently.

Cray tore the rest of the chicken in half, the bones and meat ripping apart in his hands. He threw one of the two pieces about five feet out. Almost before the meat reached the water, the giant alligator ripped into it.

He watched the man twisting on the rope. A red trickle dropped into the swamp now from the man's head.

"Penderby," Cray said, "from what I know, you caused some innocent children to plead and beg just as you're doing now. Did you show mercy?"

The man babbled now. "Please...please...no...."

Cray knelt at the edge of the porch and turned the man to face him. "Here comes your answer."

He dropped the final, grisly piece of chicken in the water inches from Penderby's head.

Cray stepped back and leaned on the cabin wall.

For a moment, the swamp seemed peaceful.

Then the monster erupted from the black water.

Screams tore the night and the cabin shook. Abruptly, the shrieking stopped as the creature's jaws snapped shut, opened and closed and tore, again and again.

Cray watched until the shredded rope swung from the porch beam.

He took the lantern from the nail on the porch wall and went back into the cabin.

The girl's voice trembled. "Is he gone?"

"Yes," he said. "You're safe."

She sat with her legs curled beneath her on the sofa.

He walked closer and sat beside her. "Are you hurt?"

She shook her head. One hand fluttered to her bruised face.

"Let me see." He turned up the lantern's light and brushed the hair from her face.

He stopped and stared at the girl.

She squinted in the flashlight's beam. "What?" Her voice showed alarm. Then her eyes widened.

"You," he said. "You're the one...."

She cringed and closed her eyes.

"You left my daughter there." His voice cracked now. "You led her to that monster that day, then you ran away and never called for help, because you wanted to protect yourself...."

Exxie was crying now. *What was that girl's name.... Seems so long ago now.* "I'm sorry, I'm so sorry...Is she...."

Cray slapped her hard. She slumped against the couch.

Still kneeling next to the prone girl, the man closed his eyes and saw slashing red across the blackness. *Pressure in my head...building, building....* He squeezed his face between his hands and screamed his anguish.

Cray scooped up the girl and threw her over his shoulder.

Chapter 34

Larue heard the man scream inside the cabin and stopped scooping the water over Forte's face. He watched the tall man pull the other one out to the porch, suspend him from the ceiling, and throw something out to the water. The water boiled and Larue knew exactly what caused it. He felt his skin tingle at the back of his neck.

"Lord have mercy," he whispered. "Mighty big gator, that one."

He put one hand behind Forte's head and reared back with the other. "Sorry, cher," he said. He slapped the man's face hard.

Forte snorted and sat up, then fell back to the bottom of the boat.

Another scream sounded, this one louder.

From the shadows, Larue watched the cabin for a moment, then turned and drew back to slap again.

A hand jutted up from the bottom of the canoe. "Okay, okay...I'm awake," Forte's voice was slurred but he was stirring.

Larue helped the man sit up.

"Who...was it...." Forte shook his head violently, trying to shake off the tranquilizer.

The old man shook his head slowly. "Don't know who. But dis I know—he wanted the man mo' than you did, my boy." He pointed toward the cabin.

Forte watched in a daze as the monster churned the water as it lunged toward the porch. The hanging figure screamed once and Forte recognized it as a man's cry.

Then the alligator was gone with its meal.

Forte turned back to Larue. "Penderby?"

"'Fraid so."

Forte absorbed this revelation calmly. Deep in the recesses of his mind he knew he would have been shocked by the horror of what had happened if not for his drugged state.

He squeezed his eyes shut hard, then opened them and concentrated on focusing again on Larue's face. "And the girl?"

The old barber shook his head. "She probably inside. Ain't seen her yet."

Forte nodded solemnly. "Help me up."

He felt the old man's arms around him and was surprised at the strength still left in limbs he had considered ancient for years. "You are one tough old bird," he said.

Larue eyed him coldly. "Mind them manners, mister smart boy."

"Yes, sir," he said. He stretched his hands over his head and felt the cobwebs beginning to clear from his mind.

An ache lurked at the base of his skull, the aftereffect of the tranquilizer. He rolled his head from side to side and tried to concentrate. *He wanted the man mo' than you did.* It made no sense. Who would even know where Penderby had taken Exxie? Lucky Battier? He was long gone with his money now; the man was smart enough to know that others in Marchetti's organization would put a bounty on his head for a while, even if only to make a show of loyalty to the late boss—all the while carving off pieces of his domain for themselves.

Who else? He squeezed his eyes shut, then opened them wide, stretching the muscles in his face. The lagoon was calm again and the gator was nowhere in sight. On the far side of the cabin, a grey heron picked its way among the lily pads searching for a midnight snack of its own. He had seen herons in the swamps for years on his fishing trips with Larue. The big birds fascinated him, their cautious stilted strolls through the swamp punctuated by the deadly quick spearing of a hapless frog with its beak. *I wonder what the bird is going to do next....*His mind was drifting.

Snap out of it. He reached up and slapped himself hard. Larue glanced at him but said nothing.

A plan, make a plan, even if it's a ridiculous one, he told himself. *Whoever you are, you are the target until the girl is safe.* He scooped water to his face and reached for his scuba mask again. The big alligator had disappeared, probably to digest in peace. Forte put the thought from his mind. He dipped the snorkel mask in the water, emptied it, and pulled it over his head.

When you have no time to plan, make your attack simple and direct. One of his Navy SEAL instructors had pounded the message into his SEAL class over and over, proving the wisdom of his words in dozens of exercises. In actual missions, Forte had put it into practice.

He picked up the waterproof tote-sack from the bottom of the canoe, unzipped it, and pulled out the H&K submachine gun. He tapped the shoulder of Larue, who was watching the cabin intently. "I'm snorkeling up to the cabin. I want you to cover me in case there's trouble." He handed him the assault gun. He couldn't make out the old man's eyes in the shadows. "And, if you have to shoot, try not to hit me. I'll be the good-looking one."

Larue nodded solemnly. "Sumpin gonna change for you 'tween here and there then, eh?"

Forte let his fingers trace the outline of his Glock through his wetsuit. He clamped the mask over his face and slithered into the water, watching for the long, dark killer he had seen in action a few minutes earlier.

He could feel the underwater vines in the shallow lagoon pull at his flippers as he made his way to the shack. The cabin seemed approachable only from the front because of the way the cypress trees stood guard to the rear like hideous sentinels in the night. Everything was black and gray and silver in the moonlight. Forte watched for any variations in the monochromatic background that would betray movement by the person who had attacked him and killed Penderby.

No choice but to go straight through the front. He approached the porch and raised himself from the water's surface just enough to peer through the screen door. No movement inside the cabin. He reached down and took off both flippers and placed them on the edge of the porch.

Pulling himself up almost solely with his upper body strength, he rolled onto the porch. He stopped, listening. He unzipped the wetsuit and pulled out the Glock.

He approached the screen door in a crouch. He glanced back toward the sandbar where Larue waited. The old man could handle the gun if need be.

Forte took a quick breath, released it. He put his hand on the handle of the door. *One, two, three....*He snatched open the door and tumble-rolled into the room. He came out of the roll in a crouch, sweeping the one-room cabin with the pistol.

The room was empty.

Wet footsteps led to the back door of the cabin.

* * *

Cray barely noticed the burning in the muscles of his shoulders and triceps as he power-paddled the canoe away from the cabin. A trio of mammoth mosquitoes found the exposed skin of his neck above the wetsuit and began feeding. Wreaths of low-hanging moss brushed against him from this thickly-wooded area of the swamp. He ignored it all and kept stroking.

The girl. He remembered overhearing two policeman talk about Exxie Graham at the station when he had first raced there after his daughter's attack. "Big trouble now and in the future," one cop had said. "Spoiled little jail-bait," the other replied.

He'd met the girl only in passing when Jenny was going out to some concert. A chauffeur had appeared at the door and Cray had followed him out to the car. The rich girl had obviously put on her charm-the-parent manners that night.

That had been only three months before the attack.

A friend inside the police department had pieced together for him the girl's involvement in Jenny's tragedy. Exxie had been the one to make the contact with the man through the Internet; he had monitored Jenny's net activities too closely for her to chat with such a monster. The girl had apparently thought it was a joke, according to some of her school friends.

When the predator grabbed Jenny to drag her off, Exxie Graham had run away.

She had never called the police for help.

Cray stopped paddling and closed his eyes against the blood-red fury that blotted out the night. *She killed Jenny, she killed her, she killed her as much as what that monster had done.* He raised the paddle over his head with both hands and twisted in the seat. Through the gnarled limbs above, the moon showed Exxie's bruised face, her eyes showing horror. A muffled scream caught in the duct tape over her mouth.

Cray hacked the paddle downward.

* * *

Forte willed his body to ignore the fatigue that had begun to tear away his resolve. *Keep going, keep moving.* He knew part of it was the tranquilizer and part was lack of sleep after a steamroller of a day that included the shootout at the restaurant, the fight with Lucky at the gym, the recovery of Fizer at Battier's house, the realization that Theodore Beal had hired Lucky to kill Marchetti.

But part of his weariness had nothing to do with the physical challenges of the day. At the bottom of it all was a crushing sense of failure at having lost Fizer at first and at having Exxie Graham plucked away from him just as he was poised to rescue her. He could almost hear the old strains of self-doubt whispering to him. *What makes you think you can protect anyone or save anyone? You couldn't save your wife, could you? You watched her die in your arms, didn't you?*

Few people would have guessed that the self-doubt attacked him still. He looked up at the moon peeking through the moss streamers. *You know where you can find relief,* the moon said. Forte slumped forward as he stared at nothing in the bottom of the canoe.

"Cher, you okay?" Larue's voice in the darkness reminded him of those nights long ago when he awoke sweating from the nightmares of crashes and formless terrors and dead bodies. The old Creole's soft voice had calmed him then. It calmed him now.

He realized he had stopped paddling.

"I'm okay, I'm okay," he whispered. *Just do what you can do, and keep doing it every minute, every hour, every day—one day at a time.* He'd heard the words so much it was like rote most of the time. Tonight he needed to feel the truth in it.

As the canoe drifted, the trees ahead parted and the moon spotlighted another boat.

A man in a canoe, his paddle held aloft.

Blonde hair hanging over the back edge of the boat.

Forte jerked his Glock from its holster and fired.

Chapter 35

Cray sliced the edge of the paddle downward with all his strength.

And hit the water next to the boat.

Water splashed high and the sound of the wood spanking the swamp's surface shattered the night silence.

The noise of the paddle masked another sound: a barking, popping noise.

The bullet slammed his right shoulder, knocking him to the floor of the canoe.

The canoe drifted sideways, without guidance. It bumped against a log, then lodged itself among the cypress roots.

Cray looked up at the tree as it bent toward him with its deformed limbs, clutching at him. He pulled out his pistol from its holster. Peeking above the edge of the canoe, he spied Forte just as his boat slid behind another huge cypress twenty yards away.

He sat up. Using his left hand to shoot, he sent three rounds at the spot where Forte had faded from sight. Splinters flew from the tree. "I saved you and then you shoot me," Cray screamed. He shot twice more and flopped back on the bottom of his canoe. His right shoulder was numb. He pressed the wound and groaned. The pain almost sent him into darkness. He shook his head violently and began breathing quick deep bursts of air, in and out.

A scuffling noise came from the rear of the canoe. Cray kicked out his legs and caught Exxie in the stomach, pushing her to the floor again.

He struggled to a sitting position again and put the pistol away. With his left hand he pulled Exxie close to him. He snatched the tape from her mouth. A scream followed. He grabbed her throat in the darkness to silence her.

"Tell him," Cray hissed in her face. "Tell him how you killed my Jenny."

Exxie gasped and flung the slime from her hair. "I didn't mean to....I was scared...."

Cray raised his hand to slap her. She stopped talking, her face shadowed.

"Just tell him," he said, his voice low.

Exxie let her chin drop to her chest. "I left her," she mumbled.

Cray shook her. "Louder," he commanded.

She raised her head. "I left her. I left her behind." All other noises in the swamp had stopped. Her voice rose. "I thought only about me. Then, she was gone." She began sobbing. "I'm sorry, I'm so sorry...I didn't know...."

Cray pulled his hand back again just as the moon rolled from behind a tree. In its glow, the girl's face showed the pain and sorrow of the past 24 hours, the bruised lips and puffy eyes that should never belong on anyone's little girl, no matter what she had brought on herself.

On anyone's little girl. Cray lowered his hand.

What have I done here? He stared at the girl's face and the features seemed to flicker. Softer, younger, more innocent. And the hair was no longer blonde. The girl smiled. "Daddy, it's okay now," the voice came to him, though the girl's mouth didn't move.

"Jenny, I wanted to make it better. That's all." Cray felt the anger ebb from him. In its place came a weariness unlike any he had ever known.

"It's okay," his little girl said. "You can stop now."

Cray smiled and the feel of it on his face seemed strange. *How long has it been?* He ran his fingertips over his features, feeling the contour of the smile. The slick blood from the bullet wound was left behind on his face. The pain was gone now. Cray reached out and touched the girl's face. " I can stop now, can't I?"

* * *

Forte saw the man slump backward and felt sure his bullet had hit him. When the man returned fire a moment later, he wasn't so sure.

He turned to Larue. "Stay here and be ready with that gun."

He carefully climbed out of the canoe and balanced himself on the cypress roots. In the moonlight he could see well enough to make his way around to the other side of the tree. As he balanced on the slime-covered roots, he listened to the man's ranting voice. *He saved me? What?* The voice seemed familiar. Where had he heard it?

The fight with Battier's men. The bum who helped him. The bum who was no bum. Forte's mind spun with the possibilities of who the man could be. Nothing. *Stop it and focus.*

Forte peeked around the tree. He could see the man lifting Exxie up now. He leveled his gun and tried to sight in on the man, but the girl was blocking his view. He could see the man's face twisted in anger, then the girl's head would block him again. He couldn't risk hitting her.

He waited for a clear shot.

Exxie's voice rang out now. *Left her behind? Who?*

Forte brushed aside the speculation about what had happened between Exxie and the man. *Only one goal now.* He felt everything fade into the background of his concentration now: Battier and Jackie Shaw and Fizer and Rosie Dent and the drugs and the mosquitoes and anything else that might run through his mind and distract him now.

It was as if the moon had shone its silver spotlight on the canoe with the girl and man sitting upright.

Forte held his pistol steady.

The girl dropped her head, crying.

The man's face was in full view now.

Forte's finger began squeezing the trigger.

And stopped.

The man's face had changed.

Forte waited and watched.

The man in the other canoe was talking softly, too softly to be heard as he reached out and touched Exxie's face.

Then he stood up, hands over his head, and stepped out of the canoe onto a mass of cypress roots. He pushed the canoe away from the tree.

Forte watched the canoe glide toward him.

Forte ducked back around the tree and waited for the girl's boat to come close. When its bow appeared, he took his paddle and pulled it toward him until it was blocked from the other man. Larue bent over the girl and cut away the tape from her hands and ankles.

Forte looked around the trunk of the tree again. The man was not moving. He sat in the crook of two giant roots, his back against the tree while his legs lay in the murky water.

The moon flickered above and Forte looked up. A grey heron flapped overhead, the only movement in the sky.

Forte stepped back to his canoe and pushed it away from the tree. He trained his gun on the man as he floated into view. With his left hand, he dipped the paddle into the water and inched forward.

The man seemed unconscious. *Is he alive?* Forte's canoe came to within thirty feet of him.

"Hold it there." A pistol was pointing at Forte. The hand that held it was trembling with pain.

Forte held steady, his own gun trained on the man on the roots.

The man spoke again. "I don't want to shoot you. You're a brave man. And you're doing the right thing." The man moaned and the gun dipped but came up again. "Just take the girl and go."

Forte lowered the Glock and put it in its holster. "I can help you."

"No." The man's voice was fading.

"You need a doctor. We can work through this."

The man shook his head. "No. It's over now."

"Yes, but...."

The man smiled. "It is over now," he repeated, his voice a whisper.

He brought the gun to his chest and pointed it toward his heart. His face seemed relaxed.

"Wait!" Forte shouted.

The man pulled the trigger.

From behind Forte came a girl's scream.

The man lay still now, cradled at the base of the ancient cypress tree as his life flowed out of him.

Forte sighed and looked up at the sky. The heron was gone now. The moon smiled down at him. *It is over now.*

He pushed his canoe away from the old cypress.

Chapter 36

Jackie back-pedaled as the orange plastic disk rose above the park in the summer sun, accelerating as it curved to the left and sailed over her head. She turned and sprinted after the Frisbee. Just as it seemed the disk would hit the grass, she snatched it up.

Fizer hooted. "Man! I thought I got you that time. Pretty fast for an old lady."

Jackie put her hand on her hip. "Old lady this!" She launched the Frisbee far above the boy's head and watched as it hit the ground and rolled thirty yards away. A golden retriever dashed from behind a tree, scooped up the disk in its mouth, and kept running. Fizer yelled and ran after the dog.

Forte watched them from a park bench. "Funny how things can seem so normal so quickly again."

Manny Leard smiled and followed with his eyes the boy chasing his dog J.D. "Is there really such a thing as normal?"

Forte grunted and slumped on the bench, taking in the clouds above. Within minutes a white dragon morphed into a pig then dissolved into abstraction.

"You think the dead can see us here?" He glanced sideways at Manny.

The old pastor's bushy eyebrows rose slightly, but he held his tongue for a moment. "I don't know if they can see people here on earth. The Bible seems to indicate that they can."

Forte nodded, still studying the clouds.

Manny turned his face to his friend, calmness in his ice blue eyes. "I've never known you to ask a question like that."

Forte tilted his head back, closed his eyes and let the August sun warm his face. "Lot of death lately. Makes you think."

Manny studied the sky. "Yes, it does. Does it make you wonder what will happen to you after you die?"

Forte kept his eyes shut. "You'll never stop with that preaching, will you?" His tone, however, was not unkind.

"No, I won't. Without God's grace, through Christ, I would not be here now to even contemplate the heaven to come. If you knew you could show a friend on death row the way to be pardoned, wouldn't you tell him about it?" Manny didn't expect an answer and got none. He dropped his head and observed his friend for a moment. "The door's always open, you know that. Mine and His."

Forte opened his eyes and took in the other man's face, the weathered sailor's visage with a grin that at times seemed to balance out all the evil in the world. "Yes, I know. Thanks."

The others approached the bench now. The dog still held the Frisbee in his teeth.

Manny stood up. "Who's up for ice cream?"

"Let's go," said Fizer.

Jackie shook her head. "I'll stay here and rest these old bones. Bring me back a drink though."

The old man, the boy, and the dog walked away.

Jackie sat down and wiped the back of a hand across her forehead. "You'd have to be crazy to run around in this heat." She curled her legs beneath her on the bench.

"He seems to be doing okay," she said.

"Yeah," he said. "Kids recover pretty fast."

"Yes, they do. And the rest of the money, if there is any...."

"Fizer says there is. We're talking about what to do with it. It will probably go into a trust for him."

"I guess Lucky Battier is long gone by now."

"Oh, there are those who will try to track him down. He seems to be able to take care of himself though."

"And the Graham girl. How is she?"

Forte let his eyes follow a pigeon above and watched as it joined its friends being fed by tourists. "Her mother called and said she was very quiet these days. Her therapist is working with her, thinks she'll be okay. Bryce Graham and the FBI are trying to track down that offshore account he sent the ransom money to. No luck so far. But it won't hurt the company if they lose the money. They had insurance for that sort of thing." The pigeons scattered when a red-haired girl of maybe four ran toward them. "Speaking of money, Verna told me a big check had come in from the Grahams."

"How big?"

He looked at her. "Big big. Real big."

"Good. We wouldn't want Forte Security to go bankrupt, since I know for a fact you have so little regard for the money." She frowned. "What about Micah Cray? At the end, he just snapped, didn't he?"

Forte thought about Cray, the relief in the man's voice across the moonlit swamp. The smile, the words *It is over now.* "I think he had come to the end of everything he had to live for."

He had come to that point after Ruth was killed. After standing at the precipice of despair, he had turned back from it. Would that dark cloud of hopelessness ever come back again? *No, it's useless to think that way. You've got too much to live for now.*

He turned and saw that Jackie was watching him.

"What?"

"You're a deep man, Mr. Al Forte," she said.

He smiled. "Scary to think about, huh?"

"Nah, I ain't skeered." Her eyes twinkled. "You've seen a lot of pain the past few days, but you've done a lot of good. If you hadn't kept after both Fizer and Exxie Graham, neither of them would be alive today."

"Well, I don't know about that."

"I do."

He chuckled. "Listen, I've thought about what you said, about the walls around my heart, about setting it free forever." He studied her face and wondered what his own face looked like to her. "I want you to know that I appreciate you having the guts to say that to me."

She said nothing, her eyes locked on his.

He paused but kept his attention on her face. A hint of a smile played across her lips. *Different, so different from anyone I've ever known.* "And I just wanted you to know...well, that...." He cleared his throat.

She leaned toward him. "To know what, Al?" Her voice was soft.

Across the park Manny and Fizer and the dog strolled back toward them. Forte turned back to Jackie.

"I want you to know that I want to move in that direction, to pull down these walls." The words tumbled out now. "Now I don't know for sure exactly what that means and what kind of timetable we are talking about here or anything else, but I just wanted you to know that...."

She reached over and touched his arm. "Shhhh, that's okay, Al. There is no timetable."

He looked down at the hand on his arm. He reached and clasped it in his own hand. Somehow it felt warmer even than the New Orleans sun above.

"No," he said, "I guess there isn't."

The jog took a meandering route back through the Quarter out to Riverwalk, then back along the river beneath the stars. He went past the French Market and kept going on Decatur until he took a left on Esplanade, out away from the tourists for a moment.

Fewer streetlights shone here, and the shadows harbored dark figures with no interest in showing their faces. He passed them by, looking for the turnoff. When he found the narrow street, he slowed his pace and searched for the rusted gate at the alley entrance. He had to rely on directions; the last time he had visited the place, he had been blindfolded.

He spotted it and picked up his pace as he sprinted toward it. Leaping high, he put one hand atop the gate and vaulted over it. Through the alley and into the courtyard he jogged, slowing again to find the apartment number. He walked up to the door of the correct apartment and rapped on it.

On the other side of the door, he sensed movement. After a few seconds of silence came the sounds of multiple locks clicking open.

A man stood in the open doorway, his face a blend of expectation and caution.

"Hello there," the man said.

"Hello, Benny," said Forte. "Mind if I come in?"

The man stepped back and Forte entered.

He remembered the interior of the apartment—the Blue Dog poster on the stylishly-cracked-plaster walls, the stacks of computer magazines, the pin-striped sofa. The young man's place seemed the same but Forte knew different. The man himself had changed. His eyes were clear now and showed none of the unabashed yearning for relief he had seen the year before.

The man smiled now. "Well, Mr. Forte, what brings you to my neighborhood?"

Forte studied the man's face a moment longer. He wondered if he had looked the same at this point in his recovery. There was that bit of strain about his eyes. He remembered seeing that in the mirror. But did the young man feel the same terror he'd had that first year, the same doubt, the same worry that everything in your life could topple over in the next day, the next minute, the next second? Maybe not, Forte mused. Then again, maybe he felt it more. It was always hard to judge someone else's recovery from the outside.

"Benny, I heard you might be looking for a sponsor," Forte said.

The young man's eyes widened and became shiny. He looked much younger now.

He nodded.

Forte held out his hand. Benny took it.

❧ The End ❧

About the Author

Glen Allison lives with his family in northeast Mississippi. He is co-founder of the Mississippi Writers Club and is the author of *Still Standing Tall*, the story of the Williams Brothers, by Billboard Books. He has written for *GUIDEPOSTS*, *MISSISSIPPI* magazine, and *MEMPHIS* magazine, among others. *NETBLUE* is the second in the Al Forte mystery series from Yoke Press that began with *MISCUE*. Glen can be reached by e-mail at glen@netga.com.

For more information, go to:

Yokepress.com

7-04

FINES 10¢ PER DAY